LANGBOURNE'S

Rebellion

ALAN P. LANDAU

In loving memory of my mother,
a very kind and gentle lady, loved by all.
Winsome Deborah Landau.
1935 – 2003

BOOKS IN THE LANGBOURNE SERIES :

(In sequential order.)

Langbourne

Langbourne's Rebellion

Langbourne's Empire

Langbourne's Evolution

Langbourne's Loyalty

Langbourne's Legacy

Also by Alan Landau:
To Brave Men

By Brenda Kate
Of Sand and Stars

Southern Africa
c. 1891
Zambezi River
Fort Salisbury
Mashonaland
Damaraland
(Belgian)
Portugese East Africa
(Portugese)
KoBulawayo
Bembezi
Fort Victoria
Matabeleland
(King Lobengula)
Kalahari Desert
Limpopo River
Walvis Bay
Bechuanaland
(King Khama)
British Protectorate
Transvaal
(Dutch)
Portugese East Africa
(Portugesc)
Namaqualand
(German)
Nomandudwane
Mafeking
Pretoria
Johannesburg
Orange Free State
(Dutch)
Kimberley
Natal
(British)
Orange River
Durban
Cape Colony
(British)
N
East London
Patensie
Cape Town
Port Elizabeth
Rail
Wagon Track

Chapter One
Mafeking 1893

Hissing and spitting with a barely concealed anger, the train pulled into the Mafeking Railway Station, clanging her ironware, and blackening her carriages with soot.

Morris and David looked out of their compartment window at the bland, miserable town that greeted them. Of the two basic colours available – beige and brown – the variety was provided only in the shades of the same hues among the trees and bushes, on the walls of the buildings, and in the clothes that the people wore.

"Is this it?" David questioned no one in particular, while Morris said nothing at all. Both of them were appalled at what they saw. It was such a contrast to the verdant colours of Port Elizabeth, with its contrasting white beaches and aquamarine sea.

Having sold their small but rapidly expanding cigarette manufacturing business in Port Elizabeth to an American tobacco company for a handsome sum, the Langbourne brothers had decided to travel into a country opening up to the north and start a trading business. They took their profits with them in the form of an official Standard Bank Letter of Credit, which they needed to deposit into another Standard Bank as far north as possible. On

the journey up they had stopped for three hours in Kimberley, the prosperous town where diamonds had been discovered, but whose discovery had compelled Cecil John Rhodes to buy up all of the diamond mine claims a few years earlier, thus forming a company that he had named De Beers.

The brothers quickly located the Standard Bank of Kimberley where they asked the manager to open an account in order to deposit their newly acquired wealth. In their haste to get back to the train, however, the meeting did not go very well, with Morris' notoriously short temper getting the better of him at times, instantly causing a dislike and distrust between the two parties. It was only because of David's calming and diplomatic manner that the manager suggested they open their account in Mafeking itself, where they had a sub-branch of their bank with all the facilities they would need. Furthermore, he suggested, it would be much closer to where their intended business would be located. David thanked the manager, shaking his hand in appreciation and with an unspoken apology for his brother's abrupt behaviour, before dashing out the door to catch up with Morris himself, who was busy striding out for the train station.

Kimberley was not a particularly beautiful town and the menfolk, comprising mostly rough and hardened miners, did not seem particularly hospitable. The brothers were therefore pleased when the train pulled out of the Kimberley Railway Station and continued northwards.

Mafeking, however, did not look much better: in fact, it looked far worse. With much trepidation, the brothers gathered up their meagre belongings and exited the coach. The platform accommodated a number of aimlessly wandering people, who seemed totally uninterested in what opportunities the day might have presented to them. As the brothers stood, utterly dejected, surveying the gentle ebb and flow of the Mafeking populace, David could not help thinking back to the day they had disembarked from the ship that had brought them to Africa and left them standing at the edge of the Port Elizabeth harbour, watching her daily life unfold in front of them.

Although they had been scared, and apprehensive about leaving the safety and comfort of their cabin, the harbour had been alive with activity. All the men seemed to have a mission in life, carrying boxes and cartons, trotting from one shed or office to another, with the occasional dog following its master. And he remembered how the people at least wore a variety of clothing with some colour and purpose. Even the African men who wore nothing but a leather apron around their loins had a bright sheen reflecting off their dark skins.

"This place is as bland and unexciting as eating unsalted newspaper," David commented.

"We won't be staying here long," Morris said under his breath, "you can be sure of that. Let's find a place to stay where we can plan a quick departure."

David looked out at the town that appeared before him and did not like what he saw. In fact, he was certain that all that he could see was the sum total of the entire settlement. "There's nothing here, Morris," he grumbled.

"I think we need to go back to Port Elizabeth or Cape Town. This place is dead, and I fear it will be twice as bad farther north in Matabeleland."

"Let's keep the Cape Town option open," Morris agreed. "Come on; it's taken this long to get here. Let's at least see what this place can offer us. If nothing grabs our fancy, we'll be back on this very train tonight, and that's a promise."

The brothers picked up their trunks and sought out the stationmaster to get some advice as to where to get lodgings and, more importantly, where to find Julian Weil's business.

Julian, because of his vast network of stores throughout the colonies, had been their best customer when they had been producing cigarettes in Port Elizabeth. They believed that it had been solely because of his loyalty to their business that their only competition, the American corporation in Cape Town, had encountered huge difficulties breaking into the market around the country.

As a result, the boys had been made an offer they could not have refused by the Americans to buy them out, lock, stock, and barrel. And now, at the young ages of sixteen and seventeen, they had a very sizeable fortune sitting in their bank account.

Having experienced poverty and hunger in their home in Ireland, they believed they had a responsibility to support the family they had left there. Their father, Reuben, had once been a successful businessman in Poland before the hardships of England and Ireland had reduced him to little short of a pauper. As they had grown to maturity, he had instilled in his boys a practical set of sound business principles. He had constantly tutored them at the dinner table, playing crafty little games which had been centred on business strategies and how to understand people, to work out what they wanted, what type of person they were, and to get what they, themselves, wanted. He wished them to succeed in life and business.

When Reuben lost his beloved wife to illness, he spiralled into a depression and lost all interest in working and supporting his family, choosing instead to spend an inordinate amount of time in the local synagogue, praying and studying religious books. Little had the brothers realised how their father's subtle teachings had become ingrained in their characters. They did not fear business. They took calculated risks and spent time talking and learning from others more experienced than they, particularly if such people had local knowledge they could use. Thanks to Reuben's tutoring and upbringing, they had accumulated a small fortune in just over a year. Their belief was that their Lord was watching over them constantly, presenting them with opportunities that they were quick to take.

Their mother, Esther, had come from nobility. She, too, had instilled a solid upbringing in her children before she died. She was pedantic about their presentation, ensuring they dressed well and remained well groomed. Table manners were important, and even after she died, their elder sister, Bloomy, continued to encourage their mother's values, correcting the boys whenever they held a fork incorrectly or put their elbows on the table. She forbade them to pass the saltcellar to a recipient hand-to-hand. Even when they were desperately destitute, Bloomy ensured proper etiquette was observed in the home, and Reuben continued to discuss business and trading with his sons.

Now, here they were in Mafeking, the northern frontier of the southern Africa colonies, and the town where the rail line ended. If they wanted to go further north to Matabeleland, they would have to go on horseback, by wagon, or simply walk. The stationmaster was not much help, but he did point them in the direction of Julian Weil's General Store, which, thinking about it afterwards, would not have been difficult to miss. It was just fifty yards along the same dirt road that edged the station. There was a sign above the entrance to the store painted in rough white paint, now beige from the incessant dust, proudly stating "Julian Weil & Co." and under that, another smaller sign saying "Sample-Room". Other than that, it was just a plain brick building with two small windows and a rusted, corrugated iron roof over the top.

Morris and David entered the gloomy interior of the building and put their trunks down on the floor, waiting for their eyes to adjust to the dim light from the bright day outside. As their vision cleared, they were greeted by a number of long, heavy wooden tables, laid out in a military-style formation. On top of the tables was all manner of merchandise: blankets, bolts of fabric, enamel pots, pans, plates, glassware, tools, and clothing. Towards the rear, they could make out food items, packets of salt, tins of food, sugar, cooking oil, and other interesting items they could not discern that were either boxed or packaged, or simply wrapped and held fast with frayed string. There was a distinct smell of soap.

"Good morning, gentlemen," a voice called out, muffled by the numerous rolls of fabric on the table near the boys. "How may I help you?" the voice continued. David peered into the gloom and saw a tall, thin man approaching, almost gliding towards them.

"Oh, good morning to you, sir," David responded quickly, so as not to sound rude. "We were hoping to find Mr Julian Weil."

"Ahh… indeed. Well, you have come to the right place. May I introduce myself to you? I am Mr Ian Taylor. I am the manager of Mr Weil's store."

"Pleased to meet you, Mr Taylor. I am David Langbourne, from Port Elizabeth, and this is my brother, Morris Langbourne."

"Ahh… the Langbourne brothers!" Taylor exclaimed, shaking their hands vigorously. "Yes, we know all about you. We stock your cigarettes! What an absolute pleasure to meet you."

"And likewise to meet you," Morris said as he shook Taylor's hand. "We are most grateful for your custom and loyalty to our business."

"Mr Weil has nothing but praise for you two. Insists we support you at all times."

"We are deeply honoured, sir," David beamed back. "However, we do bring news in that we have sold our business to an American corporation, so our business no longer exists."

"Oh!" Taylor sounded surprised. "We so enjoyed doing business with you."

"All is not lost, Mr Taylor," David continued. "It seems the tables have now turned, and we are about to become customers of yours."

Ian Taylor was silent as he took this new piece of information in. "Well," he said, beginning to smile, "I do believe I need to find Mr Weil for you."

Morris nodded his pleasure. "That would be very kind of you sir."

Within seconds of Mr Taylor disappearing into an office at the rear of the building, Julian Weil appeared, unmistakably short and slightly rounded. He calmly walked over to the boys, right hand outstretched in a warm welcome, despite his characteristic lack of a smile. Julian was in his early to mid-30s and already starting to show signs of balding. When they'd first met him in Port Elizabeth, he had hardly ever smiled, and if he had, it would have been very fleeting. Julian always looked concerned, and he had a habit of pausing to think before he spoke. Then when he did, he was succinct, seemingly uninterested in idle conversation.

"Welcome," he said calmly. "To what do we owe the pleasure of your visit to our humble town? Come in, come in. I have asked Mr Taylor to make us some tea," Julian continued, as he led them into his office, seemingly excited to see the boys, as he did not allow them a chance to greet him in return.

Once inside the rear office, they were seated on two rickety wooden chairs while their host walked around the other side of the desk and sat on an old leather office chair that swivelled. Pleasantries were exchanged, with quick quips about the journey to Mafeking. The boys began to relax while Mr Taylor dutifully poured tea for the three of them in stained and mismatched cups before politely excusing himself to tend to the shop floor. Julian's office was cluttered with papers, files, notepads, invoice books, bank deposit books, and clipboards of all manner of colour and size. In fact, there was barely a vacant spot on the desk on which to place their teacups.

Morris cut straight to business. "We sold our cigarette business to an American company, Mr Weil." Morris was similar to Julian in this way, preferring to discuss matters of importance with some urgency, while David preferred to talk about issues not directly related to any business for a short while before gently easing into the crux of the matter. He believed it was good practice for building sound relationships that would last.

"Is that a fact?" Julian mulled, allowing a frown to crease his forehead. "I did not know that. I trust you got a good price?"

"Indeed," David said. "They made us an offer we couldn't refuse."

"Good!" Julian responded simply. "My father once told me that you haven't actually made any money until you have sold something for a profit."

"Indeed," Morris nodded. "We've sold the business, and now we have some money to get into a real business venture. We were thinking of going up north, to Matabeleland, to become merchants. We have no idea what's up there, just hearsay. What might be your opinion of that idea, Julian?"

"Well, Mr Rhodes certainly has plans for that place, and I can assure you people are moving up there in droves to mine the land. Rhodes has a treaty with the King of Matabeleland; his name is King Lobengula—a big man; aggressive, vicious, and quite brutal, but very respected. Probably more feared, I should say, even by his warriors, commonly known as impi. The treaty is only for mining, so no one is permitted to settle or farm the soil. That is Ndebele country, and Lobengula won't allow Europeans to settle on his land."

"So," Morris asked cautiously, "unless you are a miner, there's no point in being a trader?"

"Oh, no, of course there is." Julian put up his hand to stop Morris on that thought. "You can trade and have a business there. The miners, their families, and the military need support, as well as goods and food and things like that; you just can't settle there permanently. I'll tell you something, though, between us," Julian leaned forward and lowered his voice. "I believe Rhodes has every intention of settling Matabeleland, and the land beyond that."

"How is he going to get this king, what's-his-name?" Morris questioned, forgetting the complicated name of this seemingly belligerent king to the north.

"Lobengula."

"Yes, Lobengula; how is Rhodes going to persuade him to allow people to settle there?"

"I have no idea!" Julian leaned back in his swivel chair, causing it to squeak in objection. "All I can tell you with confidence is that you can make good money there. It's dangerous, the conditions are tough, but any trader can make big profits if he has the money to buy goods to take with them to be sold. But be warned; it is a very long way from anywhere. If you think Mafeking is a long way from civilisation, think again. From here onwards you ride a horse, or walk. And if you are not used to a saddle, I can assure you that you will walk most of it."

"I'm having my doubts about heading up north then," Morris said, scratching his head as concerns started to flood his thoughts. Already he was not taken with the landscape and isolation of Mafeking, its sheer distance from the civilised Cape, and the thought of native warriors wielding lethal spears and clubs. All manner of deadly weapons, including European weapons, scared him, let alone the dangers of wild animals on the way.

"I'll tell you something else, gentlemen." Julian leaned forward again, his chair protesting angrily, and lowered his voice even more, causing the boys to also lean forward in earnest. "There is a very large and captive market up there."

"How so?" asked David.

"The military, and in this case, the British South Africa Company, or BSAC, will pay good money for just about anything. Money is no object; I've seen it myself," he broke off, briefly staring over the boys' shoulders. "Let's discuss this later over dinner, shall we? I have a meeting down at the military camp in a few minutes. Sadly, Mafeking doesn't have anything like The Grand Hotel in Port Elizabeth. Where are you staying?"

Morris straightened up. "Actually, we have just got off the train and were hoping you might kindly advise us of a suitable establishment at which we could stay."

"Nonsense! You will be staying in my home." Before the boys could object, Julian called for Mr Taylor, who bustled in promptly. "Mr Taylor, please gather two of the staff to carry the young gentlemen's luggage, and then please escort the Messrs Langbourne and Langbourne to my home. Please tell my wife that they will be our guests for as long as they are in Mafeking."

"Certainly, Mr Weil," Ian Taylor responded with a smile and a curt nod, and quickly led them out of the office as the brothers tried to object.

"Make yourselves at home, gentlemen!" Julian called out to them as the rather bewildered brothers followed the obedient manager out of the store. "I will join you later this evening."

The Weil residence was simple, just like the other houses in Mafeking, made of square, light-brown bricks under a rusted corrugated iron roof, with a generous verandah surrounding the entire homestead. The inside was plain and neat, with very little in the way of furniture, but pleasantly cool. The wooden floor had been polished to a magnificent shine. Mrs Weil was a lovely lady in her early thirties, and equally as round as her husband. She met them as they approached the verandah, and they took in her short brown hair, happy face, and blue floral dress. Since she was used to having her husband's impromptu arrangements and unexpected guests, she made Morris and David feel right at home from the start.

They were shown to their room, which was, again, very simple. A tall, dark-brown wooden cupboard stood against one wall, the wood of which smelt like pepper, with a small writing bureau next to it, and two single beds neatly made with crisp, white linen and sky-blue blankets. So as not to impose on Mrs Weil, the boys suggested to her that they would like to explore the town of Mafeking, and would return later that afternoon to freshen up for dinner.

It did not take long for them to completely circumnavigate the town. First, they walked back to the railway line and followed it south, in the direction from which they had come, until they reached a bridge over a small river that seemed to be where the town came to an end. Off to their right was a distinctive African village with the typical circular mud walls and thatch-roofed houses, a few plumes of white smoke billowing gently where the womenfolk were obviously cooking. On the riverbank, they could see some young women washing clothes, while naked children splashed and laughed as they played in the refreshing water.

To their left were some buildings that looked like houses, built of brick and mortar, so the brothers decided to walk over and explore that village more closely, but it was something of a disappointment because there were only about nine or ten houses, and no people. As they came out the other side of the village, they encountered an open patch of land that was being used to manufacture bricks. The kilns to fire the bricks were not working, and, again, the place seemed deserted. They walked back to the railway line, turned right, and headed north, back into town.

There was very little of interest in town. Some low buildings were either cluttered general stores, run or owned mainly by the Indian community, or simply storage sheds. Four of the sheds had the name "Weil" painted above their doors, suggesting that Julian Weil was indeed a prominent businessman in town.

There was one factory that seemed to have much activity and noise emanating from it. It appeared to be a foundry. But as the boys got closer, they saw above the entrance a sign framed in heavy, black wrought iron proclaiming it to be "Gerran's Coach Building & Ironworks".

At the northern end of the town was a hospital and what looked like a church, so the boys continued on, walking past it, and found the local cemetery. Again, the boys walked past, trying not to look at all the crosses planted in the soil. That was the end of the dirt road; ahead were simply some rough tracks where wagons, horses, and some form of human existence had travelled along from time to time. Here the brothers stopped and looked out into the brown, drought-stricken, African landscape. A low, but prominent hill off to their right appeared, but – apart from that – the land was relatively flat, dusty, and filled with pockets of dry straw.

David broke the silence. "Well, I'm guessing Matabeleland is in that direction, about a three-month walk from here. Can you imagine walking in one direction for three months?"

With their hands in their pockets, the two boys stood listening to the emptiness of the African landscape. Even the birds made no sound.

"I don't like it," Morris stated eventually, not taking his eyes off the horizon.

David shrugged his shoulders as he jingled some coins that he found in his pocket. "We can always go back," he suggested.

"I cannot see how anyone could possibly do any business out there. In any case, the isolation scares me; this place is bad enough as it is."

"I must agree. I'm not entirely comfortable here."

For another full minute the brothers stood in the bright sunlight, gazing at Africa's doorstep. The parched, unwelcoming harshness of the open land had a forbidding beauty of its own, as if to say: "Please come; you're welcome, but just beware." The more they stood, gazing at the harsh beauty, however, the more Mother Africa subtly began to draw them into her heart.

"Come on, let's go back to the Weil's," Morris said finally, and turned on his heel. They headed for the town whose only real claim to existence seemed to be that it was at the end of the railway line, a fact that weighed heavily on his mind.

Later that evening, Mrs Weil provided a very nourishing meal prepared by her loyal cook, Langton, who worked tirelessly behind the scenes in the kitchen. Langton only appeared briefly to put the food on the table, and later to take the dirty crockery and cutlery away. Julian had invited his younger brother, Samuel, to join them for the evening meal so that he could meet Morris and David.

The conversation before, during, and after the meal was intense. Morris asked most of the questions, desperately drawing on their older host's knowledge of trading in the northern territories, as well as the politics and culture of the people of the north. By the time they went to bed, their minds were swimming with information – some good, some troubling – but overall, confusing. Daylight did nothing to clear the perplexity in their minds.

Breakfast with the Weil's was another enjoyable meal, and both boys were impressed with how well the people of Mafeking ate, being so isolated from the civilised world. Julian excused himself, as he had business to attend to, and suggested the Langbournes call by his office at lunchtime. He would take them to the officer's mess in the military camp nearby so that they could meet some of his friends in uniform who had just returned from Matabeleland.

By ten o'clock that morning, Morris and David, dressed in open-neck, long-sleeved shirts and dark slacks, found themselves back at the spot near the cemetery, looking out into the vastness of Africa's north. They stood in silence, hands in their trouser pockets once again, and deep in thought.

Their characters were different, but they had developed a very strong bond. Standing in silence side by side was as good as standing face to face in deep conversation. They knew each other extremely well, and this worked in their favour. Morris made all the final decisions, yet he would take care to listen to his younger brother's counsel. David, on the other hand, accepted his brother's decisions, because he knew Morris would consider his advice and never had he found any reason to doubt his brother's acumen. They made a good team.

As usual, it was David who broke the silence. "So?" he spoke into the still air, and then let the vast openness settle its oppressive weight on them again.

Morris spoke gently into the African peace and quiet. "I don't know what to do. It's a huge risk."

"I think leaving Ireland for Africa was a bigger risk, and that turned out well. I mean, when we left Ireland we had no idea where we were heading, and we had very little money."

"Yes, David, but when we left Ireland we had nothing to lose. We were poor, hungry, and cold. We are rich now, and we know what lies over that horizon. Things are very different today."

"True," David replied, shrugging his shoulders. "I think we need to decide pretty quickly, though, because I don't think I could spend much longer in this place. I'd go demented." Morris stole a quick smile at his brother's candid opinion of Mafeking.

There was another long pause as they thought things over again.

"It's dangerous," David said casually.

"It seems things are a bit tense between the Europeans and the Matabele, but there is no sign of any conflict."

"Not yet," David observed, not taking his eyes off the horizon. "We could make a lot of money. We also could be killed and lose everything."

"True." Morris was pensive.

They continued staring into the sweeping expanse for a while before Morris finally decided. "Let's do it," he murmured.

David turned his head to look at his brother and cocked an eyebrow. He wasn't sure if he was surprised at his brother's decision or not.

Morris looked over at him. "I think let's risk it. Let's at least give it a try. Either we will walk out of Matabeleland very wealthy, or poorer and the worse for wear, but greater in experience. What do you think?"

"I'm with you, brother," David replied, and they both turned back to gaze at the northern horizon.

Nothing more needed to be said. The decision had been made, and suddenly all apprehension and uncertainty were replaced by a sense of adventure, enthusiasm, and excitement. There was a fire burning inside of them, and they could not wait to load up and go.

From way over the horizon, Matabeleland was gently coaxing the brothers, and they had answered her call.

Chapter Two

Setting Up

With a renewed purpose in their lives, the boys walked briskly back to the Weil residence and changed into business suits. The weather was not really conducive to wearing suits, but they wanted to look smart when they visited the bank and the BSAC camp. Once they were suitably attired, the brothers had time to head over to the sub-branch of Standard Bank of Kimberley.

The Port Elizabeth branch of The Standard Bank was managed by Jack Shiel, who became their good friend almost from the day they met him, but the manager of the Mafeking branch reflected the dreariness and lethargy of the town he was sent to represent. The brothers were also soon to learn that he had a condescending, self-important attitude, coupled with a vicious streak of sarcasm.

Mr Stewart Savage was a very tall and thin man, with light brown hair and a matching, thin moustache, the corners of which were twisted up and outwards, and they wriggled whenever he spoke. His office was spacious, with large internal windows in order that he might observe the daily activities on the bank floor at all times. His eagle eyes did not miss a trick. One of the tellers knocked timidly on his wood-and-glass door and waited for Mr Savage to finish what he was reading. He slowly turned a beady eye on the teller and, with a very curt nod, indicated that she could finally enter the office.

The brothers observed that moment when she mentioned that they were in the banking hall looking for a meeting with him, because his eyes flicked in their direction for a split second before he nodded and returned once more to his immensely important paperwork. The teller reported to the boys that Mr Savage would see them and they were to wait in the banking hall until he called them through.

He kept them waiting a full twenty minutes.

"I don't like this man, and I haven't even met him yet," Morris said to David, not taking his eyes off Mr Savage. "He is downright rude. Have you noticed he's been reading the same piece of paper since we got here? What is he trying to prove: that he's upper class or something?"

"Relax, Morris," David soothed, but even he was getting agitated.

Finally, after what seemed an age, Mr Savage put the piece of paper down and slowly, very slowly, walked out to meet the boys. It did not escape them that they were not invited into his office, something Jack Shiel would have done without hesitation, as well as offering a cup of coffee, no less.

"What can I do for you boys?" Savage asked, looking down his nose at them.

With a massive effort, Morris managed to hold his tongue, feeling it best not to make a difficult situation even worse, but to leave the response to David.

"Good morning, sir," his brother replied, "My name is David Langbourne, and this is my brother, Morris." When he extended his hand as well, Mr Savage shook their hands with obvious reluctance. "We have just arrived from Port Elizabeth," David continued brightly, "and would like to open an account with you, sir."

"My tellers are very capable of doing that. They will pass the application on to me for approval. If you would kindly stand in line at Counter Two," he pointed to a counter where half a dozen people stood, "my teller will give you the forms to complete."

"How long might it take for you to approve our account, sir?"

"I beg your pardon?" Savage looked down at David disdainfully.

Morris couldn't hold his tongue anymore. He spoke deliberately and clearly. "My brother asked how long it might take for you to approve the opening of our account," he stated shortly.

Mr Savage stared at Morris, his eyes glaring with fury, and adopted the haughtiest language he could muster. "I will approve it once I am happy with your credentials, sir, and as you are a hitherto unknown personage in my presence, that may take a long time: a very long time."

"We are not unknown to your bank, sir." Morris returned the "sir" with equally heavy sarcasm evident in his voice. "We have been banking with your Port Elizabeth branch for well over a year now, and the manager, Mr Jack Shiel, would be delighted to vouch for our credentials."

The mention of Jack Shiel seemed to rattle Mr Savage slightly, and he certainly had not expected Morris, a lad in his teens, to stand his ground against him. He rolled his eyes to the ceiling. "Jack Shiel? Yes, I know him."

"We are not wishing to open a new account, Mr Savage," David took over calmly, "we simply wish to transfer our account from Port Elizabeth to your branch here."

"Regardless, I still need to satisfy myself that you are of good standing. I presume you don't know anyone in Mafeking that might vouch for you?" he tested, believing the newcomers would not know a soul.

"Mr Julian Weil can vouch for us," David said confidently.

Savage started to look a little uncomfortable at the mention of Julian's name. "And I assume you are a customer of his?"

"No!" Morris said, puffing his chest out and starting to get visibly angry. "He was a customer of ours!"

Savage looked shocked. "I see," he shuffled his feet slightly in agitation, "and how much would you be proposing to deposit into my bank?"

"If I had a choice I would not be depositing anything into your bank, Mr Savage. Such a pity there is only one bank in this town." Morris looked casually out the window onto the street, as if looking for another bank.

Savage rolled his eyes again. "I said, 'How much are you are looking to deposit, Mr Langbourne?' "

"Seventy-five thousand pounds, sterling."

"Excuse me?" Mr Savage stared at Morris in disbelief.

"You heard me. Now how long is it going to take to open my account, sir?"

Mr Savage's formerly scornful attitude turned around completely. "Why don't you gentlemen come into my office and we can open your account immediately," he smiled with his teeth. "Mr Shiel and Mr Weil should be adequate references for me to expedite the process. Please come in."

David smiled sweetly, while Morris almost growled out his responses to Mr Savage's questions as the suddenly obsequious manager personally filled out the application. David gave Morris all the rope he wanted to vent his distaste for their new bank manager and did not try to hold him in check at all. Mr Savage was only too pleased to take receipt of the Bank Letter of Credit that Morris handed him and even more pleased to see them out the door, telling them that their chequebook would be back from the printers in one week.

After the brothers had exited the bank building, Morris' anger vented for a good five minutes. "And as soon as Standard Bank or any other bank opens an office in Matabeleland, we are closing our account here. There will be no questions about that!" he fumed.

David started to laugh. "Oh, Morris," he chuckled, "wasn't it funny how he changed his attitude when you told him how much money we had?"

Although Morris, too, began to chuckle and then burst out laughing at the memory, his already existing distrust of banks became even more firmly entrenched. "Come on," he said in the end, "we have a lot to arrange. I want to be loaded up and out of here the moment our chequebook arrives. We'll need it in Matabeleland, so we can't leave without it."

They then walked over to Julian's General Store for their scheduled lunch meeting. He was waiting for them when they arrived, and they immediately walked to the edge of town, where a host of tents behind a large warehouse suggested a somewhat temporary military-style establishment. As he walked between the tents, obviously familiar with the territory, Julian chatted to the boys while the routines of the day continued unabated, as no one seemed to notice his presence. Morris and David, however, took in these unfamiliar surrounds with interest, while trying to partake in what Julian was telling them.

There were many horses in the camp, and many men, both African and European, either in or out of uniform. An open, flat, dusty parade ground with a lone white flagpole was at the centre of the camp. Drooping lazily in the hot, still, air was a flag that, on first impression, seemed to be the British Union Jack. Closer inspection revealed that this flag had a white disk in the middle with what appeared to be a depiction of a yellow lion holding a white elephant tusk in its right paw. Under the image were the initials BSAC, short for the British South Africa Company, which had been founded by Cecil John Rhodes.

Morris questioned Julian. "Is this an army base?" he asked.

"No, the BSAC is not an army. It's a private paramilitary force owned and controlled by a commercial company, which in turn is owned by Cecil Rhodes. Basically, the BSAC protects the pioneers who went north and ensures that the mining treaties they hold with the Matabele nation are maintained. The BSAC is a very wealthy company. They own assets such as mines and rail networks. They also have a Royal Charter to administer a lot of land for the British. It's complicated, but you'll work it out in time."

"So why are we meeting here, if I may ask?"

"I do a lot of business with the BSAC, and I like to maintain a good working relationship with their leaders. I'd like you to meet some of them because it will help your business later. They are expecting us."

"Julian, I am very grateful for the help you are giving us, but am confused as to why?" Morris confessed, somewhat puzzled by the special treatment they were getting.

"Morris, I like the way you work. Your business ethics have been honourable, especially in your dealings with my business. And, if I may be perfectly blunt, I hope to be soon making lots of money from your custom. Therefore, I want you to succeed up north as it is in my best interest for you to do so. What's more, you are going to need all the help and knowledge you can get from these men. Life north of here is not going to be easy, of that you can be assured."

Morris and David were both humbled by his kind comments and by his honesty. At the same time, the uncertainty of their decision to go north hung over them like a dull ache. Nevertheless, they had made a decision, and they were going to make the most of this opportunity. Julian had arranged for two senior BSAC representatives to join them for lunch and, instantly, the young brothers immersed themselves in conversation with the officers.

By nature, the brothers were shy and reserved, but they had become accustomed to rubbing shoulders with the upper echelon of the business community and society when they lived in Port Elizabeth. To them, it did not matter whether the guests at their table were in uniform and had shiny brass insignia on their collars or not. Add a stimulating discussion into the equation, however, or a conversation that required one to have their wits about them, and they were in their element, particularly Morris.

Morris was very sharp, and his thought process was much quicker than the average person. He would often cut people off in mid-sentence, flashing out the next question or comment. This would cause the conversation to ramp up to a feverish pace, and capture an unintentional audience of passers-by. He did it in a polite way. He was never condescending, and always showed extreme interest in the person he was talking to. Somehow he encouraged the other person to 'want' to tell him more, and often tell more than they'd intended. Yet, it was not done for a purpose: it was just the way Morris was built. He was always interested, always keen to learn and discover, but never aiming to antagonise or provoke. His need for knowledge was simply insatiable.

Julian, meanwhile, limited his own conversation and marvelled at the social skills and confidence exhibited by these two young lads, particularly among their peers. A quiet man by nature, Julian rather preferred his own company and solitude, but – as much as he might have disliked it – success in business always required that he interact with his customers. This was one of the reasons he admired these young boys and in particular the shorter, older brother, Morris. It was plain to see he did not miss a thing.

Morris had already swung the conversation away from BSAC matters. "Tell me about this Matabele tribe up north," he prompted, "I hear they are quite militant."

Captain Marcus William Bailey, a battle-hardened soldier from the Royal Fusiliers, replied. "Indeed they are," he said, "King Lobengula has a very structured fighting force, and they are quite brutal, especially to their own kind."

"Why?" Morris interjected.

Captain Bailey leaned back in his chair and took a sip of his water, briefly flashing a smile at Morris. He was a tall man who carried himself proudly and stood straight as an arrow, his large chest causing the buttons on his tunic to strain under the pressure of his upper body strength. He was known among his colleagues for his generous black moustache that drooped well below the corners of his mouth. "Ever since their original leader, Mzilikazi, fled the kraal of the great King Shaka in the British colony of Natal," he expounded, "the Ndebele people have moved across the land and raided any tribe that opposed them. They steal their cattle and women and slaughter the men. It's just what they and their Zulu cousins have done for generations. As a result, they are the dominant tribe. In fact, the tribes to the north of Matabeleland are under Lobengula's rule, too. They are called the Mashona, or Shona people, and he exacts tribute from them; they look after his cattle, and effectively pay him taxes, if you will."

"And how does he feel about us European people encroaching on his land?"

"He doesn't like it," Captain Charles Rudge interjected. "Let's put it this way; he accepts it, but doesn't like it." Captain Rudge was more relaxed than Captain Bailey. Carrying a little more weight, his features were more rounded. The buttons on his tunic were likewise strained, but a little lower down his torso than Bailey's tunic.

"We pay him in coin, weapons, explosives, and medicine, among other things, so that we may mine for gold and diamonds," Captain Bailey continued. "And the situation seems to be acceptable on both sides. We're not finding much gold at this stage, though we know it's there."

"So what are the chances that the Ndebele people will rise up against this, what would you call it, migration of Europeans?" David asked.

"That's not likely," Bailey continued. "We have a treaty with the king. Actually, it's a concession. It is a signed document between King Lobengula and Queen Victoria, represented by Cecil Rhodes, who in turn was represented by Mr Charles Rudd, in 1888. We call it the Rudd Concession, and it gives us Europeans the right to mine in Matabeleland and all areas north of that, which includes Mashonaland. It also guarantees the king's protection of the Europeans. In return, we give Lobengula arms and ammunition and coin for his protection."

"And he abides by this concession?" Morris asked.

"Yes, he accepts it. But, as Captain Rudge said, he doesn't like it."

"So we have his protection if we go up north?" Morris pressed.

"Yes, indeed."

"And what happens if he tears up the concession?"

"Then you have our protection!" Bailey and Rudge laughed together.

Morris looked at David and raised an eyebrow. He wasn't sure if there was any comfort in this. He turned back to Captain Bailey. "So, can King Lobengula road and write?"

"I'm pretty certain he cannot."

"Then how does he know what he signed?"

"My boy," Captain Bailey turned serious and looked Morris in the eye, "the concession was translated to him."

"So not only is he unable to read or write, but he cannot even speak English?" Morris quipped.

Bailey was getting flustered. "No, of course not! The concession was translated to him and explained to him by people he trusted, over weeks of negotiation. It is a legal document and an accepted treaty between them and us. Don't worry: the BSAC has a very big interest in Matabeleland and Mashonaland. There is no way Mr Rhodes will allow the treaty to fall into ruin."

"Alright," said Morris, "I'll accept that. So, where do we go to do business?"

"Fort Salisbury, in the heart of Mashonaland," Rudge shot back, as he leant back in his chair. "It's about two hundred and fifty miles northeast of KoBulawayo."

"Why there?" David questioned.

"It's where all the development is happening. And it's a long way from King Lobengula and his impis."

With that, the decision to go to Fort Salisbury was made. The remainder of their lunch meeting took on more of a social tone, ending shortly afterwards with a hearty farewell and thanks. A little while later, they were back in Julian's office, sitting on the rickety chairs, while Julian's seat continued to squeak desperately every time he shifted his weight. The conversation went straight to business, and they did not leave until the sun was about to touch the western horizon.

Julian told them that it would take about two or three weeks to get to KoBulawayo on horseback, or three months by wagon and oxen, a distance of about 500 miles over rough terrain, rivers, and forests. From KoBulawayo to Fort Salisbury was about 250 to 300 miles farther to the northeast, depending on the route, but the journey was much easier. This would take about two months to complete. Care should be given to travel during the dry season; otherwise, the journey could take a lot longer. At this moment, however, the seasons were in their favour.

They agreed to take six wagons, fully loaded, which they hoped might take upward of a year or two to sell through the stock, thus lessening the frequency of the extraordinarily time-consuming journey. That would also give them time to monitor how well their stock was selling, and provide enough time to send a rider or messenger back to Mafeking with a fresh order to replenish the stock. Julian made some estimates on how much a wagon-load of stock would cost and politely asked if they felt they could afford it. He also asked if they needed some credit from him. Morris assured him they could afford it, and that they would pay for it up front. This left Julian secretly wondering how much they had sold their cigarette business for in Port Elizabeth, but he had the decency not to ask. After all, it would not be ethical.

As for the wagons, which would set them back roughly £100 each, Julian felt they would have no trouble selling them to the local populace, albeit at a slightly reduced price from the wear and tear they would endure on the journey up. This would allow them to recoup some of the cost of setting up the business, but the difficult part would lie in finding enough oxen to draw the wagons. He suggested they would need about six oxen per wagon, and a few spare, should there be an injury or death to any of the beasts from stepping into a hole, or simply from being attacked by predators.

The biggest scourge, he informed them, was sleeping sickness. Many domesticated animals did not last long in the wild, often succumbing to the disease and dying within a month. Truly "salted" beasts, however, would be protected, having once been infected with the sickness and managing to survive, but these were rare and expensive. Additionally, they would need a team of men to drive and control the oxen, at least one man per wagon, and another four to help control, feed, and care for the oxen, as well as rotate with the various duties.

Buying the goods to sell was the easy part. Julian had a huge inventory in his various warehouses, and he instructed his manager, Ian Taylor, to personally tend to all the Langbournes' needs.

"What type of goods do we need to buy, Julian?" Morris finally asked his trusted friend.

"Bolts of material; very sought after by the women up there. As there are no clothing shops, the women sew and knit everything, from clothing to curtaining and bedding. You name it, they make it by hand. You will need everything from pins to knitting needles, cotton and thread, buttons; the list is endless. Hardware is another sought-after commodity: you will never have a problem selling tools of any description. Cups, saucers, plates, pots, pans, knives, forks - everything! Don't take glassware; it will break en route. Enamelware is a good commodity, almost unbreakable. The going is very tough. Never underestimate how hard it is going to be."

"You say there are no shops up there?" David asked, somewhat bemused.

"That's what I am saying; there is nothing there! It's a brand new country for the Europeans. No houses, no shops, no banks, and no Post Office. There is no rail network or telegraph office, so no communication to anywhere. If you want to get a message back here, someone has to carry it by foot, horse, or wagon. When you get to your destination, you will have to build your storeroom yourself, or you could trade from your wagons."

"So, what makes people want to go there?"

"Gold."

"Oh, of course," David remembered.

Julian became serious again. "Something you need to keep in mind, gentlemen. The BSAC is funding most of the operations up there, so there is a lot of free money circulating up north. Commodities are in short supply, both for the civilians and the BSAC. It takes months to get supplies there, literally months; so you can put very high mark-ups on your sales. Profit margins are extremely healthy."

Morris looked Julian straight in the eye. "How healthy?"

"Ridiculously healthy. You mark my words, Morris: when you arrive there, you just have a look around and see how expensive it is, and what people are prepared to pay for things. You will be very glad you set up business there, believe me."

The following day after breakfast, Morris and David sat on the front verandah of Julian's home, planning their escape from Mafeking and their journey northwards. To speed things up, they decided they would each take on the responsibility of a particular task, rather than both tending to the same thing. Morris took on the job of working with Ian Taylor and deciding what stock to purchase. David would walk down to the African village and attempt to recruit six wagon drivers and four general helpers, preferably those who had experience with oxen. It would be essential that the lead driver spoke at least some English.

Morris would make his way to Gerran's Coachworks and negotiate the purchase of six wagons, with at least two spare wheels each, and tarpaulins to cover the wagons to keep the stock dry in the rains. David would find out how and where to purchase a team of oxen.

After all the advice they had received the previous day, they decided that they would also require two horses, which they would ride themselves, along with some live chickens to supply them with eggs along the journey. Additionally, they would need two rifles, two handguns, and, most importantly, two sharp and sturdy sheath knives, not just for general use, but also for protection at close quarters. Half of one wagon would be dedicated as a dry food store, although they would hunt for meat along the way. And they needed some basic medication for injury and illness along the route, not just for themselves, but for their drivers as well.

The decision-making done for one day, the boys set off in different directions to attend to their allocated tasks. Morris had by far the most productive day. He kept Ian Taylor busy discussing and selecting stock items until well after lunch, stopping for a tea break only once. He made a selection of blankets, linen, fabric, cutlery, and crockery, as well as hardware, household items, and numerous basic necessities. He was careful not to select things that had a high-bulk, low-cost factor, such as water drums and roof sheeting, but preferred to select goods that were not so bulky, so that they could carry more of them. These would fetch a higher price, ensuring a higher profit margin.

Morris was careful to choose items of interest that people, particularly the womenfolk, would enjoy, such as vanity, manicure, and pedicure kits; bathroom mirrors; and body soaps with delightful fragrances, including the new transparent Pears Soap, made in London. It was a very expensive soap, even at wholesale prices, yet Morris purchased Julian's entire supply. He selected everything he could find for infants, babies, and young children. For the menfolk and BSAC soldiers, he chose all manner of knives, razors, and wide-brimmed hats. The list was extensive. When all was decided upon, Morris went off to Gerran's coachworks while Ian Taylor retired to his desk to spend the remainder of the day costing the invoice for Morris. Morris' meticulous mind and love of numbers ensured that he already knew what the invoice would total to within a few shillings as he stepped out onto the street. He smiled quietly to himself, knowing that if Taylor's calculations did not match his, he would enjoy the challenge of proving who was correct and who was not.

David's day was not as good as Morris' had been. He spent almost the entire day in the blazing heat of the sun trying to communicate with the African villagers and had no break for either tea or lunch. Eventually, he found a man from the Tswana tribe who appeared to understand him, and who set about helping him find a team to drive their wagons. Everyone he spoke to was lethargic and not very interested, but during the course of the day, he finally managed to recruit five young men, and the Tswana gentleman whom he appointed as their leader. By then it was too late to even attempt to find oxen. He was sunburnt, parched to a crisp, dirty, and extremely hungry. David's day was done.

Morris, meanwhile, met with Mr Gerran himself and negotiated a quantity discount for six wagons. In the process, they enjoyed a refreshing cup of tea with some homemade shortbread biscuits, made that very day by Mrs Gerran. The factory had a good supply of wagons, and Mr Gerran was happy to pass ownership and delivery of the wagons on to Morris, once he secured an official letter of credit from Mr Savage at the Standard Bank, or his official cheque, should it arrive in time. Mr Gerran's business also sold tarpaulins, spare wheels, spare bearings, a repair toolkit, and drums to carry water that could be attached to the underside of the carriage. Morris wasted no time accepting what was on offer.

Feeling very pleased with himself, Morris bid Mr Gerran farewell and made his way back to Julian's home. When he was almost there, he saw David approaching and headed in his direction to tell him of his very successful day. As he got closer to David, however, he noticed he looked rather 'pink', sweaty, dirty, dusty, and in a foul mood.

"What happened to you?" Morris asked in bewilderment.

"What a day!" David sighed. "I need a drink of water very soon. I'm parched!"

"Good Lord, you stink!"

"I don't need to hear that now, thank you. How was your day?"

"Excellent, thank you. Brother, you are a wreck," Morris continued, as he crinkled his nose at David. "Have you stepped in a cow pat too? You can't enter the Weil household like that."

"Morris!" David was getting angry now. His brother was not improving his day much at all.

"I feel sorry for you, David, but…" and then he burst out laughing, and could not stop. David was not in the mood to join in and grudgingly made his way back to the Weil's home after arranging with Morris to occupy Mrs Weil at the front door while he slipped inside via the back door.

By the end of the week, they were almost ready to leave. They had a team of oxen waiting on the outskirts of town; six brand new wagons; a full consignment of goods ready to be loaded at Weil's General Store; provisions for the journey; and, most importantly, a book of 100 cheques, freshly stamped in the name of Langbourne Brothers, Standard Bank of Mafeking. Now they were ready to do business.

The brothers outfitted themselves with saddles for their new horses, which they had been taught how to ride by their previous owner. They carried two 577/450 Martini Enfield rifles for hunting, which replaced the older model they had left with their lovely landlady, Sonja Du Plessis, in Port Elizabeth, and two Webley revolvers for close protection against attacks from dangerous creatures. They had ropes, levers, spades, a hammer, some first aid equipment, fuel for their kerosene lanterns, and a selection of books to keep their many lonely nights occupied.

On the following Friday, Morris walked into Gerran's Coach Builders and presented Mr Gerran with a cheque in full payment for their six new wagons and spare parts. Thanking him for his kind consideration of the discount, he shook hands, and headed over to Julian Weil's general store, where he met up with David and they wrote out another cheque in full payment for their purchases. In total, to effectively begin a new business, it cost them just over half of all their profit from selling their cigarette business in Port Elizabeth. Moreover, since this venture would show an even healthier profit, Morris and David were well pleased with the outcome.

Weil, Gerran, and some of the BSAC officers were secretly astounded at what these boys were spending. They felt they were foolish to buy such high-end merchandise, and so much of it. But they felt it was not for them to interfere, since they had already given their advice. If the Langbourne boys chose not to accept it, it was on their young heads. Weil and Gerran certainly did not care too much: they had their money from their sales.

Saturday and Sunday were spent loading the wagons. It took a full two days to pack everything, leaving Julian's warehouses looking notably depleted. On Monday morning, the oxen were hitched up to the wagons. They had done some dry runs over the previous three days to make sure the oxen would behave and that the drivers had control of their teams. Although things were a little rough and amateurish, the oxen and drivers improved each day, until Morris believed they were ready to in-span the fully loaded wagons. Events went according to plan and, despite the beasts straining at the new and unfamiliar weight, they performed satisfyingly well.

Wearing khaki clothing and wide-brimmed hats, with a revolver and a sharp sheath knife each on their hips, the brothers mounted their horses and rode sedately down to Julian's general store to say farewell. They looked like bush-rangers, but awkward and comical with their crispy clean, freshly ironed clothing.

"I wish you a safe journey, and may you have much success when you arrive," Julian said, as he shook hands with his young friends and newest customers.

Morris beamed from under his new hat. "We thank you again for your hospitality, Julian, and we ask that you pass our thanks on to your wife, please."

"Absolutely. It was a pleasure to host you both."

"Julian," David said, "I know this sounds funny at this time, but how do we find our way? We have no map."

"Oh, that's easy. Just follow the road. There is only one road, I am told. Just stay on the track, and you can't go wrong."

"Just past the cemetery the road seems to become flattened grass. I wouldn't really call it a road."

Julian broke into a rare laugh. "That is the road! And sadly, it doesn't get any better. Just follow the tracks, flattened grass, broken twigs; over a thousand people have taken wagons and horses that way over the last few years. You won't get lost."

"Right-oh," Morris was not confident, "we'll be off, then. We'll be back when we need more stock."

"With the amount of stock you have purchased, I don't expect to see you for a good couple of years. You have almost cleaned out my warehouses!" Julian laughed again, obviously pleased with the business they'd provided him. "All the best, you two."

With that, the Langbourne's turned their horses to face north. It was easy to tell they were new in the saddle. They were stiff, and a bit ungainly. This was nothing, however, compared to their oxen, wagons, and drivers, who were quite uncoordinated, with whips cracking unnecessarily, too much shouting, and many confused bullocks.

"How old are those boys?" Ian asked Julian as they stood, arms crossed, while they watched the procession head out of town in a cloud of dust.

"About fifteen and sixteen, maybe seventeen, I think."

"I'll put money on them not even making it as far as the Limpopo River," Ian quipped.

"That Morris lad, he has a determination that I have never seen in anyone. And he is very smart. And make no mistake, David is not far behind him. They may surprise us both."

"Hah!" Ian exclaimed. "You say they may surprise us both? So you think they may not make it either?"

Julian did not respond to that question. Deep down he felt the Langbourne's had made a number of errors in judgement. They had bought too many items they would struggle to sell, and they were too young and inexperienced to handle the perils of the wild African bush. They watched as Morris' horse shied and he almost fell off. He gripped his saddle in a sudden panic, legs flailing in their stirrups as he tried to regain his balance.

"They paid for their goods in full, right?" Ian questioned his boss.

"Yes," Julian said quietly, almost sadly, before turning on his heel. "Come on; you have work to do. We need to replenish the warehouses."

Chapter Three

The Trek

The trek north got off to a rough start. The oxen were a little confused by their handlers, who were equally confused by their leader, Tebogo, who was even more confused by Morris and David's instructions. As might have been predicted, Morris became frustrated very quickly and needed constant calming by David, who displayed an inordinate amount of patience in managing to keep some semblance of order in the slow but constant forward movement along the almost imaginary route to the north. Eventually, they found it less frustrating to leave the drivers and handlers to their own devices, choosing instead to ride a little ahead of the caravan to pick out the track, clearing fallen branches and potentially difficult rocks from the approaching wagons.

Morris had named his horse "Bruno", for no particular reason, prompting David to name his horse "Splat", after the sound he had heard when he walked around its rear one morning and had nimbly avoided an embarrassing accident. Bruno, a majestic Bay, was brown with dark legs and a jet black mane, whereas Splat, a Dapple Grey, was a little taller with pale mottled patches across his body. Despite their inexperience, the boys sat well in their saddles, so the ride was quite comfortable and an especially exciting experience - for the first hour. After that, it became decidedly uncomfortable, forcing them to dismount, with a little concealed embarrassment, and walk for long periods of time. It would take a full week before their bodies and soft skin became accustomed to the saddle and the rocking motions of the horses.

The first stop to settle in for the night was welcomed by everyone, including the animals. The process of out-spanning the oxen went well, after which they were haltered to graze on the copious dry grass around the wagons, and also to prevent them from becoming lost or falling prey to lions in the vicinity. After an uneventful night, the procession set off again around mid-morning of the second day and, over the following three days, a routine set in.

Both man and beast became more comfortable with their lot in life, including Morris, who began to relax and take in the landscape that stretched out all around them. The boys took time each evening to sit by the fire with their team and learn more about each of the men, their lives, their families, and their tribe, asking Tebogo to attempt to translate for them. It was often difficult and confusing, but a knowing nod or an occasional "ahh" in agreement seemed to keep everyone smiling. Morris was sure the crew knew that these European brothers did not have a clue as to what was being said at times.

Some of the men had intricate burn scars on their face and body, almost like a form of tribal tattoo, each with a family story to go with it. Some burn scars were not intricate, often being raised welts under tight, smooth, shiny brown skin, which must have caused a great deal of pain and discomfort when they were being inflicted. Yet each man seemed to wear his particular mark with pride. The Langbournes' genuine interest in their new employees fostered respect among the men, and strengthened their comradeship and teamwork. As the crew's names were learned, so the oxen were given names and slowly, and very surely, they became more than just beasts of burden, particularly to their handlers.

It had been a fairly dry season, and the grasses and small bushes were brown, parched, and brittle. The established trees, their roots buried deep in the hard ground, had found a little water and were showing signs of greenery, their leaves relishing the bright sunlight that cloaked the countryside. As healthy as the trees were, it was obvious to David that they had a difficult time growing in this rugged country. Their branches were gnarled, bent, and broken, with twigs that scratched at their legs and drew blood if they got too close. Many of the Acacia trees had dangerous spear-like thorns, pale grey in colour, sometimes white, and as long as a man's little finger. Although David could not be certain, he was convinced that they would have poison on their tips, as they appeared positively lethal just to look at. Since they were in Africa, it would not have surprised him.

When the boys celebrated their first week of their journey, they began to develop an intense interest in their surroundings. David, in particular, took the time to study the smaller members of the African family, such as the ants, grasshoppers, spiders, and millipedes, whose hundreds of legs, he assumed, would need a very strange brain to control and coordinate them so perfectly. With so many legs that it was impossible to count, one such millipede would curl up in a tight coil if it were disturbed. Only minutes later, sensing that the danger might have passed, it would tentatively uncoil and then continue on its journey, as if nothing had happened. David enjoyed prodding these insects and watching their defensive reaction.

One evening, as they were setting up camp for the night, David watched a species of pure black centipede appear from behind a piece of bark on a tree. It had a body flatter than that of the other millipedes, and had far fewer legs which were an attractive bright orange in colour, but moved very quickly and so caught his attention. The centipede appeared very agile and inquisitive, moving rapidly in search of food. David was about to prod it with his finger to see if it would curl up like the others when Tebogo noticed what he was about to touch.

"No!" Tebogo yelled at the top of his voice.

David snatched his finger back in alarm and stared at him wide-eyed. "What?"

"Sore. Bite," Tebogo said in his broken English, pointing to the centipede.

"They bite?"

"Like snake."

"Really?" David said, standing up and backing away from the creature. "Are they poisonous?"

"Like snake. Yes, very sore." And with that, he picked up a sturdy log and crushed the bug in one simple movement. "Better you *bulala* this one. Very sore."

David watched Tebogo walk off and then stared at the hapless creature as it lay dying in the dust in its own fluid. He was sad that it had been killed on his account but felt relieved that he had been spared a very painful and perhaps deadly bite. He looked over at Morris, who was also somewhat wide-eyed, concern written all over his face.

"You think they can kill you?" David looked horrified.

"Probably." Morris was very perturbed. "Everything out here seems to be able to do that! I wonder how many of those things live around here?" he questioned anxiously, looking at the ground by his boots and suddenly feeling decidedly unhappy with their predicament.

From that night on, Morris and David chose to sleep inside one of the wagons, clearing a space under the tarpaulins, and secretly vowing to never sleep on the ground again. It turned out to be a very wise decision, as the earth in that area was well populated with a number of insects that could inflict nasty bites, the resulting infection usually only being noticed and felt the following day.

One very hot, still day, as the convoy monotonously rumbled forward, a small black parabuthus scorpion, no more than two inches long, squeezed itself tightly under a dry, fallen log. The vibrations of the iron-rimmed wheels of the six wagons and the tread of dozens of oxen's hooves reverberated through its feet and underbelly. The threat to its safety was getting closer, and the arachnid's first instinct was to hide, its need for survival overtaking all other needs. A shadow dimmed its tight crevice of protection, and a dull thud hit the ground very close by. The fingers of a human hand appeared right in front of it and lifted the roof of its lair, causing sunlight to flood its world and chase it from its confinement. The scorpion's instinct was to attack, and, with a lightning-fast flick of its tail, it punctured the skin on one of the fingers, just under the fingernail, injecting a tiny droplet of venom at the same time.

David let out a blood-curdling scream as the poison seared through his nerve endings, instantly dropping the log. Snatching his hand away as if he had touched a piece of red-hot metal he screamed again at the top of his lungs, causing Morris and Tebogo to drop what they were doing and bolt over to assist him. He had never experienced pain as ferocious as this. The fire went right up to his elbow in an instant. When they got to David's side, he was walking in circles, slapping his hand, trying to get something off it.

"Get it off! Get it off!" he screamed, shaking his hand in the air as if to shake drops of water from it.

"What?" Morris shouted at him. "There's nothing on your hand! Stop, stop, let me see!"

David held his hand out for Morris to have a closer look, but only momentarily before he started slapping it with his free hand, trying to knock some invisible creature away, then rapidly wiping his fingers against his trouser leg.

"Hold still! I can't see anything!" Morris shouted; he was actually very scared now.

"There's something stinging me on my finger, get it off!" David yelled, stamping his feet in aggravation, before screaming loudly again at the bush.

"Calm down, calm down, give me your hand!" Morris protested.

Just then Tebogo grabbed David's hand in a vice-like grip and peered at his fingers. "What you do?" he said, looking him in the eye.

David took a deep breath, tears of sheer pain rolling down his cheeks, and pointed to the log on the ground. "I tried to pick that up."

"Ghaw!" Tebogo hawked. He released his hand and kicked the log over. The small black scorpion crawled out from underneath, tail curved menacingly over its back. "Bite sore. Like snake," he said, picking up a smaller stick and crushing the insect to death.

"Can that thing kill him?" Morris asked anxiously. "Is he going to die?"

"No, but very sore." And with that Tebogo walked back to the slow moving convoy, without much sympathy for his young boss.

"Bloody hell, Morris!" David shouted. "The pain is unbelievable. My entire arm is on fire!"

"Where did it bite you? I can't even see a mark?"

"Here!" David pointed to the tip of his middle finger. There was no mark to be seen. David shook his hand vigorously, held it tight with his free hand, looked at the sky and screamed again. Morris was starting to get very nervous at his brother's uncontrolled behaviour; he had never seen David like this before. "I'm sure it injected some poison into me. The pain is terrible, and it goes right up my arm."

"What can I do?" Morris offered, starting to panic. "Come back to the wagons, and I'll see what medication we can use." He noticed the tears streaming down David's cheeks. "Don't worry; you won't die. Tebogo says you won't die."

"I don't believe him!" David moaned. "The pain, the pain! I have never felt pain like this!" David snarled between his teeth.

Once more he screamed at the trees, then, composing himself, he walked back to the wagons with Morris, who was by now in quite a state himself.

"It feels like someone has put a needle in a fire until it was red-hot and then pushed it up my finger and up my arm. Not slowly, but fast! It feels like it is still in there, still red-hot and burning. I can't believe the pain!"

Back at the wagons, Morris frantically searched through a trunk of medical supplies he had purchased. The only thing he could find for pain relief was a white powder in a bottle labelled "Codeine", which instructed him to mix one teaspoon in a glass of water and drink it every four hours as necessary. As he started to prepare the mixture, David told Morris to put three teaspoons of codeine in the mug of water, such was the intensity of the pain. Morris did not argue, and quickly did as he was told. After having administered the medication, Morris ordered Tebogo to out-span the oxen and set up camp for the remainder of the day. Having made David rest in one of the wagons, he gave David another three teaspoons of codeine an hour later, since he was still in so much pain. It took a full three hours before David announced that the pain was subsiding, and then he drifted into a deep sleep, helped along by the codeine overdose and the relief that he might not die. The following day, David was almost back to normal. Both brothers were shaken by the events of the previous day. They were developing a very deep respect for the creatures of Africa. As a result, they decided never to pick up logs or rocks with bare hands again without careful inspection first, which usually involved a robust kick. They also agreed they needed to check their shoes and clothing before putting them on in case another creature which they had not yet discovered had found its way into the cloth.

The week that followed went by without incident. Each day was much the same; a pot of tea at sunrise, something simple to eat, in-spanning of the oxen, and then the monotonous, slow drive towards the northern horizon. As incidents of the unexpected were now fewer, the boys were starting to enjoy the journey. Each day brought with it new scenery and new encounters with wildlife. Their first river crossing was filled with excitement and anticipation. It was a small river, mostly dry, with some shallow pools of water dotted along its length. Where it was dry, the sand was soft and white, beautiful to look at, but difficult for the oxen to pull the wagons through. The strength and willingness of the oxen constantly surprised the brothers as, without complaint, the animals would lean into their yokes and pull heavily, traversing the dry riverbed in surprisingly quick time.

It was the middle of the third week when Morris and David crested a low hill and, sitting atop their horses, commanded a wonderful view in all directions around them. The land was quite flat, with several low hills, just like the one they were on, stretching out as far as the eye could see. Stunted green, thorny trees peppered the landscape, while the grass was dry and light brown as if sprinkled lightly from above. They turned around in their saddles and looked back from where they had come. Suddenly it dawned on them that they were extremely isolated, almost vulnerable. There was no civilisation to be seen in any direction, apart from the faint, almost indistinguishable path made by the pioneer column some years back. They could see their caravan of wagons inching its way towards them in the distance. They looked ahead again and stared at where the rugged land met the pristine blue of the sky.

"What a contrast to Ireland," David marvelled quietly. "Is there any end to this land, the warmth, and its beauty?"

"I'll take Africa over Ireland any day," Morris agreed as he gazed ahead, almost hypnotised by the harsh beauty that unfolded before him.

The day was hot, and the sun shone brightly overhead. The boys had lost a lot of weight on the journey, their fat having been replaced with sinewy muscle, their exposed skin having turned to a healthy bronze. They both sported scraggly, unkempt beards, as there was no reason to shave each morning. They wore their clothing loosely now, shirts un-tucked, creased and stained with sweat, dust, and a little blood. They sat comfortably in their saddles, totally relaxed, and felt as if Mother Africa had accepted their presence.

Their tranquillity and sense of total isolation were suddenly interrupted by the distant "harrumph" of a lion some distance away. Although they could not see it, the noise had been ahead of them and slightly to the left. David instinctively reached for the rifle holstered in its leather scabbard and gently pulled it free.

"How far do you think it is?" Morris asked his brother, without taking his eyes from the direction of the sound, his heart nervously starting to pound in his chest.

"I guess it's about two or three miles away."

"You think it will come this way?"

"The breeze is in our face, so he doesn't know we're here. If the wind changes direction, he'll pick up the scent of the oxen and head this way for sure."

Morris bleakly recalled one night during the previous year when he had set up camp after buying tobacco from Piet van Tonder, who then farmed in Patensie, a farming area about three days' walk from Port Elizabeth. Morris' camp had been surrounded by a pride of lions that had terrorised them most of the night before the lions had broken off the siege.

Just then the lion grunted again, and this time it sounded a little louder. A shiver ran up Morris' spine, and the horses began to shift a little, obviously nervous. "I think it's coming our way," David said calmly, "and the horses have picked up its scent. We had better get back."

Morris needed no encouragement. He swung Bruno back in the direction of the approaching wagons, and both he and David rode back to safety. They were only about ten minutes from the wagons and, as soon as they arrived, they warned Tebogo of the approaching danger. David issued instructions to pull the wagons into a circular laager and to outspan the oxen, placing them inside the circle. Morris, meanwhile, located all the shanks of rope they had and set about tying crisscross lengths between the front of one wagon and the rear of the wagon in front of it, thereby creating a type of fence in the gaps between the wagons to secure them, ensuring that the oxen were well and truly penned into the circle and could not escape. The ropes would also act as a barrier should a lion attempt to enter the laager.

Once the oxen were secured, the men began clearing smaller bushes in the immediate vicinity of the encampment with machetes, and roughly cramming these under the body of the wagons while David stood watch on one of the driver's seats. Then the men hurriedly collected firewood and placed it in small piles around the laager at about ten yards from the wagons. This would be far enough to give the boys enough light to see a predator long before it reached the laager, yet close enough for someone to carefully leave the protection of the wagons to stoke the fire if it became necessary.

The whole exercise was completed in less than an hour, and the boys were well pleased with the way their team performed. Everyone felt safe in their hastily built fortress.

David walked over to Morris and pulled him aside. "You know, we have been very lucky up till now. This is how we should set up camp every night. We could have been caught totally unprepared."

"You're right." Morris shuddered at what could have been.

He was thankful they were given the chance to prepare before a tragedy occurred. He was also very aware that should something nasty happen to them, there was absolutely no help for hundreds of miles around. What also became clear was that they knew very little about the bush, even though they felt like seasoned adventurers. Yet they understood they were learning all the time, and that such incidents offered perfect training grounds for lessons in bushcraft.

"Would you mind telling Tebogo what the new system will be in future?" Morris asked. "It's too early in the day to confine the animals. They need to graze before dark, but it can't be helped today. From tomorrow we must set up our camp an hour earlier and let the oxen graze before we lock them up."

"Sure, I'll arrange that," David readily agreed and walked over to Tebogo, not just to tell him what their new routine would be, but to thank him and his men for their swift actions. David was always quick to praise people when praise was due.

It did not take long for the oxen to become restless. Even the two horses started snorting and pawing the ground. The drivers instinctively grabbed their long spears and were walking around the beasts, talking to them softly, trying to calm them down.

It was left to David to state the obvious.

"The animals have picked up the scent, Morris,"

"Thank heavens we have daylight on our side," Morris sighed, but he, too, was notably nervous and twitchy.

Just then David caught a very slight movement deep in the bushes. Without a word he pointed in the direction of where he saw it, drawing Morris' attention. They both stared in the same direction but saw nothing. "Look for movement, Morris, look for movement," David said calmly to his brother, and then suddenly they both saw it; a very slight flicker of something; that was all. Both boys raised their rifles and pointed them in the direction of the looming danger, not certain exactly of what they had seen. Another flicker and suddenly a brute of a male lion appeared from behind a tuft of grass about 100 yards away. He had a magnificent, dark mane.

"I've got it… I see it," Morris said, a cold sweat breaking out on his forehead.

"It's still upwind; it still doesn't know we are here," David said, as he watched it saunter casually towards them. Without warning, one of the oxen bellowed and caught the interest of the lion, which suddenly stopped in his tracks, dropped to its haunches, and stared intently at the laager. Then all the oxen started to bellow and shuffle about, which had the immediate effect of encouraging the lion to begin stalking the wagons, moving slightly to the right, its eyes fixated on a single spot on the laager, a spot that Morris believed was himself.

"Let off a round, about ten yards in front of him," David whispered to Morris.

When it came to matters of the bush, David instinctively and naturally seemed to take control, and Morris was quite happy to give over command. "Let's kick up a bit of dust and stones and give him a warning. On the count of three," he nodded, and aimed just in front of the stalking beast. "One, two, three!"

Two shots rang out, enveloping the boys in a cloud of thick, white smoke, while almost simultaneously a puff of dirt erupted in front of the lion, which immediately turned tail and bolted away so quickly they hardly saw its exit. The lion's agility for its size was staggering, and left the brothers shocked at how light-footed the beast was. Meanwhile, the oxen went into a frenzy, and the horses began to whinny loudly. Tebogo's men took over and set about calming the animals down. It took a while, but they managed to get the situation under control.

As darkness set in, the fires were lit as a precaution, but nothing happened during the night; the danger had been averted. It was a long and uncomfortable night for all, but they were safe. They had been very lucky.

This was not the only time they were threatened by predators on the journey. They had four frightening encounters over the weeks that followed—three more times by lions, and once by a pack of hyenas, and all during darkness. Nevertheless, their system of forming a laager worked and gave them the protection they needed.

* * *

It had been six weeks and two days since the brothers turned their backs on Mafeking, and this day was about to be a most significant day for them. They had noticed that the bush was becoming a little greener, and the trees were growing taller and sturdier. They rode out ahead of their caravan to check the route, as they routinely did, and encountered a very wide river. It was vastly more substantial than all the others they had forded. As big as it was, however, it was much like all the others: filled with pools of water that did not flow. The banks of the river on both sides had been eroded and cut away, causing a low cliff to mark its edges. They sat in their saddles above the elevated bank and savoured the magnificent view of the still pools and soft, white sand. Hundreds of antelope of many species seemed to wander aimlessly on the dry riverbed, while in the distance, off to the left, a herd of about 20 elephants appeared from the far bank and strode out onto the sand in a somewhat ungainly wobble, trumpeting with excitement at having arrived at the waterholes. A baby elephant at the rear of the herd was sprinting to keep up with her elders and looked quite comical.

David smiled at the amazing scene unfolding in front of him. "I wish I had a telescope to get a better look at those elephants," he murmured.

Morris looked over at David and grinned. "I have seven telescopes in one of the wagons. Would you like one?"

David looked at Morris in surprise. "Seven? Is that all?"

"I'd have bought eight, but Weil only had seven, so I bought all he had. We are the only dealer north of Cape Town with telescopes. And we will be so for a long time, come to think of it," he added with a broad smile.

"You really need to tell me what you bought. I still don't know the half of what you have in there."

"I will, in good time. We are not even halfway to KoBulawayo yet."

"Talking of halfway," David smiled wryly, "I would hazard a guess that we are standing on the halfway mark right now."

"What makes you think that?" Morris questioned.

"Well, they said it takes about three months to get as far as KoBulawayo, and we have been walking for about six weeks now, so that's about halfway. But they also said that the Limpopo River—"

Morris finished his sentence, "—is about halfway between Mafeking and KoBulawayo?"

"Correct! And this river must be massive when it is flowing, so I think we must be standing on the banks of the Limpopo River!"

"By Gorrah! I think you're right!" Morris beamed. "Congratulations, brother! So that over there," he pointed to the far bank of the river, "must be Matabeleland."

"Yes, that's what I would think."

"Incredible to think we have made it this far." Morris was pleased with their accomplishments.

They sat in their saddles for a moment, wallowing in their self-pride and enjoying their sense of achievement.

"So," Morris said casually, "tell me: how do you think we will get our wagons down this cliff, and," he pointed to the opposite bank some two hundred yards away, "up those cliffs over there?"

"I'm sure there's a way. I mean, a thousand others before us did it, and look, those elephants did it, and they can't climb cliffs. There's a cut-out somewhere close, I'm sure."

Suddenly they heard a faint sound coming from behind them in the direction of their wagons. They weren't sure what the sound was, but it was rapidly getting closer. The brothers looked at each other in confusion, trying to make out the sound.

"That sounds like animal hooves on the ground. Don't tell me a herd of buffalo are coming at us," David suggested.

"It sounds like it. What else could it be? And it's coming at us fast," Morris broke off. The boys quickly spun their horses around and drew their rifles, aiming at the mysterious rumbling coming at them at full gallop. They felt vulnerable with their backs to the cliff.

"As soon as they break through the bush, start firing at the ground at their feet!" David exclaimed urgently. "Maybe we can divert them!"

"And if there are lions chasing them from behind?" Morris said quickly, but David did not respond; he did not have an answer for that.

Without warning, horses with mounted riders burst through the bush. The riders were in military uniform.

"Whoa!" shouted Morris, and instantly lowered his rifle. "It's the BSAC!"

David immediately lowered his rifle, too, and Captain Marcus William Bailey and Captain Charles Rudge, followed by about twelve other BSAC soldiers, pulled to a halt in a cloud of dust in front of the boys.

"Gentlemen!" shouted Captain Bailey, grinning profusely. "We meet again! I hardly recognised you fellows with all that fuzz on your face. You weren't going to shoot at us, were you?"

Morris and David started to laugh. They all dismounted and shook hands heartily. Since the boys had been deprived of English speaking companions for over six weeks, the men from the BSAC were a most welcome sight. Also having met two of the men before, as well as the total surprise of the encounter, all added to the excitement and joy of the occasion.

Captain Bailey ordered his men to set up camp right where they were, and invited the boys to join them, which invitation they accepted without hesitation. Nevertheless, they took the trouble to ride back to the caravan and explain to Tebogo where they would be camping for the night and further instructed them to set up camp alongside. They then returned to the BSAC campsite to catch up on the news of the world, according to Bailey and Rudge. David had shot a young male impala earlier that day, so there was enough meat for everyone. The BSAC men provided rice and a generous tot of whisky each.

Despite the isolation from other people and any form of civilisation, Morris and David noticed that the soldiers always spoke good English, were exceptionally polite, and addressed each other using their rank and surname. At first, it was a bit disconcerting for the boys, but they accepted it and followed suit.

Later that evening, after the meal was done, the laager secured, the oxen haltered and fed, and the tents having been erected in the company camp, Morris and David joined the officers for a cup of tea and a social reunion.

"The men in Mafeking are running a book on you boys," Captain Bailey said in his refined English accent, which betrayed his upper-class origins.

"What do you mean?" Morris asked.

"There's a bet that you won't make it across the Limpopo River."

"You're joking!" Morris exclaimed. "Who thinks we won't make it?"

"Weil, Taylor, Gerran, and some of the blokes in camp."

"I've got £5 with Weil that you will make it across," Captain Rudge chipped in. "Looks like I just made a quick five quid out of you boys."

"Hah!" David shook his head. "Not so quick, Captain Rudge. We have not crossed the river yet. I can't believe they doubted us! Wait until I see Mr Weil again," he laughed.

"Had any problems with your livestock, or with wild animals?" Bailey asked.

"Bloody hell!" David exclaimed. "I'll face a pride of lions any day, but keep those little insects well clear of me."

"Why?" Bailey was intrigued.

"I got bitten by a tiny little insect," David indicated a space about two inches between his thumb and forefinger, "and I honestly thought I would die. The pain was the most excruciating thing I have ever felt. It was unbelievable - indescribable, actually."

"Oh, I think I know what that was," Marcus Bailey said with a scowl. "A little chap with two nippers and a long tail?"

"Yes!" David almost shouted.

"Walks around with his tail curved over his back, like this?" Marcus demonstrated with his hand over his head.

"Yes! That's the one!" David almost shouted again. "What is that creature?"

"It didn't bite you, it stung you, with the end of its tail. It's called a scorpion. Bloody nasty little creature. People tell me it's like a red-hot needle, about ten inches long, that gets violently shoved into you."

"Yes, yes, that's exactly what it felt like, and it doesn't subside for hours. Goodness me, that was the most dreadful experience I have ever been through. I honestly thought I was going to die."

"Oh, people can die from scorpions. Ghastly business, that," Captain Rudge muttered, as he took a sip of his hot tea. He also had a refined English accent, but exuded a very relaxed air about him. "What about lions? Any trouble?" he asked nonchalantly.

The group chatted happily until almost midnight, the boys relating all the incidents they had experienced during their journey, and the company men explaining that they were on their way to KoBulawayo to gather reports for Mr Rhodes before heading to Fort Salisbury, via Fort Victoria, to do much the same thing. The officers were quick to give the boys plenty of advice about the route to KoBulawayo, and suggestions on how they might better protect themselves from lions, hyenas, and other threats north of the border.

Marcus happened to mention something to the boys that both Morris and David regarded as terribly important, yet it had never been discussed before. He said that they would come across a number of forks in the road after they crossed the Limpopo River because the terrain became more demanding in Matabeleland. The pioneers before them would often find that their route became impassable, whether it was because of deep ravines, a river in flood, or woodland that was just too dense to forge through. They might have to backtrack, therefore, and find or make a new track either to the left or right of their intended route. Oftentimes the detours that were passable at one time might also come to a dead end because of a recent flood. This meant that in some places the road north could be as much as six or seven miles wide! The good news, though, was that there was only one way north. And although they might have to backtrack and try new forks, they would ultimately end up in KoBulawayo.

The road from KoBulawayo to Fort Salisbury was much clearer and easier to navigate, so the next stage of their journey would be the most difficult to traverse. Not enough people, wagons, or horses had used the route to create a definitive roadway. In just one season, an existing route could be swallowed up by nature. Unless they knew the route very well, and very few people did, apart from some of the regular company men, they could well end up at a dead end more times than they wished, and this would be most frustrating.

The boys were very pleased to receive this information, as it could have caused a great deal of consternation and doubt had this happened too often. They decided they would have to spend most of their days well ahead of the wagon convoy, exploring the route ahead and, more importantly, locating alternative routes.

The next morning they regrouped with the company men to enjoy a cup of piping hot coffee and more much-needed socialising before they went their different ways.

"Captain Bailey," Rudge calmly ventured, while peering over at the Limpopo riverbed, "might I be so bold as to suggest we assist these young gentlemen to navigate this river crossing, and see them safely into Matabeleland before we continue on?"

"Certainly, Captain Rudge. I see no reason not to. We have made good time and are ahead of our schedule."

"Well, I mention this not so much as a gesture of goodwill, which of course I would not hesitate to offer, but I have a fiver hanging on their successful crossing of the Limpopo, and I would be most comforted to know without doubt that they have actually crossed the river."

"Oh, jolly good thinking, Captain Rudge," Bailey agreed, obviously pleased. "I, too, have a wager with Mr Weil that I would take great delight in collecting."

Morris and David looked at each other, not knowing whether to be pleased with the soldiers' concern for their safe crossing or not. They accepted the offer in good faith and laughed with them, thanking them at the same time for their apparent "concern".

Since they found a cutaway not far from where they had camped, the river crossing was accomplished without incident. The oxen had strained hard through the soft sand, and even harder when they had climbed out of the riverbed, using the very same cutaway that they had seen the elephants use the previous day. David noticed that the side walls of the cutaway in the embankment were coated with what looked like a paste of dry grass that had been chopped into small pieces about two or three inches long.

"Captain Rudge?" he called over to the burly BSAC officer, who was now standing at the top of the embankment. "Do you know what coats these sandy walls with all this dry grass?"

"Indeed, the hippopotamus does, when he defecates."

"Defecates?" David asked, and got down on his haunches to pick up a handful of the chopped grass, studying it with intrigue, crushing it through his fingers. "What does 'defecate' mean?"

Suddenly everyone went quiet for a moment and stared at David. He heard a soft giggle emanate from the soldiers gathered at the top of the sandy bank and looked up at them blankly. He noticed everyone smiling except Morris, who looked as confused as him.

"Ahh…" Captain Rudge said loudly, attracting the entire assembly of soldiers' attention. "To defecate?" He paused, looking at the attention he was receiving. "It means to excrete one's bodily waste. To pass a stool." The troop of men were struggling to suppress their giggles, as they waited for Captain Rudge to finish. "It's what you do when you visit the crapper," he continued in all seriousness. "A poop, if you will? What you are holding in your hand, dear boy, is faecal matter, commonly known as… hippo shit."

David jumped up in disgust and threw the clump of dried grass away, wiping his hand in the sand and then on his trousers.

The men, including Morris, burst into uncontrollable laughter. When the hilarity had finally died down, much to David's extreme embarrassment, he sniffed his hand in disgust, which caused the laughter to ignite again.

"It doesn't smell like… you know…" David objected.

"Of course not," Captain Bailey laughed, wiping tears from his eyes. "Hippos are herbivores, and they only eat plant matter, so it doesn't smell like animals that eat meat. As hippos defecate they start to…" he burst out laughing again, holding onto his sides as they began to ache. This started his men off yet again. Bailey finally composed himself and continued, "…they flap their tail very fast, causing the faeces to spray in all directions. Quite spectacular, actually. It's how they mark their territory."

"As you walk through the bush, and if you are in close proximity to a river, you might see trees that have been splattered with hippo crap," Captain Rudge explained, getting in the last laugh. He was not as polite with his vocabulary as Captain Bailey was.

By the time the river crossing was complete, it was close to midday, and they then prepared to part company with the BSAC soldiers, all of whom were in very fine spirits, thanks to David's exploits. The company men all wished the boys much success in the next phase of their adventure before mounting their horses.

Just before Captain Bailey mounted his beautiful stallion, he handed David a small brown bottle from his saddlebag that contained a couple of teaspoons of clear liquid. "Here, guard this with your life."

"What is it?" David enquired as he took it off him.

"It is called morphine. It is a very powerful painkiller, so powerful that if you take more than the instructions on the bottle dictate, it might kill you. So hear me carefully: use it wisely. We keep morphine with us for suppressing very painful injuries, like gunshot, spear, or arrow wounds. Next time you get stung by a scorpion, just take a little of that. But I mean just a little, no more than a teaspoonful."

David was very grateful. "Thank you so much, Captain Bailey. I don't know how I can thank you."

"No thanks necessary. Just don't tell anyone I gave it to you," he said with a wink. "Make sure you always travel with morphine, especially out here."

"Where can I get more if, may the Lord forbid, we use it up?"

"I have a close friend who is a doctor. His name is Dr Leander Starr Jameson. He keeps morphine in his medicine bag. He is a personal friend of Mr Rhodes and the private physician of King Lobengula, when the king is not being treated by his traditional medicine men," he added under his breath. "You might find him in KoBulawayo, or if not there, Fort Salisbury. I'm not too sure of his location right now, but you might come across him along your journey. Tell him I referred you to him, and he will be happy to give you some morphine. He is a very likeable man, down to earth, and an exceptionally good doctor. You will enjoy his company."

With that, Captain Bailey mounted his horse, and the procession took off into the bush at a gentle trot. David and Morris walked back to Bruno and Splat and heaved themselves into their saddles, David placing the small bottle of morphine securely in the saddlebag. And then, with a renewed sense of adventure, the convoy of wagons followed the BSAC troopers.

For a full week, they had no difficulty following the trail left by Captain Bailey and his men. But on the eighth day, their spoor was swallowed by either the wind, other animals, or nature in general. They had seen some of the forks in the route, but the BSAC trail helped them immensely. It did not take long after that to realise that men on horseback could travel a fairly direct route, be it over hills or down dales, but that wagons needed to have their routes picked out carefully, often having to divert uncomfortably from the horse tracks.

They had to start making decisions whenever they saw a fork in the trail, darting down one fork for a couple of miles to investigate, then returning and pushing onwards on the existing trail to check what was ahead of them.

All the while the oxen, wagons and drivers moved forward at a gentle pace. This kept the brothers extremely busy, as they always explored together. They would have made better time if they each took a fork in the track, but they agreed that safety was their paramount concern, and that riding in pairs was a very sound tactic.

One afternoon after the oxen had been out-spanned and the laager secured, David rode up a slight rise to look over the lay of the land, something he tried to do whenever a hill or rocky outcrop allowed. He also now kept a brass-and-leather field telescope in his saddlebag, while keeping the wagons in eyesight as a safety precaution, but was increasingly finding enjoyment in the peace and serenity of the African bush.

On this particular day, the view was not so clear, as the trees were fairly dense, so he trained his telescope on a bird that flashed across his vision and landed in a tree about 50 yards away. He had always enjoyed looking at all the wonderful varieties and colours of the birdlife but had never had a good look at them through a telescope. As he brought the lenses into focus, the bird became crystal clear and seemed larger than life, as if right in front of his eyes: a lilac breasted roller. The bright lilac feathers on its breast shone in David's eyepiece, and the iridescent turquoise and cobalt blue of his wings shimmered in the sunlight. David could not help but gasp in awe at the sheer beauty of this little bird. Never before had he seen such colours; he did not even know the names of the colours—they were impossible to describe, and he could not take his eye off it. He wanted to rush down to Morris and bring him back to share in this wonder that God had created, yet at the same time, he did not want to stop looking at the feathered creature.

Suddenly, a golden-brown blur swept past his field of vision, so close that it caused David to involuntarily jerk his head back in shock and immediately yank the telescope away to see what the movement was. What he saw made him freeze in fright, and his heart skipped a beat. In front of him stood an animal he had never seen before. It was taller than an elephant, as much as two or three times taller, and its head easily as high as the treetops. David was stunned, both in fascination and fear. The giraffe gently and very gracefully walked past David, ignoring his presence totally. A couple of small brown ox-pecker birds with bright-yellow eyes and prominent red tips on their yellow beaks clung effortlessly to the side of the giraffe's upper legs with tiny talons.

When David was looking at the rear of the animal, a sense of relief swept over him as he realised it would not attack or hurt him. Instead, he started to laugh and realised he loved Matabeleland intensely, despite all the pain and dangers it threw at him. Then, chuckling to himself, he picked up his reins and turned his horse towards the camp.

As he approached the perimeter, Morris was busy lighting a fire but glanced up when he saw David approaching, and did a double-take as he realised that his brother was silently laughing to himself. Abandoning his attempts to light the fire, he stood up and walked to the edge of the camp to meet him, grinning at David's apparent amusement.

"What's so funny?" he asked.

"Morris," David laughed a little more. "Get Bruno. I want to show you something absolutely amazing. This, you are not going to believe!"

Filled with curiosity, Morris obliged. He mounted Bruno and followed his brother back into the trees. It was not long before they found the giraffe again, with several others, and they proceeded to observe them for a solid hour. They noticed their unusual markings and their strange habit of stepping with both front and rear legs on the same side of their body at the same time, without appearing to overbalance. With the aid of the telescope, they watched them eat the leaves at the tops of the trees, wrapping a very long, dark-blue tongue around the twigs and ripping the leaves off into their mouths. They watched as one of the adults approached a tree with the massive grey thorns and, without flinching, wrapped its tongue over the thorns and pulled, stripping the leaves and some thorns off the twigs, and chewing at them apparently without concern. Something unseen then disturbed these majestic animals and they galloped away in what looked like slow motion.

David then turned his attention to the trees again, as he wanted to show Morris the stunning beauty of the birdlife, a beauty they had until now missed without the help of the telescope. The lilac-breasted roller he had seen earlier was nowhere to be found, but he saw other birds. A woodpecker knocked at a hollow tree trunk, and David swung the scope in that direction. There he saw a smaller bird with a dull, greenish-grey back and wings with little patterns on them, a striking red cap on his head, and a black mark like a beard under its beak.

The telescope had opened David's view into a whole new world, a world filled with wonders of every description. It had fast become his best friend. Although fascinated by all David's discoveries, Morris was not as passionate as his younger brother. He preferred instead to pore over the invoices of their recently purchased stock, and code their cost prices into "black rhino", the secret code he had invented in Port Elizabeth. By assigning a number to each of the letters of "black rhino", two words Morris had selected which contained ten letters that did not repeat themselves, they could write the cost of an item on the sales ticket. No one would know the cost price except the brothers, whose instant knowledge of the cost gave them an advantage if they were in a position where they had to haggle. Also, they could discuss costs via public telegram without the postmaster or messenger understanding the code.

It also helped should an invoice go astray. This had happened in Manchester, when the brothers were working in a cigarette factory. They had found an invoice in a bin belonging to the company, and were able to work out the profit that the factory was making on their cigarettes, and subsequently their markup. This was a discovery that also led them to enter the cigarette business when they arrived in Port Elizabeth, a move that had proved extremely fortuitous.

When the time came that they needed to hunt for food, the brothers would leave the convoy and head either left or right of the direction of travel in search of small buck, such as impala. Without fail, they would come across an abandoned attempt that another wagon convoy had made trying to find a better track. One day they even found a wagon wheel that had been smashed beyond repair on a rock and discarded. David had mastered his aim with his rifle and would always bring down a buck for the pot without missing. His brother accepted his skill, and happily left the hunting to David, although he was sure to always accompany his sibling on hunting excursions. Every time David spotted one of the hundreds of spectacular birds, he would share his telescope with Morris, who would also admire their beauty.

One afternoon, after a successful hunt, they finally came across a bird they had been eagerly waiting to see; a massive bird that their friend in Patensie, Piet van Tonder, had warned them about: an ostrich. It was much bigger than they had imagined, and the first thing they looked for was the colour of its legs. They recalled what Piet said that day in the bush:

"In order to attract the females, the shins on an ostrich's legs turn red. If you see an ostrich with red legs, do yourself a favour and stay well clear of him, as he will carry with him a bad temper. You will be amazed at how big they can get."

The bird did not have red legs, nor could they tell if it was a male or female. As they approached, it moved away, and kept a healthy distance between them. For that reason they followed it for a while, admiring its size, and hoping to find others. The ostrich walked in a wide circle, and as they followed it, the brothers discussed its feathers and wondered what it would taste like, or how long it would take a team of men to eat all the bird's meat. David did not know where he could shoot it and make a clean kill, so they decided to let the bird live.

It started to get agitated after a while, and then David realised why; they were circling her nest of eggs. The eggs were also massive, nothing like those they had ever seen before, lying exposed on the ground.

"Let's grab an egg for dinner!" Morris said excitedly. "Just one is big enough to feed the entire camp!"

"You're brave," David chuckled. "Right-oh, let's distract the bird by getting between it and the nest, then you jump off your horse and grab an egg quickly."

"Sounds like a good idea. Let's do it."

The boys carefully walked their horses just to the right of the nest, with the ostrich becoming more agitated the closer they got to the small collection of eggs. Just after passing the nest, they turned left slightly and headed directly for the bird, cutting off her view of her nest. Morris stopped and let David walk on ahead, taking care to keep Morris and the nest out of her line of sight. When Morris felt it was safe enough, and there was a respectable distance between them, he gently slipped off Bruno and quickly strode over to the nest. He was amazed at the size of the eggs; about half the size of a football, and a creamy matte ivory in colour. Picking one up, he felt its smooth orange-peel shell, weight, and warmth. Tapping it with his bare knuckle, he could tell the shell was very tough.

Sensing something was not right, the mother ostrich suddenly changed direction. David, having been caught stealing a glance at Morris' progress, was too slow to pull his horse around. With a blood-curdling scream, the bird ran to save her precious eggs, darting almost right under Splat's neck, which caused the horse to rear up in fright.

Morris heard the sickening scream that sent a shiver of fear down his spine and made him drop the egg. He spun around just in time to see David rolling wildly off the back of his horse, which had bolted, and a crazed ostrich tearing down at him at full sprint; short, stumpy wings extended and huge legs pumping the ground so hard he could feel the vibration through his boots. The peace and quiet of the African afternoon had so suddenly been shattered that even Bruno bolted for safety, leaving Morris standing totally exposed to the fury of the maternal fowl. The nearest cover was a tree-line some thirty yards away.

David was of no help; he lay motionless on his back in the dust. Morris turned for the tree-line and ran as fast as he could, trying to undo the flap of his holster as he ran. He did not think he would make it in time, as she was gaining on him so quickly. With his heart pounding furiously, he looked over his shoulder when he was just a few yards from cover, but it was too late. The angry mother hit him with her chest between his shoulder blades so hard that all the wind was knocked out of him as he became airborne, crashing into a large, thorny thicket and coming to rest heavily against the base of its stem.

The thorny bush was his saving grace, as the ostrich was unable to penetrate its spiked defences. It did not stop her, however, from circling the bush menacingly, trying to find a way in, stamping furiously on the ground, while attempting to make physical contact with her prisoner. Morris tried to sit up, but the thorns pinned him down. He was also so winded he found it better to lie still while he concentrated on gasping for air. While his revolver was lying tantalisingly close in the dirt under the bird's feet, he thought of playing dead, hoping the angry ostrich might leave him alone, but then suddenly he remembered David, lying motionless in the dust. He raised his head and to his relief saw David sit up and look around in a daze. But this movement also caught the attention of the mother ostrich, which instantly forgot about Morris and sprinted towards his hapless brother.

"David!" Morris tried to shout with whatever air had been spared in his lungs.

Fortunately, it was just enough to catch David's attention. With eyes wide in horror, he looked over his shoulder and saw the very angry giant bearing down on him like an out-of-control locomotive. He tried to stand, but his muscles had seemed to seize up, and his body was moving painfully slowly. Having landed heavily on his back, he, too, had felt the wind being knocked out of him and his head was spinning, a splitting headache pounding the back of his eyes. He'd barely made it onto all fours when the ostrich reached him, and without missing a beat, she stamped on his back with her foot so hard that Morris heard the thud and grunt clearly from where he lay pinned in the thorn bush. David went face-first into the dirt.

"David!" Morris yelled in horror. "Shoot it!" At the same time, he tried to reach for his revolver, but his arms were so tangled among the thorns he could not break free of its painful grip. Tiny, needle-sharp and twin-hooked thorns on thin, firm, but spring-like vines had found purchase on every bit of his clothing and exposed skin. Even his left ear was hooked on a double thorn.

David reached for the revolver on his hip, but the next footfall caught him on his right shoulder blade. Pain shot through his body at the impact, stars exploded in front of his eyes and his right arm went limp. Suddenly the bird was standing on top of him, stamping furiously with both feet. David started to black out. He knew he was in critical danger, and with every ounce of strength he had left in him he forced his arm down to his revolver. He found the handgrip of the weapon, and without hesitation he withdrew it only an inch from the holster, firing three shots in quick succession along the ground. He was in no position to aim the weapon; he just hoped he might scare the bird off. That was all he could wish for at that moment, as he was utterly helpless in the attack. Luckily it had the desired effect, and the ostrich ran off in the direction of Morris. Fortunately, she had a short attention span, and when the bird reached her nest, she stopped. Then, as though nothing had happened, she started to tend to the eggs, tenderly hooking her beak under the egg that Morris dropped and gently rolling it back to join the other eggs.

The bush went silent.

It took a good five minutes for David to stir. Very slowly and painfully he pulled himself up into a sitting position where he sat still for a few minutes, checking himself over, all the while keeping a sharp eye on the ostrich some thirty yards away and pointing his revolver vaguely in its direction. His head had cleared enough for him to take in the situation a little better. Morris was half-sitting, half-lying in a bush, both arms and one leg extended at odd angles. David noticed his brother was alive as there was some movement, but he was nervous to call out in case he attracted the wrath of the ostrich again, and this time he feared he would not survive the attack. His back, ribs, and arms were aching badly, and he was bleeding. The horses were nowhere to be seen, and he was very exposed in the open grassland.

The tree-line was only about ten yards behind him. He figured that, if he could just make it to the protection of the trees and bushes, he could circle around to Morris and help him. Too scared to stand up and attract the bird's attention, David began to crawl backwards towards the nearest tree. Once he was behind the tree, he cautiously stood up, his entire body telling him in no uncertain terms that he had come off second-best in the bizarre contest. Feeling a little more secure behind the bushes, he quickly made his way to where Morris lay, heart pounding at the thought of what he might find. By the time he reached the thicket, Morris had not moved an inch.

He was lying at an awkward angle and had his back to him, so David called out in a harsh whisper, "Are you alright?"

"Careful!" he whispered as loudly as he could. "This bush is a trap."

David looked at the vines on the bush and saw what he meant. There were hooked pairs of thorns all down the length of each vine, and it now made sense why his brother hardly moved, or why he did not come to his aid while he was nearly being trampled to death.

"I'll have to cut you free," he said quietly, pulling his knife from its sheath. It was going to be almost impossible to cut through from the rear of the bush, so David almost leopard-crawled to the front, where Morris had earlier made his undignified entry. The ostrich took little interest in the rescue operation and allowed David to work unimpeded.

Morris had thorns all over him. One vine had caught him across his face and was pulling at one nostril and one eyelid. His hands and fingers were well and truly hooked, making it nigh impossible for him to disentangle himself. What made the rescue all the more difficult was that the vines were tough and very springy. Each time Morris tried to move, the thorns would dig in harder and pull back harder, lifting his skin in little raised lumps and bumps. He was literally trapped by the thorns.

David also fell victim to the thorns as he cut his way through the vines, but unlike Morris, he always had a free hand and could disentangle himself each time a set of thorns gripped him. They stung as they pierced his skin, but he was so battered and bruised he ignored the pain. His first concern was protecting his brother's eye, and then he worked on one of his arms. Once that was free, he managed to retrieve Morris' own knife, which he handed to him. Now that they had two knives working on the vines, they progressed faster, and shortly Morris was free. David quickly led the way deeper into the bush to put some distance between them and the ostrich.

Morris gasped as he saw David's back. "Oh my Lord! Are you alright?"

"I think I may have broken a couple of ribs. Why, what can you see?" he said, as he tried to reach behind his back.

"Your shirt is shredded, and you're bleeding!" Morris lifted David's shirt up and checked his back over. "It doesn't look too bad, but you've taken a pounding. The cuts are not too deep. I don't think you need sutures, just a dressing," he said, relieved at what he saw.

"That's good. But now we really have a problem," David gently pulled his shirt back down. "The horses have bolted."

The severity of this suddenly sunk into Morris. "Oh, damn!" he muttered. "This is not good."

"It's bad, Morris." David was deeply concerned. He looked around the bush, hoping to see the horses. "Our rifles are with the horses, and we need them to hunt for food, and for protection. Not only that, I'm bleeding. If a lion or hyena or some other predator downwind gets a whiff of me, we're fair game."

"Let's get back to the wagons as quickly as we can," Morris urged.

The boys began their walk back to where they had left the team, David taking the lead and limping heavily, while Morris took the rear, taking care to watch behind them for potential threats, and perhaps a sight of the horses. The wagons were only about two miles away, but they were moving forward, and David estimated they would have to walk a further three or four miles to catch up with them once they reached the place they had left the wagons earlier that day.

By the time they intercepted the track where the wagons had passed, the sun was low on the horizon, and they were getting worried they might have to walk the last mile or so in the dark. Their luck was finally turning, however, as they soon came upon the laager, barely half a mile further on. Tebogo, to his credit, had heard the three shots fired at the ostrich in rapid succession and had realised that this was not a hunting shot, which was usually just a single shot. Believing his bosses to be in trouble, he had halted the caravan and formed a laager immediately.

As the boys limped into camp, the men gathered around them, clicking their tongues, shaking their heads, and murmuring among themselves in hushed tones. These increased in volume when they saw David's bloodied and bruised back under his torn and shredded shirt. He walked over to a water bottle and took long gulps before gently sitting on the ground, grunting heavily as he did so.

"What happened, Boss?" Tebogo asked with concern.

"A bird attacked us. You know an ostrich?" Morris asked, making the shape of an ostrich's head with his hand and mimicking it, with his arm held above his head, indicating the size of it.

"I know the one. Very dangerous. Shame, shame!" Tebogo sympathised.

"We thought we would take some eggs for the meal tonight, but the bird was too clever." Morris shook his head and went to find the medicine box so that he could tend to his brother. The men started to disperse silently.

"Boss?" Tebogo turned back to look at Morris. "Where is Splat and Bruno?"

"They ran away. We need to find them in the morning."

"We find them. Maybe they dead. I was seeing footprints of maybe six lions going this way yesterday," he said, pointing in the direction of where the boys had been hunting.

Morris was horrified. He realised how lucky they must have been. "We need to try and find them anyhow, because we need to find the guns."

"Morris," David winced as he looked up, "the bottle of morphine is in my saddlebag. Believe me, we need that morphine."

"Are you in that much pain, David?"

"No, I can handle this, this is nothing. But I never want to experience another scorpion sting again. We need that bottle."

Morris looked at his battered brother sitting in a bloodied mess in the dirt. He was stunned with this statement. "You'd rather take another beating like this than get stung by a scorpion?"

David stared at Morris for a moment, then nodded his head. "Sadly, I think so."

"You know what, David? I've had just about enough of this trek. I never imagined it would take so long and be so fraught with danger," Morris confessed.

"Me, too," David agreed, as he picked at a remnant of a thorn in his arm.

"This is ridiculous," Morris sighed, lowering himself and sitting in the dirt next to his brother. "To hell with Fort Salisbury. I say we stop in KoBulawayo and take our chances there."

David looked at Morris and nodded. "I'm with you on that, brother."

* * *

Sunrise saw the men, except for David and three of the drivers who remained in camp to guard the wagons and oxen, searching the African bush for the two lost horses. They found Bruno close to the ostrich nest around mid-morning, but Splat was never found. When they returned late in the afternoon, David was relieved to learn that they at least had one rifle, which meant they could still hunt for food. But he was very sad and disappointed that they had lost Splat, and the pain relief medication that he cherished in his saddlebag. He also realised that he had lost the telescope, too, but that could easily be replaced with another from their stock, provided that Morris would accept a small loss on their potential profits.

Losing one horse also radically changed the dynamics of the trek. Now only one person could scout ahead to ensure the track was passable, and hunting had to be done on foot, as the boys stayed firm in their resolve to hunt in pairs for safety's sake. Regardless of the setbacks, the journey continued, and David recovered from his injuries remarkably quickly.

When they estimated they had about one week to go before they would stumble upon the settlement of KoBulawayo, David and Morris set off to shoot an impala for the pot. They had not gone far when they came across a sight that troubled them deeply. They had noticed some movement on the ground a short distance away and so approached cautiously, fearing another nesting ostrich. However, it was not an ostrich, but a flock of lappet-faced vultures. Their heads did not have any feathers, but were covered with ugly pink skin, creased with wrinkles, that hung loosely over their heads and down their necks. They were feeding on a dead buffalo, their large, razor-sharp, yellow beaks tearing chunks of flesh off the beast in a ravenous frenzy. So frenzied were they in their greed that at times they would fight each other over the carcass. The buffalo's stomach had been split open, and one of the vultures emerged from inside the cavity where it had been feeding. The boys backed away very quietly, and quickly put some distance between themselves and the predatory birds. Only when they were well clear of the kill did they speak.

"I can't believe what we just saw," Morris whispered, even though he did not need to whisper.

"That was horrific!" David said in awe. "I thought an ostrich was dangerous; did you see the size of the buffalo they killed?"

"They must hunt in packs, like hyenas and wild dogs. Would you have ever imagined a pack of birds hunting animals the size of a buffalo?"

"I wonder what kind of birds those are. Hideous looking things! Matabeleland is getting worse the farther north we go. What other surprises will it throw at us?"

Little did they know that the vultures were scavenging on the remains of a buffalo that had recently been killed by a pride of lions, but lacking sound knowledge of the African bush, the sight had unnerved them. Nevertheless, they continued on their hunt, looking not just into the bush anymore, but also watching the skies for man-eating birds.

The very next day, another unexpected sight caught them totally off guard, leaving their hearts in their mouths and adrenalin pumping through their veins with fright. Morris and David were walking just ahead of the lead wagon, checking for obstacles in the track when, seemingly from nowhere, six Matabele men in full war dress appeared in front of them. There was no sound or movement to announce their presence; they simply appeared in front of the boys. They wore feathers in a headband on their foreheads, black and white dappled cowhide shields held steadfastly by their sides, and the sharpened edges of their short stabbing spears glinted menacingly in the sunlight. Morris raised his hand and motioned the lead herdsman to stop, but that was not necessary, as he had seen the warriors at the same instant and pulled the oxen to a halt.

Silence descended around them, but the Matabele men did not flinch, staring intently at Morris and David. This was not the case with the Tswana herders, who shifted uncomfortably behind them. The travellers soon realised, to their horror, that they had been surrounded by more men on their left and right flanks; once again, they had been totally oblivious of the warriors' arrival.

"We need to greet them," David said calmly to Morris. "Wait here and I'll approach them."

David, who was holding their only rifle, passed it to Morris to indicate he was unarmed, even though he had forgotten he had a revolver and a knife hanging from his belt. He strode off towards the obvious leader. He had heard that the Xhosa language that they had learned from their employee and subsequent friend in Port Elizabeth, Nguni, was somehow connected to the Matabele language.

When he was a comfortable distance from the warrior, he stopped and looked the soldier in the eye. He was as tall as David and much the same age, but had finely honed muscles under his skin, which indicated that he was extremely fit, and very strong.

"I see you," David said in his best Xhosa, bowing slightly as a mark of respect. When he looked up at the warrior, he was smiling with perfect white teeth. The attempt at his language seemed to go down well.

"I see you," the Ndebele soldier responded. It was not exactly the same language, but close enough for David to understand. He smiled back.

"My name is David Langbourne, and that," he said pointing behind him, "is my brother, Morris. We are very grateful that your king has granted us permission to pass through his land." He bowed his head again in respect.

"I am Ngwenya," the warrior responded authoritatively.

"The Leopard," David repeated, as he recognised the word. "You are strong and cunning. I did not see you approach; therefore, you walk as silently as the leopard."

"Yes, I am cunning, and I have stealth. And you are stupid," Ngwenya said bluntly, the smile gone from his face.

David was taken aback by his blunt response and instantly became anxious. He thought it best to agree with him; after all, Ngwenya had a small and well-armed group surrounding him. He wondered what he had said wrong.

"I am new to this land. I have much to learn."

"You must wait for the big bird to search for food. Never take her egg when she is watching you."

David looked at him in surprise, eyebrows raised. "You saw that? You were there?"

Ngwenya chuckled gently, and at the same time his impi of men did likewise. David was very embarrassed, and Morris, who could not hear the conversation, looked at all the men around him. His concern for their safety had been replaced by confusion, with a small dose of relief. David joined in the joviality, but he was shocked that these warriors had tailed them, and no one in their party was even slightly aware. His respect for the Matabele's bushcraft soared.

"I must agree, you are the leopard." David bowed slightly in genuine respect, which obviously pleased the warrior. "My brother and I would like to invite you and your men to sit with us and share some food," he offered, not really knowing what he should do in the current situation.

Ngwenya shuffled uncomfortably and looked over David's shoulder. "Who are they?" He avoided the invitation and curtly nodded his head in the direction of the wagons.

David looked over his shoulder and noticed the drivers had huddled closer together. "They are our drivers. We engaged them in Mafeking. They are from the Tswana tribe."

"I know their tribe," Ngwenya said with a scowl. "I do not eat with them." He was again blunt, and obviously not impressed with the Tswana people.

"There were no Matabele in Mafeking; otherwise I would have certainly engaged your people. Your tribe is fierce and strong, and we can understand each other," David continued his flattery. "And these people hardly talk to me."

Ngwenya grunted in disgust, but nodded his approval of what David had said. "You may proceed on your way, Shaya'nyoni. We will meet another day, I am sure."

"Thank you, Silent Leopard. Please pass our gratitude to your King Lobengula."

Ngwenya flashed his perfectly white teeth, obviously pleased with the honourable name this white man had bestowed on him, and the respect shown for his king. He nodded, and turned on his heel to walk away.

"Oh," David stopped him in his tracks. "How far is it to KoBulawayo?"

"Near-near." And with that, Ngwenya and his men silently blended into the bush and disappeared completely from view. When David turned to walk back to the wagons, Morris was visibly anxious.

"What was that all about?" he asked.

"Interesting," David scratched his head. "Very interesting. They've been watching us for a while now."

"Really? How long exactly?" Morris was intrigued, but kept nervously searching the bush around him, looking for hidden soldiers.

"He has given me an Ndebele name—'Bird-fighter'. I'm not exactly proud of that, to be honest."

Morris stood stunned for a while as the reality of the situation sunk in. David's altercation with the ostrich had happened a week or two ago. They had been totally unaware of being followed for all that time!

As the caravan continued on its journey, the brothers took the lead and walked ahead of the wagons, as was their habit, and David filled Morris in on what had transpired during his meeting with Ngwenya. It became plainly obvious that their Tswana crew were rattled by the encounter, constantly looking into the bushes, acting skittishly, mumbling to each other in their own dialect, and not really concentrating on the track ahead. David explained how he had handled Ngwenya, offering humility and respect, and inviting him to share some food with them. He felt they had got off on the right foot. He also told him that they were getting close to their first, and now final, destination of KoBulawayo.

"How much longer?"

"Soon, soon. We are near-near," David said with a smirk and raised an eyebrow, waiting for his brother's reaction to what Ngwenya had said.

Morris just rolled his eyes heavenwards. "Oh Lord, you know what that means in Africa, don't you?"

David chuckled. They had asked Nguni that question when they were in search of tobacco farmlands near Patensie more than a year ago. "Near-near" meant anything from one day to one week's worth of travel. Time and distance meant very little to the African people.

"We could be there tomorrow, you know?" David said, still smiling.

"Do you know that when we arrive in KoBulawayo, we will only be two-thirds of the way to Fort Salisbury?" A frown creased his forehead. "Never in my wildest dreams did I believe Africa was so huge."

"Not only that," David quickly added, "we are only in the southern tip of the continent."

That night, Tebogo approached the boys and told them that they were not happy being in Matabeleland among the secretive Matabele warriors, and wished to return to Mafeking. David convinced him that the leader of the impi had accepted his passage, and had even given him a Matabele name. This seemed to settle Tebogo a little, but not totally. They were so close now, and to lose their team of drivers would be devastating, so David felt he needed to negotiate with him.

Realising that Tebogo did not know that they had decided to stop in KoBulawayo and not Fort Salisbury, as was the original plan, he suggested that, if the drivers would get them as far as KoBulawayo, which was near-near, the brothers would release them from their commitment to get them to Fort Salisbury, and they would be welcome to return to Mafeking. Not only that, they would give them one wagon and enough provisions and maize meal, their staple diet, to last them the three-month journey back to

Mafeking. As the wagon would not have a heavy load anymore, they would only need a team of two oxen, but they could take four in the event of an accident. They would be paid half their agreed wages before they started on their journey southwards, and on arrival, they would need to return the wagon and oxen, together with a letter to Mr Weil, who would pay them the full amount remaining on their contract.

Tebogo took this offer to his men, who were delighted to hear the terms of the new agreement, although Tebogo hid their eagerness to go home and told David and Morris that they had begrudgingly accepted the offer.

Ngwenya had been correct; they were close to KoBulawayo. After they had in-spanned the oxen the following day and started once more on their monotonous march, the gentle morning breeze was blowing in their faces, and with it came a very slight scent of civilisation. As they had been in the bush for so long and not smelt any form of humanity, their sense of smell was very acute.

"Can you smell that?" David turned to his brother. "Smoke?"

"There's more; I can smell fried onions," David smiled.

"Near-near, brother. Near-near," Morris almost laughed.

"Take Bruno and go up ahead. I'll stay with the wagons," David suggested. "We will need to find a place where we can set up and secure the oxen before we all arrive."

"Good idea. Will you be alright here?"

"Absolutely. Good luck; find us a good spot!"

Morris saddled up and went ahead while David walked down the line of wagons, calling encouragement and beaming smiles at the drivers and stock handlers. It was obvious they were happy and pleased their destination was in sight. It was a happy day for the entire team.

They could literally smell KoBulawayo!

Chapter Four

KoBulawayo

Four hours after leaving David, Morris rode into the sprawling settlement of KoBulawayo, pulling Bruno to a gentle walk as he surveyed all that was unfolding around him. The dozen or so menfolk he came across were not particularly well presented, their clothes looking worse for wear, but to their credit, they made the most of what they had. Although wearing long-sleeved shirts with threadbare collars and smart trousers that should have been relegated to the dustbin years ago, some men had taken the trouble to wear a necktie and polish their shoes. Most gentlemen wore felt hats, sporting a colourful feather in the hatband, even though they, too, were very well worn and often bent out of shape, with some showing distinct discolouration from their owners having sweated in the blazing hot sun.

Morris had not looked at himself in a mirror for some time, but, if appearances were anything to go by, he was in no position to criticise anyone. Most of the men he passed acknowledged him with a nod, politely cast their glance in another direction, and continued with their daily business.

Morris soon came across a tacky wooden sign coarsely nailed to a tree that someone had written upon in thick white paint: "NO WAGONS PAST THIS POINT!" He was glad he had seen the sign and realised that he needed to ensure that David out-spanned the oxen well before they reached this part of the settlement. Most of the dwellings were tented, or a combination of tents and wagons. Occasionally he passed a circular, wooden pole-and-mud hut with a thatched-grass roof. The closer he assumed he was getting to the centre of the settlement, the more people he passed. But the number of huts and tents did not intensify, and he could easily see that there was plenty of space between the habitations. The dirt track was well worn, and there were paths to his left and right that led to more tents. The main track was slightly wider than two wagons abreast, but, apart from that, only tufts of dry, wild grass and drought-stricken, scraggly bushes and trees competed with the humans.

It was not a pretty settlement; in fact, the ugliness of Mafeking would rate better, many times over. Morris was very disappointed by what he saw, and he did not quite know how he would break the unwelcome news to David. The lie of the land was exceptionally flat, and there were no mountains as in Cape Town, but he noticed some massive, grey, granite boulders and outcrops not too far away. The vegetation had less than the colours of Mafeking, and none of the established buildings, hotels, or restaurants of Port Elizabeth. As far as he was concerned, KoBulawayo was the worst place on earth!

About a hundred yards ahead, a commotion erupted in the roadway. Men were gathered around a wagon that was stationary and attached to some agitated oxen that were bleating in protest. Even from where Morris was he could tell that the argument was becoming heated. Having been deprived of any entertainment for the last three months, he picked up his pace so that he could get a good view of the unfolding drama. He stopped and dismounted next to an older man, probably in his forties, quite tall and very thin, wearing a soft khaki hat with a very wide brim that flopped gently over his forehead and ears, who showed very little expression on his face.

"What's it all about?" Morris asked, without taking his eyes off the men up ahead. They were now starting to gesticulate wildly and shout loudly at each other.

"Oh, the usual," he replied casually. "That gent with the wagon," he pointed to a very thick-set man with a large, black beard, "has just arrived, and he didn't read the sign about not bringing his wagon this far up the street."

"Why can't you do that?" Morris was curious. "I noticed the sign; it was very obvious."

The man looked down at Morris. "You also new in town?" he asked politely.

"Just arriving now," he said with a smile.

"Abe Kaufman," the man said, and extended his hand to Morris. "Welcome."

"Morris Langbourne, pleased to meet you," Morris reciprocated.

"The street ends there, and it is too narrow to allow the wagon and all the oxen to do a U-turn," Abe continued. "It happens all the time. Now the trekker will have to out-span his oxen, turn the wagon around by hand, hitch the animals up again, and then go back to where the settlement starts so that he can find a place to camp. It always causes some aggravation when this happens. Sometimes the trekkers just listen to the Settlement Administrator and abide by his rules, and at other times there are some fisticuffs. Those can be fun to watch."

Morris shrugged and turned back to watch the argument. "Odd that people don't see the sign when they come in," he offered.

"It's more of a case that they can't read; that's all," Abe said nonchalantly. "You see that tubby man in uniform?" He pointed to a man fast becoming scarlet in the face as the shouting escalated. "He is the Assistant Administrator. He can't tolerate people who bring their wagons up here without reading his sign. He's quite funny to watch, actually."

After a couple of minutes, Abe seemed to lose interest in the commotion and began to walk back down the road. Morris followed him, deciding to keep the conversation going. He wanted to find out as much about their new home as possible, and Abe seemed quite comfortable chatting with him.

It turned out that newcomers did not need permission to set up their camp: they just found a suitable spot and settled there. Because they were so pleased to have found some form of civilisation, the trekkers simply stopped as soon as they arrived from Mafeking. They could not wait to set up a home—especially if they had womenfolk and children with them. As a result, the settlement was beginning to take on a rather long, thin shape in a southerly direction. Abe's home was about halfway between the beginning of the settlement where the road ended, and the sign that prohibited people from bringing wagons any further. Since his position indicated how long he had been at the settlement, it was clear that Abe had been one of the original settlers, a "pioneer", they called him. His home was right on the edge of the road, as were most camps, it seemed. When they arrived, Abe stopped and invited Morris to join him for a cup of tea, which he eagerly accepted.

It was a simple home, consisting of one tent and a wagon, the canvas cover of which had been torn and crudely repaired with thick stitching. His wife had taken his two children to the makeshift school not far up the road, so Abe set about boiling a blackened kettle over some smouldering embers that he stoked back to life.

An hour later, as Morris took his leave, he had learned that about half a mile beyond the place where the road ended, where he had witnessed the commotion earlier, lay the royal village of King Lobengula. Very few European people ever went there, unless they were invited by the king, or formally sought an audience with him, which he hardly ever gave. Thus only a handful of BSAC officials, a doctor, and the odd missionary had been beyond the village fortifications. The end of the road was also where the BSAC camp was located, and where any form of administrative offices of the settlement was situated; the Settlement Administrator, the mines registrar, and the doctor – all could be found there.

Abe also told Morris that some of the settlers had dug wells in their camps and he would be able to get water from them. He was welcome to dig his own well if he intended to stay put for a while, as there were no rules of any significance. To that end, he could simply find a suitable piece of land in the area to set up his "camp". He was expected to register his arrival with the Administrator, or his assistant, who were BSAC officials. Then again, many people had not bothered with this formality.

Since the general terms of the concession with King Lobengula were simply to "dig holes in the earth and take whatever shiny stones they find", many of the menfolk would leave their wives and children in camp to go prospecting for gold. Only if one of the men actually found gold would they stake their claim, then return to take their wife and children back with them. Some of the settlers' wives ran thriving little businesses from their camps, selling groceries, confectionery, and other edible delights, and Abe told Morris that his nostrils would have no difficulty in leading him to the better handicraft stalls. Abe also warned Morris that all goods were very expensive, as everything was in very short supply, with the average settler arriving with only one, or very occasionally two, wagons. Morris was embarrassed to tell his new friend that he had six wagons that were about to come rumbling into town.

Morris would be allowed to trade from his wagon if he wanted to become a merchant, but he would have to do so from within his camp, as wagons were not permitted into the main part of the settlement, the practical reason for which was now obvious to him. If he wanted to mine, then he was required to register his intent with the Administrator, and if he pegged a claim, that, too, would have to be registered. Abe had spent two years prospecting for gold and had come up empty-handed. He was convinced there was very little gold in Matabeleland, if any at all, and he was now broke and intending to return to Cape Town.

Armed with what he had learned over the welcome cup of hot tea, Morris bid Abe a gracious farewell, mounted his horse, and turned south to intercept David, whom, he felt, should be no more than about an hour away. Once he had met up with his brother, he excitedly told him what he had seen and learnt. He wasted no time in telling David to not expect anything exciting or lavish, and that Mafeking was a thousand times better. He was not sure, however, if their six wagons of general goods were going to work well in their favour, or if they would become their downfall. Certainly, from the information he had gleaned, they probably had the most significant and substantial business in the settlement; but there were simply not enough people to buy what they had.

Morris also wanted to locate their camp as close to the BSAC base and administration area at the end of the road as possible. He felt that that was where everyone tended to gravitate during the day, which would help their business immensely. Not only that, Julian Weil had mentioned several times that the BSAC was a fully-fledged company and that all their men and soldiers seemed to have a great deal of money to spend. Morris suggested that, as soon as they saw the first camp on the outskirts of the settlement, they should divert right, towards the east, and circle around all the campsites, then cut sharply left and get as close to the BSAC camp as possible.

Circling around the tents and mud-and-pole houses was easily accomplished, and when Morris had decided that they were level with the main camp, they turned left and pushed in again as far as they could. Once civilisation prevented them from going any further, they halted the wagons and formed their traditional laager. The handlers out-spanned the oxen and haltered them by their ankles nearby to graze on whatever dry grass they could find. Morris was happy with their location, as he could actually see the soldiers' camp not far ahead of them, a five-minute walk between some bedraggled trees and dilapidated tents.

Once their camp had been established, David called their men into the middle of the laager and, translating with the help of Tebogo, told them that both he and Morris were very happy with their service and that they would be free to return to Mafeking on the following day. In order to give them the wagon and oxen as agreed, however, they would have to unload one of them first. As there was nowhere to put the goods, he suggested they would need to build a wooden pole-and-mud hut. Tebogo said that the men agreed to delay their return by a few days so that they could assist with building the hut as requested.

Morris extracted a brand-new enamel bucket from one of the wagons and went for a walk around the settlement, looking for water and food, while Tebogo and his men started collecting wood for the hut's walls and roof structure. David, meanwhile, paced out a six-yard-by-six-yard square outline on the dry earth adjacent to the wagon laager and, with a spade, demarcated on the earth where the hut would be built.

When Tebogo saw the size of the outline, he was horrified. "This is too big, Boss!" He stood shaking his head, looking at the outline on the ground.

David was worried he might refuse to build it. "How big is the biggest house you have built, Tebogo?" he questioned.

"Hah!" he exclaimed, and indicated a size on the ground only a quarter of the size David had marked out. "And the house must be round. No corners."

No matter how hard David tried to convince Tebogo that he needed a house as big as he had drawn on the ground, and that it had to be square, Tebogo refused to have any part of it. In frustration, David agreed that if they would simply cut down enough suitable logs to build the house and pile them on the ground close by, he would let them go, and he would build it himself.

Three days later, Tebogo and all his men left the settlement of KoBulawayo with one wagon, four oxen, three months' worth of provisions, and a letter for Julian Weil, as had been agreed. When they left, the Langbourne brothers watched them depart as they stood outside their laager of five wagons. The contents of one wagon were piled on the ground in the middle of the laager under a canvas tarpaulin, and a mountain of logs outside the laager next to a square that had been etched into the hard, dry earth.

"I'm actually pleased to see the back of them, to be honest," Morris said, as their wagon disappeared through the scrub and bush.

"They weren't the most sociable bunch, but they got us here."

"We need to find more men to tend to the oxen, and quickly."

Morris stole a look at the beasts grazing quietly a short distance away. "David…?" Morris trailed off a question.

"Sure, I'll go and look for some people. Boy, I miss Nguni. He was amazing."

"Thanks." Morris smiled at his brother. "If we don't find men to tend to the animals we will have to sell them, and I really don't want to do that just yet, or our wagons will be stuck where they stand."

"I'll be back soon," David said, as he walked off towards the main part of the settlement. "Look after the fort for me while I'm away, will you?" he called back with a smirk and a wink.

It took exactly one week to build their warehouse. Standing beside their circular laager of wagons was a very rough-looking square building made of small tree trunks, branches, wire, rope, and a rough, thick layer of hardened brown mud that had been unceremoniously slapped between the gaps. The walls were about nine feet high and on top of the walls was an A-frame roof, clad in rusty, secondhand, corrugated-iron sheets. The apex of the roof was filled in with wooden poles cut roughly with an axe from the surrounding bush and, once again, all gaps were filled with mud. The only door and both windows were made of thin branches held together with nails and string that did not hinge open, but had to be removed completely to either enter the room or allow light in.

The corrugated-iron roofing was purchased from a friendly young man from Birmingham, England, called Philip Innes, who had a general hardware store on the west side of the settlement. His store was mostly out in the open and looked very scrappy, without any semblance of order, yet he knew exactly where everything was, and what he had in stock. David enjoyed walking around his yard and found many items of interest that he took a mental note of, should the need for such items arise one day. Phil was about ten years older than David, had fair hair and hazel eyes, and was a most interesting person, proving to be the source of a wealth of information on any and every topic that was discussed. And he was certainly not shy to strike up a conversation, causing David to really enjoy his company.

One morning, David picked up a rusted nail and studied it between his fingers. Philip went into an intense discussion on how nails were made, who invented them and when, and how best to use nails to get the most strength out of them. He advised David to never use new, shiny nails, as they had a reduced grip when nailed into wood; but rusty nails would grip the wood grain exceptionally well with their rough surface.

As for the corrugated-iron roofing, new sheets without holes or dents were simply not available. But Phil had enough secondhand sheets to suit David's purposes. They were in poor condition: dented, rusted through in places, punctured with holes from a previous building, and cost four times more than new sheets. But that was all there was available for about 600 miles around, so David bought what Philip had. The brothers needed a roof that would keep at least most of the rain out.

The boy's warehouse looked very ungainly, but for a building in the middle of the African bush, nestled between tents and wagons, it was a masterpiece of construction, and the brothers were very proud of it. It was by far the largest construction of its kind in the settlement and began to attract a lot of attention from curious settlers, who would constantly interrupt their work to have a friendly chat, introducing themselves, and asking what the brothers were doing and what they would be selling. Meanwhile, they were attempting in roundabout ways to steal a glimpse of what was hiding under the tarpaulins in the wagons. The settlers were a friendly bunch, Morris decided, and he tried hard to reciprocate the welcome friendliness. But he tended to become annoyed if he was busy trying to complete a task and was interrupted with their curiosity, which occurred fairly often.

David had engaged six young Matabele boys, sometimes referred to as Ndebele boys, to tend to their oxen. They were naked apart from a small animal skin that they wore around their waists. It became very obvious to both David and Morris that these Matabele lads had a strong affinity with animals, showing love and affection to each and every one of the oxen, chatting in their own language as if the oxen could understand them, and at times it almost seemed as if they did.

As soon as the brothers deemed the building to be complete, they began to make tables and shelves on which to store their stock, again using whatever they could find. The legs of the tables were made simply of wood cut from the surrounding bush. The table tops were thin branches tied together with string, and none of the tables were level or straight. This did not worry the boys one iota: all they cared about was that they could store their valuables off the ground and out of the rain, and that potential customers could view the stock that they had available.

By the time the warehouse was completed, there was not an ounce of fat left on their lean bodies. The muscles in their arms, back, and chest were sinewy and rock-hard. Morris always worked with his shirt on, but David preferred to hang his shirt on a tree and so developed a much bronzed look. They were both in excellent condition and thoroughly enjoyed the challenges of setting up their new business. David was exceptionally agile and fit, often bounding up their handmade ladder onto the rooftop with ease and confidence, while securing the iron sheets in place. The ladder was made of very coarse wooden branches with the bark still attached, and at one place, about halfway up, sprouted a small twig with green leaves growing off it.

Once the roof had been completed, one lone sheet of corrugated iron was left over. Reluctant to let anything go to waste, and as a finishing touch to their prized building, Morris took the sheet and laid it on its side propped up against some trees. Then, with a four-inch paintbrush that he purloined from their precious stock, he proudly painted the words "LANGBOURNE BROS." in a cheap, lime-based whitewash paint, a product he found in Phil Innes' yard.

Morris stood back and admired the large sign that now bore their family name. He was filled with pride and called David over to have a look at his handiwork.

"Very nice, Morris," he said. "But that's a very big sign, isn't it?"

"It's huge, and it's our name. The whole country will soon know we have arrived," Morris smiled. "It's so weird to see our name painted on a sign like that."

"Out here in the African bush, too," David marvelled, as he looked through the trees and shrubs at the settlement around them. He was also immensely proud of their achievements.

"I've been thinking," Morris said seriously. "Come, let's sit in the shade; I need to have an indaba with you."

The two walked over to a tree that gave some patchy relief from the sun and sat on two rocks they had placed there when they'd first arrived. The rock seats and the shade of the tree had become the central point of their camp, and it was where they would sit to drink a cup of tea or eat their daily meal. In African culture, to sit under a tree and have a very important meeting was called an "indaba", usually convened only by the chief of the village, and now Morris needed to have a serious discussion with his brother, and an indaba seemed to be a fitting summons. It was an unspoken, yet accepted understanding, that Morris was the chief of their little family in Africa.

"I've been thinking," Morris began as he took a seat on his rock. "I think we may have brought too much stock with us."

David cut him off with a chuckle, "Oh really? Funny you should mention that."

"I'm being serious. Everybody wants to know what we have in there," he said, pointing to the wagons. "And they are always commenting on how many wagons we have and how big our warehouse is."

"Well," David gestured around him, "have you noticed that nobody has more than two wagons, and we arrived with six?"

"Yes, that's what I was getting at. It seems we have enough stock to last us years." Morris paused to look at the wagons.

".... and years and years," David extended his brother's sentence. "Either Julian Weil took advantage of us, or you just got carried away in his warehouses."

"All right, brother, I realise that. But now we have to find a way to sell the stock as quickly as possible, and I have an idea." Morris looked at David from the corner of his eyes and smiled, cocking an eyebrow. David knew from that look that his brother was onto something.

"And what might that be?"

"We have five wagons there which we could sell for half as much again in KoBulawayo, even though they are worn down a bit."

"More than half as much what they cost us, at least three quarters more," David corrected him. "I've checked."

Morris shrugged his acceptance of what his brother told him. "Alright, so, regardless we will make money out of the wagons. Now, there are about a thousand people in this settlement, and next year there may be two thousand; who knows? But still, it is not really enough to allow us to sell through what we have and make a lot of money quickly. But," he paused for effect and straightened up, "there are about another thousand people in and around Fort Salisbury, about five hundred around Fort Victoria, and a couple of hundred in other outposts and regional mining areas like Belingwe."

"So?" David encouraged his brother to continue.

"Listen to me," Morris urged, shifting his weight on the rock. "What I think we should do is turn this building into a Sample-Room, not a warehouse. We need to display samples of the variety of stock we have. We must become a wholesaler, like Julian Weil, and also sell to other general dealers and traders. We should encourage traders to buy from us, and we must give them enough of a discount so that they feel they can make good money selling on to other people. Normal customers don't get any discount. I also suggest we offer our wagons to traders who want to trade far away from KoBulawayo. We lend them the wagons and the oxen, and they pay us for the use of them. There's a term for this, but I can't remember what it is," he added, scratching his head. "They can then stock up with our goods, take a wagon, and sell their wares in the various outposts and forts. When they come back we can resupply them once they have paid us in full for what they have sold; less their discount, obviously. If we do this, our stock will find its way all over the countryside, and not just lie here."

"Will there be enough profit for us doing it this way?" David questioned, but he already knew that his brother had done the arithmetic and that the answer would certainly be a "yes".

Morris just laughed. "Have you seen the prices of things here? Some stuff is as much as four to six times more expensive than what we paid Weil. We could discount a trader half the price and still make a fortune. Oh, don't worry: there is a lot of money to be made, make no error."

"So, how much do you want to charge for the use of a wagon? I'm assuming this includes six oxen with each wagon?"

"Oh, let's say about one-twelfth of the cost of the wagon?"

"That's expensive, don't you think? And why one-twelfth?" David questioned.

"Twelve months in a year." He shot a glance at David. "It is affordable for a trader who does not have a lot of money or a wagon and needs a start in life, but after only one year we would have paid for the wagon. After two years we would be able to buy a brand-new wagon just from the payment we get from it, and then we would have two wagons. Another year and we will have four wagons, then eight and so on. We could build a fleet of wagons in very little time."

David looked at him in silence for a moment. "How did you work this out?"

"It wasn't difficult," Morris stated simply. "From what I have seen, we will have to give these traders a lot of credit for the stock, as they certainly could not afford to fill a wagon, which is what they would want to do if they are going to travel so far afield. It also means we will not see any real profit from our business for a while. But when the money starts coming in, it will be worth the wait. And above all, it gets our business spread out around the country almost immediately. We will have to sign an agreement with each trader we engage so that they agree to our terms."

"Which are?"

"Basically that they agree to pay us the full amount for everything they sell at the price we agree when they return to re-stock, less their discount, and they agree to pay us for the use of the wagons at a set and agreed monthly rate. Also," he continued, "that they agree to return the wagon to us in reasonable condition and replace any oxen they may lose along the way. Finally, they must agree to pay us interest on an annual basis. Our guide will be the rate that the Standard Bank in Kimberley charges, but we will discount that rate to make it easier on the traders. In that way, we are making our money work for us, as well as our goods, wagons and oxen."

"I wonder if anyone will agree to these conditions?" David said slowly as he thought this through. "What you are telling me is that we will be making money in every aspect of our business, not just in profit through our sales, but by lending out our stock, wagons and animals?"

"If you want to be truly successful in business, you need to have every part of your business make money for you. Father taught us that, remember?" Morris smiled at David. "Just think, if we can lend out the wagons at a price, we won't need to feed the oxen, or employ people to look after them. Suddenly our oxen and wagons are now making us money, not costing us money, and the money we make from lending out our wagons is many times better than selling them outright!"

"But it's risky," David objected. "What if a trader runs away with a wagon full of our stock?"

"It is a risk," Morris defended his idea, "but sometimes you need to take a risk to succeed, and I think this risk is worth it. The BSAC act as a police force as well, so there is some form of law and order out there. You're good with words, David, so you will need to draw up all the documents and agreements. I'm good with numbers—you leave that side of it to me."

David shook his head in admiration at his brother's ingenious way of looking at business. He looked at the corrugated-iron roof sheet that proudly boasted the name of their business in stark white paint against the blackened and rusted roof sheet.

He nodded at it. "There's enough room under the letters to write 'sample room'. Have you got any leftover paint?"

Morris smiled broadly and stood up. David also stood up and followed his brother over to the new sign that so proudly bore their name. Morris dipped the paintbrush into his paint pot and wrote 'Sample Room' in bold letters under their business name. When he was done, they stood back to admire the work again. David insisted that "sampleroom" should have been one word, but Morris argued, not very convincingly, against it. After much discussion on the spelling of "sample room", Morris declared he was not going to change it for anything. As it was, he was just about out of paint. But to keep David happy, he agreed to put a dash between the two words with the last splodge of paint.

Just as he had finished the conciliatory dash, there was a loud bellow from behind them that made the boys spin around in fright.

"Langbourne Brothers?"

Standing before them were three BSAC officers. They all wore tight-fitting, dark-blue tunics with light khaki-coloured trousers. Each also had a leather sash over their right shoulder that wrapped around the left side of their torso. They wore slouch hats with wide brims, the brim above the left ear being pinned up. Morris froze in fear as his memory flashed back to a cold morning in Ireland when three police officers had found him working in a pigpen and had arrested him for questioning over the apparent murder of his employer. It turned out to be an accident, but the ordeal had shaken Morris to the core.

"Yes, sir," David freely volunteered, not noticing the fear that overtook Morris. "I am David Langbourne, and this is my brother, Morris," he pointed to Morris as he walked over to meet the men. "Please forgive my shirtless attire."

"Not at all. We can see you are hard at work," said the captain, who also appeared to be the highest ranking official. He did not smile or appear welcoming, rather ignoring eye contact, and, darting his eyes over the new building and their wagons, made no effort to hide what he was looking at. "So, what brings you to the settlement?"

"We arrived a week ago, sir," David began to explain. "We intend to trade as wholesalers to the general dealers."

"Has anyone granted you permission to build and trade here?" the captain scowled. David was a little taken aback at this response. It suddenly dawned on Morris that this captain was the same man he'd observed when he'd first entered the settlement. This was the man who was arguing with the illiterate settler who had brought his wagon too far up the street. Sensing that the situation was becoming a little uncomfortable, Morris felt he needed to pander to these officials and quickly took over from David.

"Not yet, sir," he said pleasantly enough. "We hope to seek permission and register our intentions with the relevant administration office once we complete our building, which we have done this very hour," he explained, pointing to their new building. Before the captain could argue with what he had said, Morris quickly continued, "We had considered approaching the administration office before we began building our Sample-Room, but felt it would be unfair to register our building without the administration office fully understanding how big it would be or what our intentions actually were. By completing the building first, we could invite the administration officers over for an inspection."

"Perhaps you would kindly do us the honour now, sir?" David continued, realising what Morris was up to.

"Perhaps I might," the captain replied, frowning as he stared at the building. "Ordinarily you should have registered your arrival and intent with us first. What if we decide to allocate you a different area?"

"Then we will relocate, sir," Morris said humbly. "We most certainly do not wish to fall foul of the administration. Please, allow us to show you around."

The captain nodded, and the boys took the three soldiers for a quick walk around the building, before removing the door to allow them access to the gloomy interior. Captain Seward was a short man with a stocky build that was enhanced by the extra weight he was carrying. He was about 40 years' old; had short, curly, dark hair; walked with quick, determined steps; and – the boys noticed – had a distinct limp in his left leg. His constant scowl and tight lips gave him the appearance of being angry, and that expression, coupled with his small eyes that never stopped darting from one place to the next, disconcerted the brothers.

Once inside, Captain Seward stood still and looked over the single room from top to bottom. The rickety tables and shelves stood silently, as if to draw attention for his inspection. One of the other officers stared up at the corrugated roof and spoke for the first time.

"How many African men did you use to build this place?"

"None, sir," David answered promptly. "My brother and I built it ourselves. We had a team of Tswana men with us but they refused to help us build it, so they have been given permission to return to Mafeking. Before they left, however, they cut some timber for us, which helped a great deal."

"Well, I'm not surprised they refused to help you," the captain commented as he shook one of the makeshift tables, which threatened to come undone.

"Why?" David asked.

"Because they will not build or live in square houses. Only round houses."

"What's the problem with square houses?" Morris queried, somewhat confused.

"Good Lord, boy!" Seward exclaimed. "You have a lot to learn about these people. This tribe believes that evil spirits live in the corners of a room. You will note that all their thatch houses that are made of poles and mud are circular so that the nasty spirits have nowhere to live or hide. Have you not seen that?"

"Well, now that you mention it..." Morris trailed off, stealing a nervous glance at a corner of the room.

The captain fired off another of his abrupt questions, which once again caught the boys off guard. "What goods will you be trading?"

Morris wasn't sure how to answer, but decided it was best to be very open with the man. "General goods, such as: soaps and detergents, cloth, some dry foods, household utensils, some clothing, kitchen equipment, telescopes…"

"Telescopes?" Seward interrupted, his dark eyes burning into Morris and his frown intensifying.

"Yes." Morris signalled to his brother. "David, please fetch your telescope for the captain to have a look at."

David bounded over to the rock he had been sitting on earlier and collected his prized possession, returning quickly to hand it to the captain.

The officer studied the shiny, smooth brass and the intricate stitching on the leatherwork. His frown instantly disappeared, and a small smile crept into one corner of his mouth. "Marvellous piece of workmanship. How do you use it?"

Visibly relieved, David began to show the captain how to pull the telescope to its full length, then the technique of bringing the telescope up to the eye while observing the target he wished to look at. All the while, the other two officers watched and listened to David in awe. Captain Seward pointed the telescope towards the doorway, and it did not take long for him to focus on an abandoned rusty bucket against a tent some 60 yards away. When he took the telescope away from his eye, he realised how much closer it had appeared to be through the lenses, and just how clear the vision was. He started to chuckle, which quickly became a raucous, infectious laugh that had everyone involuntarily laughing along with him.

"Marvellous invention! I love it. I must have one!" he exclaimed, handing it to one of the other officers. "Here, have a look." Suddenly all the joy in his face was replaced by the deep frown and thin lips once again. "How much are they?"

Morris was confused by the captain's rapidly changing facial expressions. "They sell for £12, sir, but we have a policy to offer goods to all members of the BSAC with a discount of one-eighth of the price. So in your case, that would come to ten pounds and ten shillings."

Captain Seward jutted his chin out, screwed his eyes up and glared at Morris. "You just worked that out in your head?" he snapped.

Morris looked at this strangely intimidating man with a confused look on his face, but David intervened. "He's good with arithmetic, sir. Extremely good."

The captain shot a stare at David, then suddenly the scowl disappeared, the smile returned, and he began to laugh again. "Well, I'll be. Fancy that," he chuckled, and turned back to Morris. "All right, young man, I will take your word for it. The moment you open for trade, please kindly reserve one of your telescopes for me, and be sure to let me know when it's available for purchase."

"Certainly, sir," Morris replied cautiously. "Your name, please?"

"Oh, my apologies. Captain David Seward, assistant to the Administrator, Dr Jameson."

"Dr Jameson!" David said excitedly.

"Indeed. Why, do you know him?" Seward asked, screwing up his face again in what looked like a flash of anger that overtook him.

"Oh no, but we met an officer as we crossed the Limpopo River some seven or eight weeks ago, and he suggested we make our acquaintance with the good doctor if we crossed paths with him."

"Who is this officer?" he scowled, his incomprehensible eyes burning into David.

"Captain Marcus Bailey, sir."

Once again the intimidating frown on Captain Seward's face faded and the thin lips were replaced with a broad smile. "A good man and a damn good soldier. I know him well." Seward puffed his chest out. "Shoots straight as an arrow, wins all our shooting competitions, he does. I will ask Dr Jameson to come by your shop in the next day or so. I think he will be quite keen to acquire one of your telescopes for himself."

"Thank you, Captain Seward," David acknowledged with gratitude.

"Good day to you, boys," Seward said as he turned on his heel to leave.

"Captain?" Morris quickly stopped him. "Do we have your permission to stay here and trade?"

"Of course, of course," he chuckled, smiling again. "Anyone who offers BSAC personnel preferential prices is very welcome. Heaven knows things here are frightfully expensive, and very scarce, as it is. Welcome to the settlement of KoBulawayo, boys. I'll register your arrival for you," the captain promised jovially, and then took his leave, the two other officers following him silently out of what was now officially the Sample-Room.

"What an odd fellow," Morris said softly to David as they stood in the gloom of their new building.

"Yes, most unusual. I couldn't quite work him out. Anyhow, we have permission to stay where we are, thankfully."

"Most peculiar," Morris stared out the doorway shaking his head, seemingly not hearing what David had said.

"I wish he would stop calling us 'boys'," David muttered. "So, we are giving the BSAC a one-eighth's discount then?"

"Yes," Morris snapped back into reality. "I've just decided that. One-eighth's discount to the military, and two-eighths to traders."

"Morris, you're not making this easy for me," David complained.

"Oh, it's easy, you'll work it out. Come on; we have some wagons to unload. We start trading tomorrow," Morris commented nonchalantly as he exited the building, with David following close behind and scratching his head in consternation.

"Oh, and how much did you pay Weil for the telescopes?" David suddenly remembered to ask.

"Three pounds and six shillings."

David stared at the back of his retreating brother and slowly shook his head. "And he's selling them for twelve pounds?" he mumbled to himself in disbelief.

Chapter Five

Trading

The following day was spent filling their new Sample-Room with various goods from the five wagons and the pile of stock stashed under the tarpaulin that had originally been on the sixth. Morris took charge of what was unloaded and in what order, with David happily carrying the goods into their new home. Each time Morris gave David something to put into the Sample-Room, he explained what it was, or what it was used for, how much it cost, and what the selling price would be. He also took this opportunity to call out the various prices using their "Black Rhino" code, and in no time the boys were comfortably using letters instead of numbers in their conversations. Morris worked carefully, but in a fashion that did not make sense to David. Not only was he giving goods to David, but he was also jumping around the various wagons and moving stock between them at the same time.

"What are you doing?" David asked his brother as he entered the laager.

"I'm trying to arrange the stock so that we have a sample of everything in the Sample-Room, but at the same time trying to empty at least one wagon so that it will be available should we find a trader who needs a wagon."

This explanation satisfied David, and he continued with the task he had been given, still watching Morris scurry around the wagons like a hungry rat looking for food. By late afternoon, one of the wagons was empty, the pile of stock on the ground no longer existed, and the Sample-Room was filled to capacity with at least one or two samples of everything that was stored in the remaining wagons. When David returned to the laager, Morris handed him two square boxes made of tin, both of which were painted in bright red, yellow, and blue circles, and each measuring about eight inches on each side.

"What are these?" David asked, tucking one under his arm and turning the other over with both hands, studying it carefully.

"It's a jack-in-the-box," Morris smiled. "We paid 'k' shillings and 'r' pence each for them, but we could sell them for 'b' pound and 'n' shillings."

"A jack-in-the-what?" David asked, creasing his brow. He noticed a small wire handle sticking out the side of the box.

"It's a child's toy. Here, give me that other one." Morris took the cube that was under David's arm. "Hold it like this," he demonstrated, "and crank the handle. It plays a tune."

David began to turn the wire handle on the box he was holding and, incredibly, the tune of "Pop Goes the Weasel" started to play in a plucky metallic tone. "By Jove, this is amazing, Morris! Listen to that tune, I know that song!" David looked up at Morris, smiling from ear to ear.

"Keep cranking the handle till the end of the song!" Morris urged, smiling sheepishly.

As the last note was struck, the lid of the box exploded open and a figurine of a laughing clown burst out of its captivity. David got such a fright he involuntarily screamed, opening his eyes so wide Morris thought his eyeballs would fall out. He dropped the box, took a quick step backwards and tripped over his own heels, crashing unceremoniously onto his rear in a cloud of dust. From there he sat and glared at Morris, who was laughing so loudly that he was forced to kneel down on the ground, tears streaming down his cheeks, before David, too, began to laugh. In no time at all, both brothers were sitting in the dust, laughing uncontrollably. Knowing that he had to save the jack-in-the-box before any damage could be done, Morris managed with a great effort to bring his laughter under control and picked up the toy. But almost immediately, he burst into uncontrollable laughter again, setting David off once more.

"Where the Dickens did you get that from?" David gasped through bouts of laughter. "That is so funny!"

"Weil had them in one of his warehouses," Morris explained, as he pushed the clown back into the box. "He had other toys for children, so I thought I'd buy some because I am sure no settler would have thought to bring toys, and I am certain there must be hundreds of children here," Morris giggled. "Brother, you were funny! I could watch that a hundred times over and never get tired of it," he said, as the boys stood up and dusted themselves off.

"Just you wait, I'll get you back, Morris," David laughed.

Suddenly a voice from behind them cut through their humour.

"I see we missed out on some hilarity."

The boys spun around to see Captain Seward, standing pompously in his tight-fitting uniform. Beside him was an important-looking man in a smart suit, clean-shaven, with a neat moustache and well-groomed hair.

"Captain Seward," David responded, still smiling and stifling a laugh that attempted to escape. "How good it is to see you again, sir."

"Boys, I'd like to introduce you to Dr Leander Jameson, Administrator of the settlement here at KoBulawayo."

"Ahh…" David's face lit up notably. "What a pleasure to meet you, sir!" he said, as he extended his hand to greet him. "I was hoping we would meet. My name is David Langbourne, and this is my brother, Morris."

Morris likewise shook hands with the doctor and introductions were made. Dr Jameson was a very welcoming man, and the boys instantly took a liking to him. He had an open face, a friendly smile, and was quick with his wit. They led Dr Jameson and Captain Seward to their Sample-Room and showed them what stock they were carrying. The BSAC men did not hide the fact that they were very impressed with the Langbourne range of products and the size of their warehouse.

"Captain Seward tells me that you will be giving members of the BSAC preferential pricing. Is that correct?" Dr Jameson asked.

"Indeed, that is correct, sir," Morris confirmed. "We understand that the BSAC does much to protect and serve the population up here, so of course we feel we should give something back in return."

"Well, that is very kind of you, Mr Langbourne," the doctor smiled. "I wish more traders in the settlement had the same sentiments as you two."

"We befriended Captain Marcus Bailey when we were in Mafeking,"

David changed the subject, "and we coincidentally crossed paths with him seven or eight weeks ago as we crossed the Limpopo River. In fact, he helped us cross the river, because – apparently –bets were placed in Mafeking that we would not make it across the Limpopo, and he wanted to make sure we succeeded." David flashed a smile.

"Yes, Captain Seward mentioned to me that you knew Marcus."

"I had the misfortune of experiencing the angry end of a scorpion on the trek. When we met Captain Bailey at the Limpopo, he very kindly gave me his supply of morphine in case something like that happened again."

"Oh, yes, he mentioned that to me as well. I have replaced his supply already," the doctor smiled. "Scorpions can be a bit of a bother, I believe."

"A bit?" David laughed. "It's the worst experience I have ever endured. Unfortunately, a few weeks later, an ostrich attacked us and my horse bolted. Never found the poor animal again. The problem is, the bottle of morphine was in the saddlebag, so I lost that, too. I was wondering if you would be so kind as to allow me to purchase some more from you?" David asked in all sincerity.

Dr Jameson was very amenable to helping them out, and readily agreed to dispense a little medication for him. David's luck was with him, as Dr Jameson was about to run out of the medication, and was waiting for a re-supply to come from England. He explained that King Lobengula suffered from dreadful gout, and he was the main consumer of his supply. As a result of the pain relief the king experienced from the morphine, he was able to remain on good terms with him.

Dr Jameson was curious about their ostrich incident, so both Morris and David related the somewhat embarrassing event to both officers. Captain Seward appeared relaxed and chuckled along at their misfortune. Dr Jameson was more curious to have a look at a telescope. When he saw a sample, he agreed to purchase one without hesitation, as Jameson felt it would serve his purposes extremely well in the bush when he was scouting for danger and looking for direction. The boys agreed to hand-deliver two telescopes the next day, one each for Captain Seward and Dr Jameson, and at the same time, the doctor would dispense the morphine. As they were about to leave, Captain Seward asked what the boys were laughing at when they arrived.

"Oh, I showed David a jack-in-the-box we have for sale." Morris smiled and began to giggle again as he recalled David's face when the clown jumped out on a spring.

"What is a jack-in-the-box?" Captain Seward enquired, screwing up his face with a stern scowl as he so often did.

"It's a child's toy, a box with a handle on the side and—"

Dr Jameson quickly cut Morris off. "Show Captain Seward what it is, Mr Langbourne. It's much better to show him than to explain it," he said with a wink that only Morris could see.

"If you believe so," Morris said cautiously to Dr Jameson.

"Oh, I insist. Please," Dr Jameson encouraged, nodding his approval with a candid smile. He obviously knew what a jack-in-the-box was.

"Certainly," Morris responded with a knowing smile of his own. David passed the toy over to Captain Seward. "Here, hold this box firmly and crank this small handle."

The captain raised his eyebrows as he began to crank the handle. As the tune began to play, he started to smile with his thin lips. "What an amazing toy this is," he gushed. "It makes music. I recognise the tune!"

"Play it to the end," Dr Jameson insisted, and the captain responded by cranking faster.

Suddenly the clown burst out of the box. Captain Seward got such a fright that he let go of the box, shaking his hands wildly as if a battalion of army ants had infested his fingertips. At the same time, there was a look of utter horror on his face, and the weirdest high-pitched scream exploded from his throat. David reacted fast and caught the jack-in-the-box before it hit the ground and Dr Jameson threw back his head, letting a loud belly laugh escape. He doubled over and laughed even harder when Captain Seward's face went scarlet with embarrassment. David and Morris weren't sure whether they should laugh or not, and there was a brief moment when only the doctor was laughing, but only a brief moment. The boys could not contain themselves and joined in. Realising that this was all done in jest and no malice was intended, Captain Seward saw the joke and he, too, joined in the good-natured hilarity.

The jack-in-the-box was unintentionally a huge icebreaker for the boys, and the events of that day ensured a very cordial friendship among the BSAC and the Langbourne brothers. With characteristic embellishment, a skill that Dr Jameson was quite good at, he made equally sure that his assistant's embarrassing mishap was retold in the officer's mess. Morris and David Langbourne's business thus became well known around the settlement in very short time. Trade started in earnest, with men and women of the settlement visiting their Sample-Room in a constant stream.

Although the settlers brought a lot of curiosity as to what the Sample-Room might contain, the sales were not particularly good at first. After the first week, however, their sales started to pick up, which made Morris very happy and relieved. He insisted that they never sell an item in the Sample-Room because that was exactly what it was – a sample – but rather from the stock on the wagons, and so kept the Sample-Room item on permanent display.

"If the customers can't see the item, we can't sell it," he would tell David over and over, and he was very strict with this rule.

"But what if it is the last one?" David objected.

"We just tell the customer we will order another one for them. Unless it is a very slow-moving item and we never want to stock it again. Then, by all means, sell it off."

It was a quiet Wednesday afternoon, and there had not been a customer for over an hour. Morris thought that now would be a good time to try and find some traders that might want to take up his idea of setting them up for wagon trading. He left David in charge of the shop and walked off across the tented settlement to see if the first man he met, Abe Kaufman, would be interested.

Morris found him at his campsite, sitting in a rickety chair at an equally rickety table, combing through some dirt that he had emptied from a tin pail that lay on its side at his feet. When he saw Morris approach, he stopped what he was doing and welcomed him with a warm smile and a firm handshake. Abe called to his wife, who emerged from the wagon looking rather dishevelled and frustrated, a thin film of perspiration glowing off her forehead. He introduced her as Sharon, and she welcomed Morris warmly, offering to pour him some coffee. Morris thought she was a lovely lady: slender with long legs, black glossy hair down to the small of her back, and sharp facial features. She also had a friendly smile, with bright blue eyes that sparkled against the faint blush of pink on her cheeks.

Sharon pulled two empty wooden boxes up to the table, where she asked Morris to sit while she prepared the coffee. Abe, meanwhile, told

Morris that he had just returned from a week's worth of prospecting to the east. He had given up on gold and was now looking for gemstones. He had found nothing out there, but what he did think promising he brought back in sacks to go through with a fine-tooth comb, which was what he was doing at the moment.

"And any luck?" Morris asked cautiously.

"You must be joking!" he laughed. "There is absolutely nothing out there. Just dry, parched land, with the odd Ndebele village and a bit of game. No, I think Cecil John Rhodes was dreaming when he thought this country had vast mineral wealth."

Sharon, with enamel cups of piping-hot black coffee, joined the men at the table and listened in on the conversation quietly.

"I've just about had it with this country. This trip I have just returned from was my last. Sharon runs a small business from here, mending clothes and cutting ladies' hair, and if it weren't for her we would be stone-broke," he said in resignation. "We are planning to return to Cape Town shortly."

"I've come to offer you a proposition," Morris said seriously. Both Abe and Sharon Kaufman looked at Morris curiously. "My brother and I have set up shop on the east side of the settlement, not far from the BSAC camp. We brought with us six wagons of stock and supplies. Now that we have put most of our stock inside the Sample-Room we have a spare wagon. Instead of selling it off, we would like to see if someone like you would entertain the idea of becoming a wagon-trader, buying our stock and borrowing a wagon for a small fee, and then selling to settlers in others settlements, forts, or mines."

Abe put his hand up to stop Morris. "Hold on. I have no money at all. I couldn't even afford to buy a bucket of stock from you, let alone an entire wagon-load."

"I'm aware of that, Abe," Morris replied calmly. "This pertains to most of the people who live in this settlement, from what I can see. No, what I'm suggesting is that we give you whatever stock you'd like on credit. You only need to pay us after three months, so we would expect you to return after three months."

"And what if we cannot sell any of the stock we choose?" he interjected.

"We will take it all back, very simple. But we will tally up what you do sell when you return and you pay us for that, less one-quarter of the full price, which is your profit."

"And the wagon?" Abe pressed.

"We will charge you for the use of it. The cost will be one-twelfth of the normal cost of a wagon per month and includes six oxen to draw it. Unless, of course, you already have a wagon." He nodded at Abe's wagon with the big tear in the canvas. "Then you can use your own wagon."

"That won't work," Sharon cut in for the first time. "I need that wagon to run my little businesses."

"One-twelfth of the cost of a wagon per month, you say?" Abe turned back to Morris.

"Yes, you just have to return it to us when you are finally done, in much the same condition we gave it to you."

"Sounds fair," Abe said softly, and looked at his lovely wife. "Ever think we would be traders?" he asked.

"It will certainly be better than being prospectors, that's for sure," she murmured.

"You know I can't pay you until I get back from trading?" Abe continued.

"Yes, I'm well aware of that. But I trust you, Abe, and trust is important to me. Sharon," Morris turned to the lovely lady on his left, "you say you repair clothes. Do you make clothes as well?"

"Yes," she smiled, "but not in KoBulawayo. I'm a good seamstress, but you cannot find decent fabric in this place."

"Well, we have an entire wagon full of bolts of material. And some really good quality stuff, too. Why don't you two come down to our place and have a look at what we have?"

Sharon Kaufman began to smile, her pure white teeth glinting in the sunlight. She realised that their difficult life in Matabeleland was about to take a very positive turn for the better. Abe began to look a little uncomfortable, looking at his wife and Morris, trying to find something to say. He did not need to say anything, as Sharon seemed to be taking over the discussion.

"Come on, Abe, let's go over there now," she beamed. "Are you alright with that, Morris?"

"Absolutely!" Morris said as he stood up, and the two walked off chatting happily, while Abe followed behind, mumbling indistinctly to himself.

* * *

Three days later, as Abe set off for a mining area near the village of Belingwe with one wagon loaded with Langbourne Brother's stock and six oxen with which to pull it, Sharon began making dresses for the womenfolk of the settlement. After another two weeks had passed, Morris had hired all five wagons to some of the Indian and Greek communities, who eagerly took off into the heartland of Matabeleland, going even as far as Fort Salisbury. David drew up the agreements and the various terms to suit the wagon traders, while Morris recorded the inventories that went with each of them. The Sample-Room was functioning just as Morris had wanted, with traders and the general public selecting their goods from the displays, and with the saleable stock being retrieved from storage.

Business was going according to plan and was booming. It also seemed to apply to Sharon Kaufman, judging by the numerous visits she made to the Langbournes' to buy more fabric and pay for the fabric she had previously bought on credit, using the money she earned from her customers. The next unforeseen problem the brothers came across was that, with all the wagons in the countryside, a great deal of unsold stock remained behind that could not be stored in the Sample-Room. David then hired a team of men to chop timber for him, and another warehouse of equal size to the Sample-Room was hurriedly constructed by Morris and David as time allowed. Until it was completed, all their stock was stored under tarpaulins on the ground beside the Sample-Room, which made business irritatingly difficult.

It was a very busy time for the young men altogether, but they excelled in their work and loved every moment, revelling in a strong sense of achievement at the end of each day. Once the warehouse was complete and a routine had been established, Morris and David went down to Sharon Kaufman's tent and asked her to give them each a haircut so that they would look presentable to their customers. With their new tidy and fresh look, clean-shaven and well presented, they served their customers and engaged easily with them. David's happy and positive outlook made him well liked by their customers, and as a result, he performed brilliantly in the art of selling. The brothers' all-round teamwork and eagerness to serve, the good variety of stock, and the genuine welcome they provided their customers gave them a remarkable reputation. Sales were strong, profits were healthy, and the boys had never been happier.

* * *

It was the end of June, and winter had set in. The days were comfortable, but the nights had a bite to them. The boys had moved their bedding into the new warehouse and slept there at night, in the midst of their dwindling stock, where it was a little warmer. They had been trading for almost three months now, and it was becoming increasingly evident that they already needed to buy more goods from Julian Weil. The hardship and monotony of the journey to KoBulawayo still weighed heavily on their minds, and therefore, the subject was avoided.

That night David finally broke the silence on the subject. They had just crawled under their blankets and blown out the candle. It was pitch-black in the warehouse, and David was thinking about how he and Morris had shared a room in Ireland. David had slept against a wall in Ireland and decided to continue the tradition in Africa. That evening he had noticed that the warehouse stock was looking extremely depleted.

"You know we will have to get re-supplied soon, don't you?" he spoke into the darkness.

"Yes. I can't bear the thought of going back, though," Morris sighed. "We could always sell whatever we have and return to Cape Town and start afresh there,"

"No, we are making very good money here. We could never do this in Cape Town. If you want me to go back to Mafeking, I'll be alright with that," David suggested. He was not too concerned about going back, as he loved the bush. He loved doing business and mixing with the community, too, but the African bush had a very special appeal to him.

"I've been giving this day a lot of thought, actually," Morris said, and David heard him shift into a sitting position in the dark. "If you don't mind, I think you are better suited to go back. You know the bush better than me anyhow. Take Bruno, and perhaps accompany some of the BSAC men whenever someone goes back to Mafeking. I'll stay here and look after the business."

"Alright," was all David needed to say.

"And then I would like you to do something else."

This time David sat up, wondering what Morris was going to come up with. "Go on," he encouraged.

"When you get to Mafeking, you must arrange another six wagons of stock, similar to what we brought with us the first time. Then I'd like you to catch the train back to Port Elizabeth."

"Port Elizabeth?" David exclaimed excitedly.

"I thought you'd like that idea," Morris chuckled. "Yes, go back there and catch up with our friends. But what I would really like you to do is find Nguni, and ask him if he will come back to Mafeking with you and lead the wagons for us up to KoBulawayo. That way you won't have to spend a gruelling three months trekking here; you can get back more quickly. We both trust him implicitly, and I need you here."

"I must say I do miss him," David said. He was getting really excited at the prospect of returning to Port Elizabeth and having a top-quality meal at The Grand Hotel, catching up with their good friend and manager of the Standard Bank, Jack Shiel, and even visiting their ex-landlady, Sonja Du Plessis, for whom he had a very soft spot.

"If Nguni can lead the wagons up here, there would be no need for you to follow them up. Let's assume it takes you two weeks to get to Mafeking on horseback, another two weeks to get to Port Elizabeth and back by train, and then another two weeks to return from Mafeking. You'd be away for about six weeks in total."

"So when do you want me to leave?"

"The sooner, the better. We need to find a group of BSAC soldiers you can join. I certainly think it would be ill-advised for you to do it alone. The way I work it out, we should have our resupply within four months of you leaving for Mafeking, and even that would be cutting it a bit fine in the light of our current stock levels."

David sat in silence for a while. His mind was racing with thoughts of what he had to do in Mafeking. "I'm assuming you want me to take the cash and cheques with me and bank them when I go through Mafeking?"

"Yes, but before you do, I need you to visit Gerran's Coach Builders and organise the wagons. Then get someone to put your purchases near the wagons so that you can load up as soon as you return from PE. Whatever you do, don't let anyone load the wagons when you are not there. Don't trust anyone. Check all the stock into the wagons personally. If things don't go according to plan, for example, if Nguni won't help, use your best judgement; I certainly can't help you from here. It's all your decision as to what happens from the moment you leave. I know you'll manage well."

"Thanks for your confidence in me, Morris," David smiled in the dark.

He was touched that his brother thought so highly of him. Morris seldom gave compliments, and never undeservedly. "Morris, you know that if I buy and stock six wagons, we may not have enough money. It took more than half of we had to bring the first six wagons up here."

"I have thought of that. But what you take down from here, our profit, so to speak, should be adequate."

"A lot of our profit is still unrealised and out in the bush somewhere with our traders. Do you reckon we have enough cash from warehouse sales to make up the difference?"

"Yes, I believe we will have enough, don't worry."

"Alright, if you say so," David shrugged. He knew better than to argue with his brother over money and mathematics.

"Oh, one more thing," Morris paused. "I'm going to write a letter to father and the family, which I need you to post as soon as you can. I'm going to ask Father to take Louis and Harry out of school at the end of the year and send them here. They are old enough now. Are you alright with that?"

"Sure!" David exclaimed. "What a sterling idea!"

"If we get any busier, we will need help, and as it is, I don't like the idea of working the shop on my own, or, for that matter, you going back to Mafeking on your own. It's not going to be easy to organise everything by yourself. In any case, there is no better help than family, not so?"

"Absolutely," David eagerly agreed. "I miss them anyhow. But please do me a favour, Morris, please don't tell Father I was nearly killed by a bird," he chuckled.

Morris started giggling in the dark. "Don't worry, I won't. Now go to sleep. See you in the morning."

Morris fell asleep very quickly, but the excitement of being able to visit old friends and familiar places kept David awake for quite some while.

In the morning, before most of the settlement began stirring and lighting the breakfast fires, Morris and David walked over to the BSAC camp and found Captain Seward strutting about, inspecting wagons and horses, having just hoisted the company flag on the flagpole in the centre of the parade square. He always looked busy, and he reminded the boys of a bumble-bee, constantly inquisitive, always on the move, with his short legs setting a quick pace. He was happy to greet them so early in the morning and advised them that there was indeed a small column of horsemen, "The Mail Run" he called it, leaving for Mafeking within the hour. Neither of the brothers had expected to leave so soon.

During that hour, David had Bruno saddled, changed into his khaki bush clothes, packed a small bag of town clothes, and put his trusted Martini Enfield rifle into his saddlebag. Along with three months' worth of cash and cheques that Morris handed him in a grubby envelope and, most importantly, his telescope and a small bottle of morphine, he was set to go.

As the brothers led Bruno to the parade square, Morris handed David the letter that he had written to his father. It was in an unsealed envelope. "I wrote that in haste, and in point form, because I have not had sufficient time, so I have not sealed the envelope. I suggest you write a proper letter using some of my points on your journey. I have no idea where Father has moved to, but you will see I have addressed it to the old cottage. I'm sure someone will forward the letter to him."

Previously they had sent a fairly large sum of money home to the family in Ireland, part of the proceeds of the sale of their small, but prosperous cigarette business, with instructions to find a more comfortable place to rent. The brothers had no idea, therefore, where their family might have moved to, assuming that their father had even received the money. At the time of leaving Ireland, their family had been living in a dilapidated old cottage in a farmland district near Dublin, and conditions had been very uncomfortable and poverty-stricken.

Another request they had made of their father on sending the money had been to put their two younger brothers in a decent school. Because communications were tediously slow, with the mail taking about three months just to get to England, they had no idea if their money and requests had reached their father at all. There were four men on the parade square standing by their horses when they returned, and Captain Seward was fussing around them, issuing last-minute instructions and fretting over the horses and saddlebags.

"Are you ready to go, Mr Langbourne?" Seward motioned to David when he approached.

"Yes, sir, as ready as I'll ever be," he smiled back.

"Good show. All right, gentlemen, safe travels. Away with you."

Morris watched David mount Bruno and settle into his saddle, then stepped forward and extended his right hand. "Go well, brother."

David leant down and gave Morris' hand a firm shake. "Thanks, Morris. Look after the fort for me, will you?" he said with a broad smile and a wink.

With that, the troop of men took off at a gentle trot, David waving a salute over his shoulder as they disappeared from view. Captain Seward looked at Morris, who was staring at the spot where David disappeared and detected a bit of sadness in his face. He felt strangely sorry for this young boy.

"Would you like to join me for a cup of tea in the officer's mess?" he asked Morris, snapping him back to reality.

"I'd be delighted, sir," he smiled. "If it is allowed, that is."

"If you're with me, it's allowed. Come on; I'm thirsty."

"Thank you very much, Captain Seward."

"Good!" The scowl disappeared instantly and was replaced with a friendly smile and a chuckle. Morris' heart warmed. He hoped he had found a friend.

Chapter Six

Trading

The BSAC men set a reasonably hard pace, taking their horses to a gentle trot on flat ground, walking them down hills, and dismounting on steep climbs to keep their equestrian transport as fresh as possible. They took a route to Mafeking that was unfamiliar to David, as the journey he had taken previously was with a convoy of wagons favouring level ground, whereas on horseback the route was a lot more direct. They would stop for short breaks under the shade of trees wherever possible, or where they crossed flowing streams to water their horses.

David found the first three days exhausting and rather uncomfortable, but he never complained. By the end of the fourth day, he had settled into his saddle and the way of the ride. They expected the ride back to Mafeking to be about eighteen days in total. Whenever they stopped for a rest, David would pull the telescope from his saddlebag and scan his surroundings, looking at rock formations, birds, or simply trees. If there were an animal in sight, he would study its behaviour intently, always making new and intriguing discoveries that thrilled him.

The four company men were slightly older than David, but friendly to the lad. Since they all had the same rank of corporal, seniority was based upon the time that they had been employed with the company. Their leader for this expedition was also the tallest man; the tallest man, in fact, that David had ever met, and he went by the name of Grant Dent. He was well over six foot tall with short, dark hair, and sporting a neatly trimmed goatee on his chin. As well as being very tall, he was well built, with a large chest and broad shoulders. Although soft-spoken, he was a natural leader, and any time Grant would walk up to a group of people they would take note. David suspected that even if Grant had been of a junior rank, he would still have been their leader, as he somehow commanded respect, even though he did not seem to look for it. Grant had a sharp mind and an uncanny ability to make quick decisions that his fellow officers never questioned. He had a very open and friendly face that people warmed to easily. He was, in David's mind, a gentleman, and the typical gentle giant.

The three other soldiers in the group were built similarly to David: slender, with tough muscles ready for hard work. They were fit and bronzed and, in usual military fashion, were dressed exactly the same. It was probably because the soldiers were of the same rank that they called each other by their first names. Formalities were abandoned once they left camp, and the small group of five men spoke among each other mostly at night, around the campfire. Riding in single file, made it difficult to hold a conversation during the day, so very little was said while they were on the move. At around noon on the fourth day, the men were resting under the shade of a tree when David pulled out his telescope and scanned a grassy hill off to the east about fifty yards away. He never knew what he would find, but looking through the lenses always took him into a new and fascinating world, a world only he could see. On one occasion he had studied a tiny tree that had started growing on the side of a rocky cliff, so high up that no man or animal would ever be able to reach it. Yet, through the lenses, he seemed to be sitting right beside it, admiring its perfect leaves, bent trunk, and the gnarled roots that clung desperately to a crack in the rock. He had looked at the tiny, tenacious tree for ages, lost in a world of his own.

On this occasion, however, he had noticed a couple of small birds that were too quick for him to observe closely, when a slight movement in the grass caught his attention. He watched it for a while, but could not quite work out what it was. He continued to watch the swaying of the grass until he saw the movement again. Gently lowering the telescope, he called softly over to Grant, who was slouching against the trunk of a tree with his eyes closed.

"Grant, would you mind coming over here, please? I need to talk to you." Something in David's voice alerted Grant, who casually stood up without question and sauntered over to where David was, before sitting on the ground next to him.

"What's up, David?"

"I believe we are being watched by some Ndebele warriors, over there." He nodded in the direction of the grassy hill.

Grant carefully looked at the hill but could not find anything out of the ordinary. "What am I looking for? I can't see anything unusual."

"You won't see anything without a telescope. They are masters of camouflage and stealth. I spotted one of the feather headdresses the impi wear. I can't see any others, though. My brother and I came across some impi when we travelled to KoBulawayo. They had been following us for a week, and we had absolutely no idea."

"Right-oh," said Grant softly. "We had better get a move on then."

"Are they dangerous? Will they attack?" David asked calmly.

"No, I doubt it," Grant said as he stood up and made a show of dusting his trousers off. "They are probably just spying for the king, but I don't trust them. There are a few factions in the tribe that want us out of their land, but King Lobengula is holding them back because of some pact he signed with Cecil Rhodes. I'm not sure how long the king can control them, though. In any case, I don't like being watched. Well spotted, David." Grant stretched his arms and pretended to yawn.

"Right, lads, time to go. Mount up quickly," he said calmly, but authoritatively, and walked over to his horse.

The men, sensing some urgency in his voice, did not question him, and instantly did as they were bid. For the remainder of the day they rode hard, only stopping to set up camp as the sun was touching the horizon.

At that time, the Transvaal Republic, or Zuid-Afrikaansche Republiek, was an area controlled by former Dutch and French Huguenot settlers, who had broken away from the British Cape Colony to seek their independence, and whose authority was bounded to the north by the Limpopo River. When the men crossed the river, and entered the Transvaal at almost the exact spot where David had passed several months before, Grant seemed to relax visibly. The subtle tension had rubbed off on David, so he, too, felt more relaxed once they had crossed into the Republic. The rest of the journey was uneventful, and after another 12 days of riding they crossed the western ZAR border into Bechuanaland, then a protectorate of the British Empire, and entered the dry, forlorn-looking town of Mafeking.

David parted company with the men just before they reached the BSAC camp, shaking hands with them all in a hearty farewell. He had forged a strong friendship with Grant and hoped they would cross paths again in KoBulawayo. Not wishing to impose on Julian Weil and his lovely wife, he sought out a homestead that offered temporary lodgings, which Grant had recommended as quite comfortable and reasonably priced. Once David had checked in, he took a bath in light-brown, tepid water. Ignoring the murky colour of the water, he was very grateful to be able to wash all the dust and dirt off his body. Without wasting any time, David then changed into more formal clothing and went straight to Julian Weil's place of business, where he found Ian Taylor duly tending to the store.

Ian was pleased to see David, and to learn that they had made it to KoBulawayo relatively incident free. While they were talking and exchanging pleasantries, Julian walked in from the street and he, too, was surprised but pleased to see David.

"Welcome back, David. How wonderful to see you!" he said without smiling, as was his wont. "You made it there all right, I trust?"

"Yes, indeed, thank you," David acknowledged. "Unfortunately, it would appear you lost your bet with some of the BSAC officers." David could not help but get that dig in.

Julian squirmed but flashed a rare smile. "I must admit I had my doubts, but well done to you both: a masterful achievement. Nevertheless, I certainly did not expect to see you back in Mafeking so soon."

David accepted his congratulations and then continued, "About three months ago we sent our Tswana men back with one of our wagons…"

"Yes," Julian interrupted him. "It arrived a fortnight ago, together with your men."

"I hope you did not mind us imposing upon you like that, but we were at a bit of a loss as to how to deal with the situation. I'm assuming Morris' letter explained what occurred?"

"Indeed, and it was no imposition whatsoever." Julian waved a hand, generously dismissing David's apology. Julian excused them from Ian Taylor and took David into his office to explain all that he had arranged.

The wagon had been placed at the rear of one of his storage sheds, and the oxen sold off. The money received was used to pay the men as instructed by Morris, and the remainder banked in the Standard Bank at the Mafeking sub-branch. Julian then offered David a place to stay while he was in town, but he graciously declined, saying that he was on his way to Port Elizabeth after he had placed another order with Weil and Co.

Julian was extremely surprised to learn that David wished to place another large order with him so soon, and offered the full service of Ian Taylor at his disposal. Seizing the opportunity, David explained that he would like Mr Taylor to have the wagons that he would purchase from Gerran's coachworks delivered and stored on the premises while he was in Port Elizabeth. Although Julian offered to load the wagons with the selected stock, David diplomatically declined, explaining that it was essential that the loading wait until his return because Morris was so fastidious with stock and numbers that David did not want to make a mistake, and would therefore personally load everything himself. Once arrangements had been made and Ian Taylor briefed as to what David would be relying upon him to do over the next week or so, David took his leave and went over to Gerran's coachworks.

He entered the factory and introduced himself as Morris' brother. Mr Gerran warmly welcomed him into his office, and they agreed on a price for five more wagons. As was his custom with good clients, Mr Gerran offered David a choice of tea or coffee, with some extremely delicious shortbread that his wife had baked that very morning. His hospitality was exceptionally fulsome, but then David was a very good customer, buying in large quantities, and paying cash up front.

As the meeting was drawing to a close, David helped himself to another piece of shortbread and took a mouthful. Savouring the buttery-sweet taste, he mentioned to Mr Gerran how wonderful the biscuits were, and wished his brother could sample them.

"Oh, he has," Gerran beamed back. "He loved them very much. Just about cleaned me out when he was here. Everyone loves my wife's biscuits."

David was just about to put the last half of the biscuit in his mouth when he stopped. "Oh, he did, did he?"

"Yes, indeed," Gerran smiled back happily.

Huh! David thought to himself. *While I was trying to find oxen and hopelessly attempting to employ a team of men in the blazing hot sun with no food and water, stepping in mud, dust and cow dung, Morris was in here snacking on tea and shortbread!* He popped the last of the shortbread into his mouth and washed it down with the last of his coffee.

"It's been a pleasure doing business with you, Mr Gerran. I will be back tomorrow with the cheque. Please send my most sincere compliments to your wife for the shortbread."

With that he went back to his lodgings, whistling a little ditty, and greatly looking forward to a good night's rest in a real bed.

Whereas it had taken Morris one day to select six wagons' worth of stock and calculate in his head almost the exact value of what he had bought, it took David three days to select his stock and calculate the value with Ian Taylor. Since he enjoyed the benefit of rail transport, Julian Weil's sheds had been replenished since Morris had last decimated his stock levels so thoroughly and the wholesaler had no major problem, therefore, in providing what David needed. With the added advantage of having almost three months' hands-on trading experience in KoBulawayo, David also knew what was selling well and what was not. Just to begin with, he bought every jack-in-the-box that Weil and Co. had, while telescopes were also very high on the priority list, along with brass compasses, brass scales for weighing certain goods, bolts of ladies' dress materials, and fragrant soaps. Mirrors were equally popular, as was every type of enamelware. David discovered a dusty carton under a pile of timber planks in the corner of one of the warehouses that seemed to have been lost for some time. Even Mr Taylor did not know what was in the carton. They opened it and found 120 packs of Bicycle playing cards, manufactured in America.

"How much are these?" David enquired.

Ian spent the next fifteen minutes consulting his inventory and files.

"Ah ha!" he finally exclaimed. "They are one shilling a packet."

"So I make that £6 for the carton?" David enquired.

"Correct," Ian nodded his agreement.

"This is old stock, Ian. Who knows how long it has been here. You'll struggle to sell it. Give it to me for £5, and I'll relieve you of the whole carton. I'll bet Mr Weil will be really pleased to see the back of it."

Ian thought about it for a moment and then agreed, entering it in his ledger, while David secretly smiled at the success of his negotiating skills.

When all was said and done, David thanked Ian for his help and left him to gather all his purchases into one place and tally up the invoices. His next stop was the railway station to book a ticket to Port Elizabeth via Kimberley and Cape Town. He was in luck, as the train departed at five o'clock the following morning. He then made his way to the Standard Bank and hurriedly deposited their takings. It did not amount to anything substantial, and he, unfortunately, bumped into the manager, Mr Savage, who insisted on almost interrogating him about the status of their business in Matabeleland after glaring at the meagre totals on his deposit slip. David did not feel the conversation went well and was pleased to leave behind the sarcastic innuendoes and veiled criticisms of Mr Savage.

Later that evening, David sat at the small writing-desk in his room and extracted the letter that Morris had written in haste to their father in Ireland. He read through the letter twice, then, folding it up and putting it away, he wrote his own letter in his best handwriting to replace Morris' hasty attempt. David decided to post the letter when he got to Cape Town, believing that, if he posted it in Mafeking, it would have to go via the Cape regardless, but on a much later train. This would be the quickest way to get the letter off to Ireland, he was sure. After curling into bed and blowing the candle out, David fell into a deep sleep almost immediately.

The rail trip to Port Elizabeth went via Kimberley and Cape Town, stopping at a number of smaller settlements in between, which made it a rather protracted journey for David. He did not mind, however, as he revelled in the camaraderie and friendships he formed with his fellow passengers.

When he got to Cape Town it was freezing cold, grey, and wet, and the wind was uncomfortably blustery, a complete contrast to what he had experienced during their previous visits. He had always felt he could quite comfortably live in Cape Town, but this day he could not wait to leave. He had a few hours to spare before his connecting train to Port Elizabeth departed, so, carrying with him the little luggage he had, he quickly found the Post Office and posted his letter home to Ireland. He had not anticipated the icy conditions of Cape Town at that time of year, and therefore had not thought of packing any warm clothing. Leaving the Post Office, he hastily entered the first men's outfitters he came across and purchased a pure wool black overcoat. It was frightfully expensive, but he did not care; he was frozen to the bone.

Arriving in Port Elizabeth on the following day, David was elated to see the familiar platform of the station, and a sense of homecoming enveloped him. It was smiles all round as he greeted everyone he saw, even though he did not know them from Adam. The Standard Bank was closed, as it was too early in the day for them to be trading, so he walked past their darkened glass doors and headed directly for The Grand Hotel to check in for the duration of his stay. He was certain his previous landlady, Sonja Du Plessis, would have loved for him to stay in her lodgings, but it was more convenient for David to stay in a hotel, and, after all, he hated imposing on people, and it was probably more appropriate, too.

As he entered The Grand Hotel, the nostalgia of the day the brothers had first landed in Africa in 1891 flooded back to him. Nothing had changed in the reception area: the mounted animal heads were still hanging from the walls in their customary positions. The thick carpet still muffled his footfalls on the wooden floor, and the musty smell emanating from the library continued to mingle with the stale smoke left behind by the patrons of the bar and the dining-room on the previous night. Everything remained exactly the same as it had been, each and every day, and he loved this old, majestic establishment. It had been home to the Langbourne Brothers business and it still remained a home for him.

An African waiter, dressed in his impeccably white uniform, walked past the entrance to the dining-room and glanced into the reception area. He did a double-take as he realised that the figure of the man standing at the unattended desk was someone he knew.

"Hawu!" he exclaimed. "Boss Randorn!"

David looked over at him and smiled. It was the hotel's barman. "Shadreck!" David responded, very pleased to see the man. "How are you?"

"I am fitness, Sah!"

"You are 'fitness'?" David repeated somewhat surprised, and then laughed heartily at the comment. "I am fitness, too, and very happy to see you. How is your family?" he queried, shaking his hand and enquiring about him, his family, his cattle, and village members, as was the polite custom of the Xhosa people, all the while quietly marvelling at the differences between the Xhosa and the Tswana tribes.

After a few minutes of exchanging news with each other, on Morris and the country called Matabeleland, Shadreck went to find Mrs Bunting, the manageress, to allocate him a room. She was in a warehouse behind the kitchen, and when she heard that 'Boss David Randorn' was in reception she shrieked in delight, so loudly that David could hear her from the reception desk. It made him feel good to be so well-liked in Port Elizabeth.

Mrs Bunting had a soft spot for David; his kind, gentle, and polite mannerisms, and to top it off, he was a handsome lad, smartly groomed and exceptionally well dressed all the time. His cute smile made the fairer sex melt in his presence. She came into the reception area almost at a run and enveloped him in a huge bear hug, kissing him on the cheek and making a fuss over him. David was quite taken aback at all her attention and affection but lapped it up all the same. Mrs Bunting allocated David a room on the upper floor with a private bathroom, and then ushered him to his room, inviting him to come down to breakfast, which would be served in the dining-room in half an hour.

David wasted no time in running himself a hot bath and relaxing in the soothing water, easing the aches in his joints and muscles that the train journey had inflicted upon him. He thought of Morris in Matabeleland having to contend with a wintery cold wash standing by a tin bucket of dirty water but did not dwell on that thought for very long. A quick shave, a change of fresh clothes, and he was a new man, ready to face the day.

Breakfast was huge and scrumptious. David's belly was not used to eating the vast quantity and variety of delights Mrs Bunting provided, but he could not help himself. By the time he had washed the food down with a cup of strong, sweetened coffee, he was uncomfortable and bloated, though very content.

His first port of call was to see his friend, Jack Shiel, at the Standard Bank. Jack Shiel had enjoyed their company and had found Morris' sharp brain, acute business acumen, and quick ability to grasp what he was telling them simply amazing. David was not far behind Morris in his business abilities, and he knew they would make an impressive team in the business world. Being a bank manager, he was able to provide a wealth of information on the business, commercial, financial, and shipping sectors and he had freely shared this knowledge and expertise with the boys when they had first arrived in Port Elizabeth. The brothers had made it a practice to have regular dinners with him and ply him with questions, seeking advice and guidance, and drawing on Jack's immense experience. Jack, for his part, found their conversations stimulating, and enjoyed their company in every respect. Not only had Jack become a very close friend of the boys, but he had also become their mentor.

Jack was delighted to see David and pumped his hand vigorously, slapping him on his shoulder with his free hand. Coffee in his office was not an option, it was compulsory. At that time, only sixteen years' old, David was on a high with all the attention from the people around him, especially the adults' attention. Along with the top-quality food and luxurious comfort he received at The Grand, life could not have been better than in Port Elizabeth.

Jack brimmed with excitement and expectation. "So, tell me about Matabeleland," he prompted. "Are you trading yet?"

"Yes, we are, but it's different up there, Jack," David said, turning a little serious. "It's hard work, that's for sure, and it's one hell of a long way. You simply have no idea how far it is or how big this continent is. The Tswana people are helpful enough, but don't seem to be too keen to do much. And then everyone is scared stiff of the Matabele, nobody trusts them. But I can tell you something; I think they have reason to be. The Matabele are born warriors, and, my goodness, do they know their bushcraft! They are fit and strong and bred for war, so they are a dangerous tribe, that's for sure." David shook his head in awe, before changing the subject to business.

"Morris decided that we should become wholesalers as well as traders and that we would also supply the public directly, all working on a pricing structure that he calculated. I guess it's similar to how we sold cigarettes here in Port Elizabeth. I imagine we bought too much stock in Mafeking because Morris might have gotten a little carried away in Julian Weil's warehouses."

"Oh dear," Jack sounded concerned. "You know that is not good for business? Your cash flow will take a knock."

"Yes, but Morris had a plan, and it's working! It's a long story; I'll get back to that in a minute. We built a Sample-Room out of timber and corrugated iron sheeting. It's the biggest building in the settlement!" David laughed at their unexpected achievement.

"I think you two are crazy," Jack said, genuinely frowning in concern. "You built it?"

David started laughing again. "Yes, Morris and me; on our own. It's not pretty, but it does the job. You're not going to believe this, but we built a second warehouse the same size next to it!"

"Why did you do that?" Jack asked.

"We took six wagonloads of stock up with us. We needed a place to store all the excess stock. Anyhow, it's also our bedroom and home now." And with that David started laughing again. Jack tried to join in, but his attempt at a laugh was feeble.

"So, have you sold your wagons?"

"Oh no, this is the plan Morris came up with. We have also become suppliers to wagon traders. We lend our wagons out to traders, for a fee..."

"You rent them out?"

"Ahh, that's the word. We didn't know what you called it to lend out for a fee."

"Yes, rent, or lease. Go on," Jack urged, intrigued by David's story.

"So, we have five wagons that we have rented out to traders, and they buy our stock, on credit, and go out into the country selling from their wagons in other settlements, forts, and villages, whatever they find. When they get back, we tally up what they sold and give them a discount, which is their profit."

"Very clever," Jack said, thinking this through. "But you know there are risks involved. What if someone takes off and never comes back?"

"Yes, we know. It is a big risk. But Morris feels it is one we should take. In any case, it certainly moved our stock; we have just about depleted all our stock levels already, and that's why I am here, to buy another six wagonloads."

"Another six?" Jack exclaimed. "I hope your wagon traders pay you. You'll be in big trouble if they don't."

"And that, Jack, is the risk we are taking. We could ask them to pay for the stock before they leave, but nobody has that sort of money, so we are almost forced into giving credit."

The conversation went on for well over an hour and over another cup of coffee. Jack had many misgivings about Morris' ideas and plans, but he admired the bold risks the older brother was taking. He quite correctly assumed that the boys had used up most of their money, and cash flow was now their biggest enemy. David also discussed the miserable bank manager they now had in the form of Mr Savage. Jack confessed that he'd had dealings with the man in the past and was quite pleased he was based in Mafeking, and nowhere near Port Elizabeth.

As the meeting drew to a close, David enquired after another of their good friends, Danie Coetzee. Jack told him that he was still in town, but that he had resigned from Weil & Co Procurement and was moving to Johannesburg in a fortnight to join his uncle in an accounting firm. He and Jack finally arranged to meet again at The Grand for dinner at six o'clock, and David promised to call in at Danie's workplace in the following five minutes to catch up on their friendship and further invite Danie to join the two of them for dinner.

The reunion with Danie was filled with smiles, laughter, and the good humour that long-standing friends enjoy. He told David that, within a week of the boys leaving Mafeking to strike out for KoBulawayo, Julian Weil had come to PE for a few days and had been ecstatic over the volume of goods that the boys had bought from him. In fact, Danie had spent almost a full four days re-ordering stock from England to replenish the warehouses in Mafeking.

"Well, I've just made yet another dent in his inventory," David laughed, causing Danie to raise his eyebrows in astonishment.

They agreed to meet with Jack at The Grand Hotel at six o'clock, and David departed to walk down to the harbour, looking for Nguni; someone he was very keen to see. It wasn't difficult to spot him among the throng of workers, because he was by far the biggest man and was shirtless, as always, carrying the largest hessian sack on his shoulders. From a distance, Nguni saw David and broke into a wide smile, flashing his perfectly white teeth that contrasted starkly with his dark skin. David waved to him in acknowledgement of the eye contact and then pointed to the ground he stood on. Next, he pointed to the sun and drew an arc to where it would set, and then again pointed to the spot where he stood. Nguni immediately understood that he would be there when the day was over and that David wanted to see him, so he nodded, smiling broadly all the time, before walking into a warehouse with the massive sack over his shoulders.

Satisfied that they had understood each other, David strode off towards the lodging that he and Morris had called home during the initial stage of their adventure in Africa. It was an old, ramshackle, wooden house with an overrun garden that had served not only as a place to put their head down at night, but was also where their cigarette factory had been born. The only reason he went to that old house was to see Sonja Du Plessis, the lady who had become like a mother to them, and a lady both boys were extremely fond of. Her hospitality and kindness had been so genuine and sincere that the boys paid off the debt that remained on her house before they left for Matabeleland.

David walked up the rickety wooden steps onto the verandah and knocked on the door. He heard her call out something, followed by her footsteps approaching. When Sonja opened the door, her face lit up.

"David, David, David!" she squealed. "You're back!" And she launched herself at him, hugging him tightly, shaking him from side to side. David hugged her back, so very pleased to see her. "Come in, come in," she urged. "Let's have some tea, but where's Morris?" She suddenly became concerned. "Is everything alright?".

"Yes, yes, everything is well" David quickly replied. "Morris is still in Matabeleland. We have a business there now, and he is looking after the shop while I am away."

"Wonderful!" she exclaimed, ushering him inside and putting a blackened kettle on top of a wood burner. "Tell me your news, now, and don't leave out a single thing."

David and Sonja subsequently chatted the afternoon away, laughing at times and giggling often. David told her all about the trek to the north, the building of their Sample-Room, the scorpion sting, and even confided in her about his unfortunate incident with an ostrich. She laughed delightedly at this story, though she tried very hard at first not to. When she expressed genuine concern, however, about the dangers they faced from wild predators, David told her about his fascination with birds, and how his telescope opened up their world to him.

"You know, Sonja, you say you are concerned about dangerous animals. Well, let me tell you, the further north you go, the more deadly they become. Morris and I saw a flock of birds that hunt in packs."

"Birds that hunt in packs? Well, I never!"

"Yes, incredible. We always kept a watch on the ground for lions and hyenas and leopards, snakes and the like, but over the Limpopo we have to keep a close watch on the sky as well." David squirmed in his seat.

"Never?" Sonja looked worried. "How big are these birds?"

"Oh, they come up to about my thigh," he said, tapping his upper leg with an open hand. "But we came across a flock of about twenty of them that had killed and devoured an entire buffalo!"

"They killed a buffalo? The birds killed a fully grown Cape Buffalo?" She looked shocked. "Did you actually see them kill the buffalo?"

"No, it was already dead when we got there, but they were all over it. One was even inside the hollow stomach of the animal. A formidable species of bird, I'd say."

Sonja stared at David in disbelief, before bursting out into laughter again.

"What?" David looked hurt. "What did I say?"

"You silly-billy!" she said between her laughter. "Those were vultures. No bird hunts in packs from the sky. Vultures feed off dead animals. They wait for a predator to kill an animal first, then they scrap off whatever is left!" She laughed again. "I can see why you must have thought the vultures killed that buffalo, though. How funny is that?"

"Well, that's what it looked like to us, Sonja," said David, trying to defend his pride.

"At least you don't need to be worried about a silent attack from the sky anymore," she said seriously, and then burst out laughing again.

The sun was starting to dip close to the horizon, so David had to excuse himself, as he did not want to keep Nguni waiting. He told Sonja that he would be in town for a few days and would like to see her again before he left. After bidding her a fond farewell, accompanied by another hug, David made off for the harbour to meet his old friend, Nguni.

Nguni was waiting at the agreed spot, draped in a traditional cream blanket with vibrant threads of red, green, and yellow woven into the edges. He was an impressive man, tall and well built, with a friendly, happy face. He stood on the exact spot that David had pointed out earlier that day and did not move, but preferred to let David walk up to him. When they met, they clasped each other's right forearms in a warm and sincere greeting. They were both smiling, and it was obvious they were very happy to see each other.

"I see you, Nguni," David almost laughed.

"I see you, Boss David," he replied, allowing his joy to escape in a hearty chuckle.

"You are looking strong and well, Nguni. Your wives must be feeding you well," he joked. "How is your family?" David engaged in the customary tradition to discuss matters of importance before anything else.

Nguni told David that his three wives were well, that his children were growing strong, and that he was well pleased with their development. His youngest daughter had stolen his heart. The crops were good, the cattle fat, and all was well in his life. He asked after Morris, and David told him all his news, including the building of a huge Sample-Room that he was very proud of. He deliberately avoided telling him that it was square, with four corners, in case the superstition of the Matabele was much the same in the south. Nguni asked if David's skill with a rifle had improved, and David was pleased to say he was now very good at hunting, and never missed his target. This pleased Nguni, who then became very interested in the journey they had taken.

"It is a very long way, Nguni," David said, shaking his head as he reflected on the massive distance they had covered between Mafeking and KoBulawayo. "It takes many days to travel on the train just to get to a town called Mafeking, in Bechuanaland. It is very far. Then you must walk for three months with ox wagons to get to KoBulawayo in Matabeleland, passing through the country called the Transvaal."

"It is very far," Nguni agreed, as he looked over David's shoulder towards the north, trying to imagine the distance.

"But that is why I have come back to Port Elizabeth. To ask you if you will help me take another six wagons from Mafeking to KoBulawayo."

Nguni stood proudly and beamed with delight. "I will help you, Boss David."

"It is very far, and it will take many months for you to go there and many months to come back. I need you to discuss this with your wives and your village elders first, before you agree. Will you do that for me, Nguni?"

"Yes, Boss David, I will do that," he agreed, but both men knew immediately that the big man would be taking this job.

"I would like you to bring five of your best men, too. There are six wagons with six oxen on each wagon. These men would also need to get the approval from their families and the village elders."

"I will ask them, Boss David," he agreed, before a look of concern crossed his face. "Are there no African people in Mafeking to help you?"

"Yes, there are many Tswana men, but they are different to the Xhosa. I prefer the Xhosa. I understand your language, and you are my friend, whom I can trust."

Nguni was touched by what David said. "Five of my village are not enough for so many oxen. You need more."

"Then the extra we will choose from the Tswana."

Nguni was comfortable with that and David explained that he would put them on the train with him and they would travel to Mafeking together. There they would find extra Tswana men, buy oxen, and load the wagons. After three days of trekking, and ensuring everyone was comfortable with the journey, David would leave the group and ride by horse to KoBulawayo. When Nguni and his team felt they were "near-near" to KoBulawayo, he would need to send a runner into the settlement, and David would ride out to meet the convoy to guide them to where the Langbourne Brothers business was located.

Once the wagons had been unloaded, David would send the men back with one of the wagons and four oxen, loaded with provisions for the three-month journey, in much the same fashion he had dealt with Tebogo and his team, plus enough money to buy tickets for the train back to Port Elizabeth. In all, Nguni and his men could be away from their families for a good five to six months. David negotiated the remuneration he expected to pay Nguni and his men, and he quickly agreed to the offer.

These arrangements were pleasing to Nguni, as he saw it as an exciting adventure, and something he could later talk about with his children over the evening fires. He would discuss this with his wives and the elders of his village, and bring an answer to David the next day. They parted company having enjoyed their reunion, and David made his way to The Grand Hotel to freshen up before meeting Jack and Danie for dinner.

Chapter Seven
Rumblings

David's three days in Port Elizabeth flashed by faster than he had wished, and the return journey to Mafeking went without incident. Whenever the train pulled into a town and stopped to take on water and coal, David took Nguni and his men on a quick walk around whatever settlement they were at, not only to show them what existed in their country, but also to give them some exercise. In some towns and settlements they were ignored altogether, and in others, they attracted some curious stares from the locals.

As soon as they arrived in Mafeking, David set to work without delay. The first move he made was to take Nguni and his men to the warehouse, where he and Ian Taylor would be loading the wagons, to show them where he would be during the day. Then he sent them off to the African township on the western side of the settlement to get a feel for 'things'. One of these 'things' was to find lodgings and food for the team. That was the priority: finding oxen and extra men to help with the drive north would come the following day. Meanwhile, David arranged that they would meet him back at the warehouse just before sunset to fill him in on their discoveries. David and Ian then began the onerous task of checking off the Langbourne Brothers purchases and loading the six wagons.

At around four o'clock that afternoon, Nguni returned to the warehouse without his men. He was smiling broadly as he always did, so David greeted him joyfully, speaking in Nguni's native tongue.

"I see you, Nguni. You look happy."

"I see you, Boss David. Yes, I have obtained happiness."

"That is good for me to hear, Nguni. What is it that has made you happy?"

"I have found my brother. He lives here."

"Really!" David exclaimed. It was fantastic news for David. "What is he doing in Mafeking?"

"He is working for a mine nearby. There are many Xhosa here. My brother's family will look after us and feed us, and they will show us where to find the best oxen."

"Oh, brilliant, brilliant!" David almost laughed, turning to Ian, shrugging his shoulders and smiling at him as if saying, 'How about that?' Ian just looked at him, totally confused, as he did not understand a word of their conversation. David turned back to Nguni – he wanted to hug him!

"Nguni," he said, "this makes my heart very pleased. I am very happy for you, and I am very happy for how you are helping me. Go now, and spend some time with your brother. We will meet again here in the morning."

They bid each other farewell, and David returned to the task at hand with renewed energy and boundless enthusiasm, which did not please Ian Taylor, who was already wilting under the pace David had set and just wanted to go home. When it began to get dark, David reluctantly agreed to call it a day and parted company with Ian, making his way to the same lodging he had stayed the previous week.

Four days later they were set to go: the wagons were loaded, all accounts settled, oxen purchased, and, most importantly, David now had a group of 14 trusted men to drive the caravan of six wagons northwards, all Xhosa men that Nguni had found using his family connections. David was well pleased with the arrangements and more than ready to leave. But before they turned their backs to Mafeking, he asked Nguni to introduce him to his men.

Nguni's brother was first to be introduced, and David rightly assumed that he would be the second-in-charge. He looked a little like Nguni, just slightly shorter and not quite as well built, but still an impressive specimen of humanity in his own right.

"My brother is known as 'Daluxolo'," Nguni smiled proudly, clicking his tongue halfway through the name.

"I see you, Daluxolo," David greeted, clicking his tongue just as Nguni had. "I can see you and Nguni have the same mother."

"I see you, Boss," Daluxolo replied, pleased that David could pronounce his name properly. "We have the same father, but a different mother," he corrected David.

"Oh, I see," David smiled at his error. "So what does Daluxolo mean? I do not know this word."

Nguni replied in English, "It means 'The Calm One' or 'The Peaceful One'. My brother can talk to the oxen when they are unhappy, and he makes them happy again."

David smiled at Daluxolo and returned to their native tongue. "I thank you for joining us on this trek." He then introduced himself to the remainder of the team, making sure he spoke briefly with each man and welcomed them onto the team. He would later sit with them in the evenings around the fire in the laager and learn about the men and their families.

When the caravan departed from Mafeking, David stayed with the convoy for the three days as planned. As they sat around the fire on the third night discussing family matters, something they always tended to do, David spoke up when there was a pause in the conversation.

"Nguni, I have a serious matter that needs discussion."

"Yes, Boss, we are listening," he said in his unmistakable baritone voice, briefly lifting his hand to silence the gathering.

"At sunrise, I will leave you and ride fast to KoBulawayo to join my brother Morris, who needs my help. Are you ready to lead and protect this convoy?"

"Yes, Boss," he eagerly asserted.

"Good. Tomorrow I will give you a letter that explains who you are, and to whom these wagons belong. I don't think you will need it, but if anyone from the BSAC asks you, then you must show them this letter."

He explained how they would find their way to KoBulawayo, how the track crossed the Limpopo River, and how he would have to navigate the various forks the path took, but that they still made up just one road to the north. In an attempt to help Nguni to understand, David said he would try and follow the same route he had taken about four months ago with the first lot of wagons. If he remembered a fork that came to a dead end, he would snap two twigs in a tree at the height of a man's head when sitting on his horse, to guide him down the correct fork. They both knew this might not work for a number of reasons, and so Nguni was to use these bush signs as a guide, no more. He simply needed to press north.

David described the terrain ahead, and instructed the men on how to change a wagon wheel, should the need arise. He warned Nguni that the Matabele warriors might be watching him when he got closer to KoBulawayo, but that they would not harm them. After three days of explanations, instructions, and practical exercises, David was comfortable that Nguni and his close-knit team of men could handle the job well.

On the following day, as the sun rose, David took off with Bruno, carrying his rifle, and with his meagre possessions packed safely in his saddlebags. His blanket was secured to the back of the saddle, but this time David kept the small bottle of morphine in a pouch on his belt. He had also tied a piece of string to the telescope that he slung over his shoulder. Now, if for some reason he lost his horse, his two prized possessions would stay with him.

As David travelled towards the Limpopo, he began to feel his isolation, his vulnerability, and the vast expanse of the African continent as he had felt it never before. It was uncomfortable and disconcerting, while a fierce sense of loneliness overcame him in great waves that left him with butterflies in his stomach. He felt so very insignificant in this unforgiving land, but despite it all, he was determined to press on. He knew that, if he had an accident, or was injured in some way, the chances that he would die in the bush were very probable. It was a fear that gnawed at him constantly.

One morning he came across the log he had attempted to move when the scorpion had stung him. Given the dryness of the area, the signs of the log having been shifted were still visible. Seeing this familiar object so far from anywhere and in such total isolation, was as if he had seen a good friend again, a family member perhaps, even though it was just a log. It reminded him that he really had been there and that Africa would wait for him forever if it had to.

As wild and inhospitable as this continent could be, it was also loving and tender. It was real, it never changed, and he was now a part of it. The awe of Africa overcame David and with a comforted heart, he dismounted and sat in the shade of a tree. He revelled in the peace and quiet of this land, listening to the sounds of the things that lived in it; the rustling of the leaves in a breeze, the whisper of the dry grass, the occasional click or shrill call of an insect, and the chirp or cry of a distant bird. He touched the earth with an open hand and felt the texture of the soil, the stones and dust, and sensed the heat it gave off.

The place was arid and dusty, and, apart from a few green leaves giving very sparse shade, all around him lay a mixed scene of brown, beige, and mustard. In the distance, the air shimmered under the hot, African sun. Although he thought he could see lakes of cool, clear water, he knew they represented an illusion. Despite having experienced one of the most shocking and painful events of his life on this very spot, it gave him a welcome sense of peace, comfort, and belonging. He decided to name this place "Nomandudwane", which meant "the place of scorpions". There was no reason to give it a name, it was just a spot on the earth that held a special place in his heart, and he felt good about it. He decided that, if circumstances allowed, this was the place he would like to be laid to rest when he died, such was the peace he felt.

In a symbolic gesture, David unsheathed his knife and crudely cut off two inches of leather from the end of his belt, placing it, together with two shiny one-shilling coins, under a large stone that lay against the log that had once been home to the scorpion. The piece of leather was symbolic of him personally being there, and the two coins represented each time he had passed by. He gave thanks to Nomandudwane for allowing him to visit a second time, then he mounted his horse and struck out for Matabeleland, his heart inexplicably cheered.

Morris had just finished serving a lady customer and was entering the sale into his cashbook when Captain Dave Seward walked into the Sample-Room.

"Good morning, Captain Seward," Morris greeted him genially, but formally.

"Morning, Mr Langbourne," he responded. "Good morning to you, madam." As he stood aside to let her through the open doorway and doffed his slouch hat, she smiled and nodded her thanks.

"Good to see you, Captain," Morris smiled. "What brings you down to this neck of the woods?" he smiled at his own pun.

The captain took off his hat and tossed it onto a table loaded with samples of detergents and personal care products. "Blimey!" he exclaimed, "I had to get out of the office. All hell's breaking loose down there."

"What happened? Did someone drive his oxen and wagons up the street again?" he joked.

"If only. That would be easy to deal with," the captain sighed. "No, it appears the Matabele have decided to have a go at the Shona tribes farther north. They're giving them a good hiding."

"What do you mean?" Morris was concerned.

"They're giving them a thumping. They do that every so often. It seems to be the way they do things here. From what I understand, the Shona have decided they will not pay King Lobengula any more tribute, or taxes, simply put." Captain Seward pulled up an empty wooden crate and sat on it carefully. "As a result, the king is decidedly unhappy, and has sent his impi off to the north to knock some heads together."

"Is it bad?"

"Is it bad?" Seward exclaimed again, then chuckled. "It's bad enough. We received a report last night from a rider who said there were a couple of hundred Shona that had been killed already."

"A couple of hundred? Killed?" Morris was perplexed. "That's a bit excessive, wouldn't you say? That's more than a hiding in my books. That's a massacre!"

"Oh, yes, it certainly is. But the king can be ruthless when his authority is challenged. He'll be killing the men and taking the women for the use of his warriors, not to forget rounding up all the cattle for themselves. He is a very brutal king to those who oppose him, and that is why we like to keep on friendly terms with him. This entire debacle is taking up all of Dr Jameson's time, and so he has made me the Acting Administrator." Captain Seward sighed again. "It's hell in the office today, I tell you." Then he looked up sharply. "Do you know what 'KoBulawayo' means?"

"No."

"It means 'The Killing Place'."

Morris was both fascinated and shocked at what he had just learned. Captain Seward had come to see him for a little reprieve from the commotion in the camp and to buy some codeine for a splitting headache he had developed from all that was going on. Before the captain left, however, he invited Morris to join him in the officer's mess for a meal that evening. He was in need of some company that was not BSAC connected.

At about five o'clock Morris secured the Sample-Room door with the rusted piece of wire he always used to hold the door in place and went into the warehouse to freshen up and change into something suitable for the officer's mess. Shortly afterwards, he was with Captain Seward, sipping a whisky that had been diluted with lukewarm, slightly muddied water, and was not enjoying it at all. To his credit, he pretended to enjoy it, but nursed it carefully to make it last the entire evening. Whisky was about the only spirit available, and it was in plentiful supply in the settlement. Captain Seward was in a jolly mood and, despite the whisky, the evening was proving to be exceptionally enjoyable. Seward invited some other officers to join them and, as a result, Morris found himself relishing the potential friendships that were being forged that evening.

Suddenly, Captain Seward's face turned to a serious scowl as he looked toward the entrance of the tent. Dr Jameson had entered, and his eyes were sweeping the room, looking for someone.

"Oh dear," the Captain said quietly, "this looks like trouble."

Morris looked over his shoulder in time to see the doctor lock eyes with Captain Seward and start walking briskly over. The captain stood up, causing all the officers, and Morris, to stand as well.

"Sit, sit," Dr Jameson said as he reached the table. Pulling up a spare chair, he sat down next to his Acting Administrator. "I'm sorry to interrupt your evening, gentlemen, but we have a problem that needs urgent attention and action."

"Oh dear," Captain Seward sighed again. "I could see it in your face the moment you walked in, sir."

"Would you like me to leave, Dr Jameson?" Morris offered politely.

"No, please stay, Mr Langbourne." He motioned to Morris to remain seated. "As some of you know, King Lobengula sent his army, his impi, up north to extract tribute from the Shona people. We think that happened over a week ago. Word is that the Matabele have slaughtered hundreds of the Shona people already, and the news we got today is already slightly out-dated." He paused to ensure everyone at the table was listening, which they most certainly were. "A rider has just come into camp with a message to say that the Shona tribes believe that the BSAC, well, in their words, 'our Queen', is here not only to protect the European settlers but to protect the Shona as well. They are calling on us to intervene, and stop King Lobengula's impi from killing their people."

"Oh hell," Captain Seward groaned. "That will put us between a rock and a hard place."

"Indeed it will," the doctor sighed. "If we don't protect the Shona, then they will turn against us, and that will make our endeavours north of here extremely difficult, if not impossible. Cecil Rhodes has ordered me to keep the Shona favourable towards us."

"And if you attack the Matabele impi they will turn on us, and every European in Matabeleland?"

"Exactly," Dr Jameson agreed.

"But, sir," one of the officers at the table intervened, "if the Ndebele turn on the Europeans, then we will be significantly outnumbered. Significantly!"

"About one hundred and fifty to one. Yes, I am aware of that."

Morris was stunned and confused by what he was hearing. His eyes were wide open and his mouth agape, but he could not contribute to the conversation because he had no knowledge of matters military. All the same, being outnumbered by 150:1 was simple enough to understand.

"But the conflict is between the Matabele and the Shona. It's not our war, surely," the officer objected.

"I agree, it's not our war, but it's now been thrown into our lap since the Shona have brought us into the dispute. We have no choice but to back them," Dr Jameson responded, shaking his head. "Gentlemen, I have orders from Mr Rhodes. So, like it or not, we are going to the aid of the Shona."

Without exception, the men at the table were dumbstruck. The doctor continued, "Captain Seward, I know the hour is late, but I will ride north at sunrise to liaise with Captains Bailey and Rudge, who are in Fort Victoria at present. I will need thirty good men to come with me, and I would like this to be arranged forthwith."

"Yes, Sir," Captain Seward snapped.

"Also: send four men to Mafeking on the postal run with our fastest horses at first light. I will write an official letter, which I need you to give to the riders, addressed to Colonel William Bedford in Kimberley, requesting reinforcements. This message must get through at all costs. Are we clear?"

"Yes, sir," Seward snapped again, his lips thin with anguish at the sudden change in their circumstances.

"Excellent. One last thing: I am promoting you to major as of this moment. Congratulations, Major Seward," the doctor stated formally, then stood up.

Involuntarily, everyone at the table, including Morris, stood to attention as Dr Jameson walked out of the smoke-filled tent.

Major Seward looked at Morris, who was somewhat perplexed, and then at each of the other officers at the table. No one moved. "Please sit," he said calmly to his colleagues and Morris. They all took their chairs, except Major Seward. He remained standing to attention, took a deep breath, and puffed out his chest, looking at the gathering of men who were eating and socialising around the tent.

"Officers!" he yelled at the top of his voice. Silence reigned immediately, followed by the sound of a smashing glass as an officer dropped his whisky in surprise.

After Major Seward had everyone's attention, he took in a deep breath. "Listen up!" he bellowed.

Just before first light, Morris ran down to the parade square, hoping to catch the postal riders before they left for Mafeking. He'd endured a restless night, thinking about David out in the bush, all alone while the Matabele were on the warpath. The memory of their having encountered a group of Matabele warriors on their journey to KoBulawayo had plagued his thoughts during the night and had unnerved him. The Matabele carried short stabbing spears, just over a yard in length, which were very effective in close combat, and no match for the traditional long spears. It did not escape Morris' attention that a good quarter of the spear was made up of tempered iron that was honed to razor sharpness and glinted menacingly in the sunlight. He had been told that when they speared a man with that blade, they twisted it as well, making sure it was extremely difficult for their enemy to survive, and this thought worried him immensely. As he walked onto the parade ground square, he saw four men standing by four horses. Major Seward was giving them last-minute instructions. Morris picked up his pace and literally sprinted to the small group.

"Captain Seward, I mean, Major Seward," Morris corrected himself. "I apologise for the interruption," he said sheepishly.

"No problem, Mr Langbourne." Formalities were once more established in front of the company men. "What can I do for you?"

"My brother David is riding this way on his own. I estimate he would be approaching the Limpopo River very shortly. I have a letter that I would like to ask your men if they would kindly pass to him, should they encounter each other. I am asking him to return to our wagons and travel up with them. I think it is safer for our wagons, considering what is going on out there."

Major Seward looked at Morris for a moment. Seeing the desperation in his eyes and hearing a quiver in his voice, he winked at Morris and then turned to the leader of the troop. "Corporal, kindly take possession of this letter from Mr Langbourne and deliver it to his brother, should you find him en route."

"As you wish, sir," the corporal readily agreed.

"Thank you so much, sir." Morris handed him the envelope. "Thank you, too, Major Seward," he said, as he backed away slightly.

"Right-oh!" Major Seward stood to attention as he looked at the riders, a deep frown crossing his brow. "Make haste, now. What you have in Dr Jameson's folder is crucial to the safety of this settlement. Whatever you do, make sure you deliver that message to Colonel Bedford in person. Do you understand?"

"Yes, sir!" the corporal almost shouted.

"And if you and that letter get eaten by a crocodile as you cross that damned Limpopo... You!" he said abruptly, pointing to another of the riders, "you will verbally take the same message to Colonel Bedford, you understand?"

"Yes, sir!" the other soldier barked, snapping to attention.

"And if you are eaten by a lion, what are you going to do?" he demanded, pointing to the third soldier, squinting his eyes.

"I will personally tell Colonel Bedford the same message, sir!"

"Good, I see I have made myself quite clear." He smiled at the soldiers. "Godspeed, gentlemen, and good luck."

With that, the men saluted, mounted their horses, and broke into a canter as they exited the parade square.

* * *

David arrived at the Limpopo River late one afternoon. He had lost track of how many days he had been riding: a week, perhaps a bit more, but he wasn't too concerned. His spirits lifted when he stopped on the sandy cliff edge that marked the southern bank of the river. He was at exactly the same place where he and Morris had met up with Captains Bailey and Rudge when they had overtaken their wagon convoy. Signs of their old camp were still visible in the sand, along with signs of other parties having also used this location for their overnight stop. There was a definitive area in the sand that was used as a fireplace; charcoal and light grey ash remained where the fires had burnt out.

David dismounted and knelt by the ashes, holding his hand over them, searching for any heat. It was cold, and judging by some dry vegetation that had fallen on top of the ash, it had not been used for quite some time. Enjoying the familiarity of the site, David decided to make camp and began gathering firewood. The ground was sandy, soft, and cool, and he knew that this was a perfect place to spend the night. Darkness came quickly in the winter months. Once he had eaten some salted and dried meat, something the Dutch communities called "biltong", and had washed it down with a mug of hot tea, he prepared for the night.

Just as he was about to climb under his blanket, he noticed a small fire burning on the opposite bank of the river. Having had his curiosity aroused, he pulled out his telescope and focussed in on the fire. Although the fire itself was clear to see, it was hard to make out what or who was around it. It looked like three or four people sitting and not doing anything much at all. Then a figure of a man stood up and walked off to the side. David thought that, if there were four men, it would probably consist of a BSAC dispatch, heading to Mafeking, more than likely with a bag of post and other documents. He folded his telescope and settled in for the night, deciding he would cross the river at first light to see if he could converse with them while they had their morning coffee. He was very keen for some conversation.

Before the sun came up, and as the sky was turning from black to mauve and purple colours, David rolled up his blanket and saddled up Bruno. By the time he had led his horse down a cutaway in the cliff and arrived on the far bank of the Limpopo, the sky had already begun to change from the deep purple of early dawn to rich shades of red and orange. He found the men where he thought they would be and he was right; they were BSAC soldiers on their way to Mafeking. After introductions were made and coffee poured, they sat around the fire to warm up.

The news from up north was not good. David was worried about Morris being stranded in KoBulawayo, right next to the royal village. The soldiers, however, firmly believed the European population there would be well protected by the BSAC. In fact, they were on their way to Mafeking to alert the top brass to send reinforcements and weapons as quickly as possible.

"It may well be that nothing comes of it," one soldier reflected. "It's simply that the Ndebele are knocking some Shona heads together. The problem is that, if we intervene and give the Ndebele a slap on the wrist and tell them not to harass the Shona, they might – just might, I say – take exception to that, and have a go at us. We want to make sure we are ready in the event of something going wrong."

"And if they have a go at us, how many of them are there?" David asked.

"They estimate about six thousand. Two thousand with rifles and four thousand spearmen, roughly."

"And how many BSAC soldiers are there?"

"I think we have about four hundred men out here," he shrugged and took a sip of his coffee.

"And this doesn't worry you?" David was shocked.

The soldier simply shrugged and sipped his coffee. There was a moment of silence as they all pondered the implications that were hinted at in the brief exchange.

"Oh, I have a letter for you from your brother." The soldier put his cup down and rummaged in his saddlebag for the envelope. "Here." He passed it to David.

David put his cup down and tore the envelope open. There was a hasty letter from Morris written on one sheet of paper.

* * *

4th July 1893

Dear David,
It seems that the Ndebele are rising up against
the Shona in the north of the country. They have
agreed not to hurt the European community, but sadly,
it seems the British forces are politically compelled to
intervene. I fear that this will cause the entire country
to dissolve into war. The BSAC would be hopelessly
outnumbered, so I do not see a positive outcome whatsoever.

I do not know where or if this letter will find you. If you
do get it, however, you must make your way back to the
wagons and stay with them. Do not let them cross the
Limpopo River until this is over. Wait at the river crossing,
and I will correspond with you as I am doing now. When I
learn more of what is happening here, I will keep you advised.
I thank the good Lord that the wagons are not in
Matabeleland at this time, and sincerely hope you too
are not on this side of the Limpopo.

Your loving brother,

Morris Langbourne

David folded the letter and put it in his top pocket. The men were staring at him expectantly.

"Well," he declared, "it seems my plans have changed slightly. My brother wants me to travel up with our wagons now." He did not say he would be stopping at the Limpopo again. "Would you mind if I ride along with you until I meet my wagons?"

"Of course not, we'd be delighted." And with that, the men broke camp, and the ride south commenced in earnest.

One morning, as they crested a rise, David noticed a movement on the side of a hill in the distance well ahead of them. It looked like a small column of horses coming down the slope towards them. David's power of observation was acute and, having given a sharp whistle to catch his attention, the leader immediately brought his horse and the procession to a halt and swivelled in his saddle to look at David.

"Horses up ahead I think, coming towards us," David called over to him and pulled his telescope out. All the men looked out in the direction of where David was looking. They could see a faint puff of dust indicating where they might be, but it was too far to determine what it was.

"Four riders," David called out. "Looks like BSAC men. They're coming this way."

"Good-oh!" their leader smiled back. "Well spotted, that man! Let's crack on and meet them."

It was just over an hour before they met each other. The leader of the other team was unmistakably big, and David's heart leapt in excitement.

"Corporal Grant Dent," he said under his breath, long before the two processions joined.

The two groups dismounted and the men shook hands after formal military style salutes were conducted. News of the trouble in the north was exchanged, and some discussion took place among the men. David did not say anything, feeling like his brother that it was not his place to discuss military matters.

Just before they set off again, David pulled Grant to one side. "Grant, please do me a favour. Please let my brother know that I received his letter and that I will do as he says. I will stay with the wagons and set up camp at the Limpopo crossing."

"Certainly, David, I'll do that for you," Grant smiled back, reassuringly.

Holding the reins of his horse, he walked with David back to Bruno, out of earshot of the others. "I'm troubled by what I have just heard." He looked at David with his piercing eyes.

"I must say I feel the same. I don't think Dr Jameson has any idea as to what he is dealing with. Those Ndebele warriors are well trained, ruthless, and filled with a somewhat unusual courage."

"Yes, I agree. I have a lot of respect for them. Anyhow, look after yourself, and I'm sure we will cross paths again. By the way, your wagons are doing well. We overtook them a few days ago."

"Thanks, Grant. You look after yourself, too." David shook hands with him; then suddenly thought of something. "Wait, I want you to have this." David reached over his back and gave Grant his precious telescope, still attached to the very grubby piece of string. "You'll need a telescope. It might get you out of a lot of trouble one day."

Grant refused to take it at first, but David convinced Grant he should, as he had access to another from the stock in the wagons. Very gratefully, and with a little embarrassment, Grant accepted the telescope before mounting his horse and commanding his troop to fall in behind him. As they departed for the north, David and his convoy resumed their journey south.

Two days later, David was reunited with his procession of wagons. He was ecstatic to see Nguni and his team, along with the rest of the crew. The four company men carrying the critical message for reinforcements stopped only long enough to say farewell to David, but the wagons did not slow their progress one bit, forging northward, grinding steadily on. David handed Bruno over to one of the Xhosa men and caught up with Nguni, who was about 30 yards ahead of the lead wagon.

"I see you, Nguni!" David smiled, and they clasped hands.

"I see you, Boss David. You look strong, but I have concerns not all is well with you."

"I am well, Nguni, but it is not well to the north, in Matabeleland. Boss Morris has sent me a message with those men to say the Ndebele and Shona are fighting now. It is his wish that we do not cross the Limpopo River until they stop fighting."

"Hawu!" Nguni exclaimed in disgust, shaking his head. "I hear the Matabele like to spill the blood of men. Boss Morris is right: we must stop at the Limpopo River."

"It is a long way, Nguni. Many, many days. We will walk together."

Nguni smiled. "It is good. I have happiness in me, then."

When they passed Nomandudwane again, David re-enacted how he had got stung by the scorpion, with much embellishment and exaggerated gesticulations, providing some amusement for the men. Entertainment was hard to find in the vast expanse of Africa, so any form of comic relief was most welcome. When the convoy was out of sight of Nomandudwane, David secretly placed another coin under the rock by the log to give thanks for his safe passage. It had become a small, but important, ritual for David.

One month later they arrived at the sandy cliffs of the Limpopo River, where they stopped under the shade of some large, leafy trees and placed the wagons in a defensive laager. The camp they built was a little more permanent than usual, with David pulling tarpaulins and extra ropes out of one of the wagons and improvising them as tents for shelter. A metal bucket was unpacked to draw water from the pools in the Limpopo, which still was not flowing, but in no time they were settled and protected from the elements, and from the wildlife.

The six-week trek to the Limpopo had gone without incident. David believed it was because Nomandudwane had accepted his gift and allowed them a safe journey. He extracted a wooden crate from one of the wagons and walked to the edge of the sandy cliff, where he put it down and sat upon it. Expanding his new telescope, he looked out over the river and quietly scanned the far bank for any movement.

It looked very peaceful in Matabeleland.

Chapter Eight

Intervention

Although trade was brisk, it was also proving frustrating for a lone trader. Every time Morris made a sale in the Sample-Room, he would quickly nip into the warehouse right next door and rummage through boxes, find the items needed, then dash back to the Sample-Room to exchange the goods for cash or cheque. He noticed a pattern forming in that, almost every time he came back from the warehouse with his customer's goods, another customer had arrived, and the process repeated itself. He did realise it was a good problem to have; the annoyance was that he would spend a lot of time out of the Sample-Room, leaving his customers unattended, which he thought they might find a little rude.

What really irritated him, though, was when a customer asked how many of a particular item he had in stock. He would usually have to check, which necessitated him dashing out of the Sample-Room again, finding the particular item, counting how many he had, and then dashing back to his customer. And if that customer then decided they did not want it, his short temper would be tested to the full. He tried hard to always appear calm and friendly, despite any inner turmoil, knowing his reputation in such a small populace was the key to success. A sales technique he tried, which proved to work well for him when a customer appeared to be testing his patience, was to return from the warehouse with the item the customer enquired about in his hands, and place it on the counter. He would then finalise the sale with a convincing "that will be six shillings and sixpence", or whatever the price was, and the customer, feeling he had made Morris assume he wanted the item, paid up and took the item, more out of embarrassment than anything else.

An elderly lady had come into the store one afternoon, and Morris found his patience stretched to the limit. He finally assumed that what she really wanted was some company, which explained the incessant chatter. She also asked him many questions about his goods and, what irritated Morris, was that he could not answer nearly every one of her questions, so he had to spend a good deal of time dashing back and forth between the two buildings. Finally, a solution presented itself: every time Morris needed to confirm the quantity of a particular item, he would check the warehouse, write the quantity on a scrap of paper, and then place the tally under the item displayed in the Sample-Room.

By the end of the week, every item in the Sample-Room had a scrap of paper lodged under it. Each time an item was sold, Morris would adjust the stock value. All the values were encrypted using the brother's secret "black rhino" code, which enabled Morris to include the cost and retail prices in the same exercise. The system worked beautifully and provided another advantage for his burgeoning salesmanship. He could tell the customer exactly how many he had in stock of a given item immediately, making his sales pitch more professional and organised. He would always smile when he caught the customers trying desperately to decipher the codes.

When Morris was running short of a particular product, he would use this to his advantage and invariably his customers would buy extra, keeping one "for later", as they had no idea when the next supply would come in. The sporadic supply of everything in the settlement, apart from whisky, which was abundant, led to a culture of hoarding, which, again, was great for business.

Since the new system radically reduced the time spent running between the two sheds, Morris was immensely pleased with himself. What made him most proud of his idea, though, was that when David finally returned from Mafeking, he, too, would know within an instant exactly how much stock there was and what he could sell it for, from the very instant he walked into the shop. The system was efficient and informative. He had even compartmentalised and mapped the storeroom into shelf number and position on the shelf so that everything could be located immediately just by reading the scrappy note under each item in the Sample-Room. Morris knew his brother would be impressed.

One afternoon, a middle-aged lady came into the Langbourne Brothers Sample-Room looking to buy some provisions for a long trek back to Mafeking. She struck up a conversation with Morris, telling him of their disappointment in their migration to Matabeleland. They had heard that the land was rich in gold and, with much excitement, her husband had given up his job and moved up here with the family to prospect for the precious metal. The problem was that very little was found, and with one setback after another, they had lost everything and were returning to the Cape Colony to start anew. To top it off, there were rumblings in the community that trouble was brewing between the African tribes and that, the family felt, was the last straw.

"I'm sorry to hear that," Morris sympathised. "I have just recently arrived, and both my brother and I have given up a lot to be here."

"But you are wise to come up as a trader. You might do all right. Had you been a miner, I would have had grave doubts about your future." She shook her head slowly. "By the way, would you like a housemaid?"

"A housemaid?" Morris asked, surprised. "What would I do with a housemaid?"

"She's a lovely lady. She can cook and clean, and even iron your clothes."

Morris politely declined the offer. "Oh, I'll be fine, thank you. I'm quite happy cooking over my fire, and I can get by without ironing my clothes."

"I would strongly suggest you iron your clothes, Mr Langbourne," she said with a stern look. Morris began to feel uncomfortable and embarrassed, quickly stealing a glance at his shirtfront, checking to see how creased it was. "There is a fly in these parts that they call a *putzi fly*. Have you heard of it?"

"No." Morris looked worried.

"It lays its eggs in wet clothing when it is hanging out to dry. A few days later, when you are wearing those clothes, they hatch, and the larva, which looks like a worm, buries itself into your skin and causes a very painful infection. My husband had six of these maggots bury themselves into him one day," she leant closer to Morris and whispered, "in his backside!"

"I had no idea," Morris confessed, slowly putting his hands behind his back and surreptitiously examining his posterior.

"By ironing your clothes, you kill the eggs. Anyhow, she can iron well, and she can even make delicious shortbread."

"Shortbread? What's her name?" Morris suddenly could not wait for a maid to start working for him.

"Nkosazana," the lady smiled.

"That means 'Princess' in Xhosa," Morris smiled knowingly.

"I didn't know that. But we call her Nkosi for short. We brought her up from Cape Town, so yes, she is Xhosa. She has found her sister and a brother here, so she doesn't want to come back with us. Would you like to meet her?"

"Yes, please," Morris almost begged.

"Would you like to buy my charcoal iron and my wood fired oven? I'm not taking those back with me. You'll need an oven to make shortbread."

"I'll take the oven, thanks, but not the iron. I sell irons; I have eight in my warehouse."

When the lady walked out of the shop, Morris just smiled and shook his head. "She's a better salesperson than I am," he said out loud, "she just got me to employ her maid and buy a second-hand, wood-fired oven, neither of which I really wanted!"

When Nkosazana started working for Morris and cooking simple meals, including shortbread and fresh bread, Morris began to put on a little weight.

Nkosazana was a slender young lady in her mid-twenties, and, as was characteristic of the Xhosa women, she had beautifully smooth, light-chocolate skin that was totally blemish free. Her high cheekbones and the perfectly white teeth that enhanced a wonderful smile made her a very attractive woman. She moved slowly and gracefully, and there was an air of royalty about her. She spoke a little English, but Morris chose to speak to her mostly in her own language, which pleased her and caused her to smile every time Morris tried to use a word that included one of their consonantal plosives, or "clicks". He was not nearly as good with the Xhosa language as his brother David.

When Nkosazana made a batch of shortbread, she would always make far too much, so Morris decided he would offer some to his customers while they shopped in the Sample-Room. Customers began to realise that they might get free treats when they shopped at the Langbourne store, so business picked up yet a little more for Morris. The other effect this had was that the customers would stay a bit longer and chat openly with him, particularly the BSAC men. This gave Morris a chance to get a great deal of information out of them regarding the state of affairs in Matabeleland. Most civilians would not have been too concerned with what was happening beyond the settlement boundaries, but because Morris had a vast majority of his stock and all his wagons out in the field, and all unpaid for, he had a keen interest in everything that was happening in the outlying districts. The British South Africa Company men were by far his biggest customers and an invaluable source of information.

Morris was busy rearranging some stock one morning when he looked up to find a very large man standing by the doorway, patiently waiting for him to finish what he was doing. Morris was startled because this was the tallest man he had ever seen, and he had not heard him walk into the shop.

"Oh!" Morris jumped in fright. "I'm sorry. I didn't hear you come in."

"I'm sorry to alarm you, Mr Langbourne. My name is Corporal Grant Dent," he said in a soft voice. "I have a message from your brother, David."

Morris was visibly excited to hear this news. "Oh, wonderful! Is he alright?"

"Yes. He asked me to let you know that he got your message, and will wait at the Limpopo River until you call for him."

"Oh, what a relief! I cannot thank you enough for kindly relaying that news to me," Morris sighed. He was so excited and relieved to hear from David. "Do you have time for a coffee and some shortbread? It was baked this morning," he encouraged.

Grant smiled and accepted Morris' hospitality. They sat outside under the patchy tree where the two rocks had been replaced with two empty wooden crates. Nkosazana brought them both some steaming coffee in enamel mugs and some fresh shortbread with a light dusting of sugar covering it.

Morris took an instant liking to this gentle giant of a man. He plied him with questions about David and relished Grant's answers. He told Morris that David rode with them down to Mafeking, and how he had spotted a group of Ndebele warriors watching them from a distance with his telescope. He also told him that he had passed their six wagons as they were heading north, and that he had intercepted the mail run heading south with David in tow. The mail run, carrying a message to Colonel Bedford for reinforcements, had found David at the Limpopo, where he had received Morris' message to return to the wagons.

"The wagons," Morris interjected, "did you see who was leading them?"

"They were all African men; no Europeans were with the wagons."

"No, I mean, could you tell what tribe the leader of the team was from?"

"Oh, him? He was definitely a Xhosa man. A very big fellow at that."

"Nguni!" Morris exclaimed, slapping his knee in delight. "Good man! He did it."

"They were all Xhosa, come to think of it," Grant said, scratching his head, trying to remember what he saw.

"They were all Xhosa?" Morris said incredulously.

"Yes," Grant replied, raising an eyebrow, wondering where this was going.

"Well, I never..." Morris trailed off. "So, tell me, where are you from? What brought you to this strange land?"

Together they talked for a good half an hour before Morris changed the subject to company matters.

"What's happening out there with the Ndebele and the Shona?"

Grant shook his head and looked at his empty coffee cup for a moment. "It's pretty bad, it seems. The Shona have taken a bit of a hiding at the hands of the Ndebele; I believe a couple of hundred have been killed so far. The postal run is being reduced from four to two men in the future so that more of us can be channelled into active service. Reinforcements are needed rather desperately. I have been called into Major Seward's office later this morning, so I have a feeling I am being pulled off the postal run to go up north. I can't say I am looking forward to this."

"But aren't you men outnumbered?" Morris was very concerned.

"Very much so. As far as the entire country is concerned, I am told there are about 700 of us and about 100,000 Ndebele. Of the 100,000 Ndebele, they estimate that some 20,000 thousand have guns and the other 80,000 consist of spearmen."

"What? Forgive me, but I really don't think you have any hope of winning this fight. Who gave them guns, for heaven's sake?"

"We did, in exchange for mining concessions. We do have some things going for us, however. The Ndebele have not been trained to use the guns properly, and we have a newly invented and very powerful weapon called a Maxim machine gun. It has never been used in battle before, but it can fire about 600 bullets per minute. It will give us an advantage."

"If it works," Morris said sarcastically. "Still, 700 against 100,000 doesn't sound like good odds to me, even with a machine gun. How many of these new Maxims has the company got?"

"Three, I think."

There was an unpleasant, awkward silence as they pondered the implications.

"Well, I must be off," Grant broke the long silence and stood up. "Thanks for the coffee and biscuits."

"I thank you for passing on the news about my brother and the wagons. You have no idea how important that is to me. Listen, I have a new maid, Nkosazana," he pointed to the young Xhosa lady, who was vigorously washing one of his shirts on a washboard over a bucket of extremely soapy water, "and she is fattening me up. I can't make her cook small quantities. Please, if you ever need some company or a meal, I would welcome your presence."

"Thanks, Morris," Grant smiled. "I may well take you up on that offer."

"You must, I insist," Morris urged, as they shook hands and Grant departed for Major Seward's tent.

The following day was fraught with problems that pushed Morris to the edge of his always limited tolerance. The door to the Sample-Room fell apart when he opened the shop in the morning, with a heavy piece of wood falling onto his toe, which put him in a foul mood. As he sat down for his mid-morning coffee, the jack-in-the-box triggered itself, giving Morris such a fright he spilt most of his coffee all over his cash book. And then, to top it off, one of the tables they had built to display their bolts of material finally gave in under the weight and two of the legs collapsed, causing the rolled fabric to scatter across the dirt floor. By now, Morris was ready to explode.

Nkosazana helped Morris stand the rolls of fabric on their ends and she began to dust them off gently while he set about repairing the display table before they both lifted the bolts back into place. Once that was done, Morris banished the jack-in-the-box to the farthest corner of the shed and then set about checking the stability of the remaining tables and shelves. By mid-afternoon, the day seemed to be improving, topped by a delivery of a hand-written note from Major Seward inviting him to join him in the officer's mess for dinner, an invitation Morris accepted immediately.

Major Seward was in fine spirits when Morris met up with him, and they enjoyed a simple but delicious meal together.

"Your Corporal Dent called around to see me today," Morris smiled. "He brought me good news about David."

"Oh, jolly good. All is well, I trust?"

"Indeed. Your men found David and passed my message on to him. I must thank you again. David is waiting at the Limpopo crossing until this matter with the Ndebele is sorted out."

"A good place to wait, I would agree," the major said as he took a sip of his whisky. "By the way, Corporal Dent is now Captain Dent. I promoted him today. A first-class man, he is. He will make a fine officer."

"Major, I know it's none of my business, but has the BSAC engaged the Ndebele yet?"

"No. The doctor is negotiating with them up near Fort Victoria. He has told them to leave the Shona alone."

"So perhaps we may get off lightly after all?"

"Between you and me, I don't think so. There is so much confusion and tension from both sides. The doctor is waiting for reinforcements from Mafeking and Kimberley, yet he has orders from Rhodes to protect the Shona. The Ndebele have orders from Lobengula, and one of those orders, thankfully, is that his warriors must not harm any European. All three sides have been put in a very precarious position. I believe the Ndebele have been given their last warning to stop attacking the Shona. Everyone is on tenterhooks right now."

"Has Captain Dent gone up to help?"

Major Seward raised an eyebrow and stared at Morris from slit eyelids.

"You're very perceptive. Yes, I sent him up there on the double. We will need every able-bodied man to be there, if trouble starts. The problem is, it takes two to three days to ride from here to Fort Victoria, and the same to ride back. News is always delayed by about two to three days, and reinforcements take two or three days to get there. It's a real bind."

Just then an officer approached their table on the double, stopped, and saluted. Major Seward dabbed his lips with a napkin. "At ease, Corporal. What is it?"

"Rider from Fort Victoria, sir. He wishes to see you urgently, sir."

"Show him in, then. Thank you, Corporal."

"I'm afraid you will need to come outside, sir. He has been wounded in battle and has been whisked to the infirmary."

"Blast!" Major Seward sighed in despair. "I fear it has begun."

Morris began to close up shop over the lunch break because he wanted to nip down to Sharon Kaufman's camp to see if she had heard from her husband. It worried him that a very large portion of his stock was out in the lands with his wagons. He was also increasingly worried about the safety of his traders because, without their business, he was in a dire predicament. As soon as he had secured the door, Major Seward arrived.

"So sorry to have abandoned you last night, Morris. A nasty state of affairs, I'm afraid," he said, walking up to the old wooden crate under the tree and sitting down. Morris joined him.

"Is everything alright?" Morris questioned, knowing full well what the answer would be.

"The messenger last night is a friend of mine, Captain Charles Rudge," he sighed, and leant against the tree, crossing his legs in front of him.

"I know him. We have met twice before. How badly is he wounded?"

"A good man, yes," Seward stared into the distance momentarily. "Oh, thank the good Lord he will be fine. An Ndebele warrior threw a spear at him, and he only saw it at the last second. He put his right hand up to protect himself, and it went right through his hand and glanced off the side of his face, nearly taking his right ear completely off. Lucky for him the doctor was on hand to patch him up. The problem is, he won't be able to fire a gun for a while, so they sent him back with news from Fort Victoria.

"I thought King Lobengula had ordered his men not to attack the Europeans."

Major Seward told Morris that the entire incident was very confusing. Nobody was sure who started it. It appeared that a group of BSAC soldiers had stopped a group of Ndebele from raiding a Shona village and that had enraged the Ndebele. A shot had been fired, a spear thrown, and the next moment all hell had broken loose. It looked as though six to eight Ndebele had been killed in the ensuing melee, and that Captain Rudge had been the only casualty on their side. Captain Dent had secretly gone to their position with a troop of men to deliver one of the three Maxim machine guns to the doctor, who had retreated to an outcrop of hills, expecting the Ndebele to mobilise their reinforcements very soon. Another troop with a Maxim was also heading their way but from another direction.

Morris was deeply perturbed. "Aren't you worried that the royal village is not even a mile away through those trees?"

"Yes, I am, if the truth be known. That is why the third Maxim is staying right here," Seward admitted. "Anyhow, I must be off. I just wanted to personally apologise for last night."

"No apology necessary, Major," Morris replied. "I totally understand. Another day perhaps."

"Indeed." Seward smiled at Morris with thin lips and took his leave.

David put on his hat, picked up his rifle, and slung his new telescope over his shoulder. "Nguni!" he called. "I'm going to hunt for some meat. Would you like to come with me?"

Nguni walked up to David and looked out over the river into Matabeleland. "I think today you must take Daluxolo. He knows the land here better than me," he said slowly in his deep, baritone voice.

"Then so it shall be, Nguni," David responded politely. "I thank you for telling me this."

David soon found out that Daluxolo shared his passion for the African bush and the wildlife within it. He provided a wealth of information about the animals, insects, birds, trees, and bushes, and was incredibly knowledgeable when it came to bushcraft. He could tell what animal had left a footprint on the ground, how big it was, and how long since it had passed by. A piece of bent grass or a broken twig told Daluxolo a detailed story, and he began to tell these stories to David, who soaked them all in, committing them to his notebook at night with a pencil that he kept sharp with his sheath knife. Daluxolo showed David what berries he could eat, what seeds were poisonous, and what roots, bark, and leaves could be used for medication to treat a host of ailments. It wasn't long before David and Daluxolo would venture out into the bush every day, leaving Nguni and his men to tend to the oxen and their camp. It pleased Nguni no end that David was becoming such a good friend of his brother.

One afternoon, when they were returning from a hunt, David saw a flock of vultures sitting in the branches of a dead tree. He pointed them out to Daluxolo and related his story about how the first time he had seen them he thought they hunted in packs. Daluxolo laughed at the story, as he could understand why David would think that.

"Those birds have big claws, and their beaks are like sharpened knives for cutting meat off an animal," he told David. "But they are a very important bird in this land. Every tribal king gives them his full protection. They are a symbol of life because they never take a life; even the life of a small rat they do not take. Instead, they eat only from animals that are already dead. They also symbolise power. I am told there is a tribe somewhere, many miles from here, where it is their custom that to be a man one must take a feather from the vulture, but they may not kill it. The feather must be plucked when the bird is alive and strong."

"How do they do that, Daluxolo, when the bird is so powerful himself?" David questioned his tutor.

"It is very, very difficult. First, the boy must dig a deep hole in the ground, so deep that he can stand in it, but no wider than his shoulders. Then he needs to kill a small animal, like the impala, and place it right on the edge of the hole he has dug, before climbing into it himself and covering his head with some branches and leaves. And then he must wait a long time. When the vultures smell the dead animal, they will come and sit on trees nearby to look for danger, just like those birds are doing now."

He pointed to the tree where the forlorn vultures perched. "When they think it is safe, one by one, they will fly down to the animal. But once they taste the meat of the animal, they forget everything around them and eat with anger, even fighting themselves at times. It is during this time that the boy must reach up and take a feather off one of the birds. If he is not careful, then they will attack him, too.

"Then once he has his feather he must wait for nightfall, when the birds will leave before he can go back to his village. When he wears that feather, he becomes a man. But if he cheats and wears a feather from a dead vulture, he himself will die, and be eaten by other vultures where he lies on the ground."

David was fascinated by that story and knew he would never forget this captivating tale of life in the wild. When they returned to camp, he wrote it down in his journal with all the other stories Daluxolo had told him. He felt a need to attempt that challenge himself, not so much to prove his manhood or test his ego, nor even to pluck one of its feathers, but to bring himself to within inches of one of Africa's most ferocious birds.

Every two or three days, the BSAC postal run would pass through David's camp in one direction or another. On some days they would camp for the night; on other days they would press on, stopping only for a rest and to share the news of the tension further north. They also spoke of the reluctance for anyone down south to rally up reinforcements, believing that the talk of "tension" was just a lot of hot air, based on unwarranted fear.

One morning, David woke to the monotonous start of yet another day. He had been sitting by the river for over two weeks, and news from passing soldiers on the mail run indicated that the tension had reached breaking point. After Dr Jameson and his men had intervened and defended the Shona in the violent confrontation that had resulted in Captain Rudge's stopping a spear with his hand, the Ndebele were angry. They needed to assert their authority over their kingdom, something the doctor had anticipated might happen. King Lobengula's impi had now gathered around Dr Jameson, and an attack seemed imminent. Meanwhile, the doctor had received reinforcements in the form of about 300 extra reservists and volunteers from Fort Salisbury, farther north, and two Maxim machine guns from KoBulawayo to the south. The stage was set for a showdown, which did not look too promising for the BSAC, and there was nothing David could do but wait it out.

"Daluxolo!" David called to his new friend, "I want to see if I can get close to the vultures, like the boys of that tribe you told me about. I do not wish to claim a feather, that is for the men of that tribe, but I do wish to look at these important birds very closely without disturbing them." Both Daluxolo and Nguni were shocked at his statement.

"That which I told you can only be done by that tribe." Daluxolo was concerned. "Those birds are very dangerous. It is not wise."

"You know I like all animals, but especially the birds. I would very much like to study such a respected bird from close quarters."

The two Xhosa brothers nodded their understanding. "It is good. Then so be it," Nguni announced with grave authority.

David found a suitable area in a small clearing, but digging the hole was hard work: the ground was baked solid There were many stones and rocks that jarred every bone in his body when his spade slammed into them. Yet, he denied any help from Nguni and Daluxolo, saying it was something he had to do alone, although he wished his pride had allowed their help. It took half a day to reach five feet deep, and by then David was exhausted. His own height was just a little more than that so he stopped digging, accepting that he would dig no deeper.

Having shot an impala for the pot later that evening, he carried the remainder of the carcass early on the following morning to the fox-hole that he had dug and laid it down right up against the lip of the hole. He collected some branches and twigs and laid them carefully to appear randomly around the dead animal and the hole, before jumping in and loosely covering his head.

Then he waited, for a very long time

When the sun finally began to set, he emerged from the hole, disappointed that nothing had happened. As he stretched his aching muscles, he peered at all the trees around him, but not a bird could be seen. When he later walked into camp, Nguni and his team could see the disappointment on his face, so they chose not to discuss it. Nguni distracted him instead with the news that a BSAC mail run had passed through and left a letter for him at which David was elated, all despondency evaporating immediately. He gratefully took the letter from Nguni and opened it.

* * *

15th August 1893
Langbourne Bros. KoBulawayo

Brother David,
I regret to tell you that a war has broken out near
Fort Victoria. Latest reports are that the Ndebele warriors
attacked Dr Jameson's camp two days ago. Reinforcements
from Mafeking have not arrived, so the BSAC are grossly
outnumbered.
I met Captain Grant Dent (yes, he has been promoted) who
passed your message on to me. I also gleaned from him that
all your men are Xhosa. I do not know how you did that, but
I congratulate you nonetheless. Grant has been sent to assist
Dr Jameson in Fort Victoria. I am concerned for his safety.
Captain Charles Rudge has been wounded, but not too seriously,
thank the good Lord. He is here in KoBulawayo now. His
military leadership will be most welcome in the community.
Business is still brisk, but we are desperate for more stock.
Although I long for your arrival here with the wagons; if the
Ndebele win this war, which I fear is more than likely, they will
surely attack KoBulawayo next. Yet you may rest assured in
knowing that, if I believe this might happen, I will flee the
settlement immediately and meet you at the Limpopo River.
We will then have to make a plan to relocate our business
somewhere in the Cape Colony.
I will keep you informed with developments.
Your loving brother,
Morris

* * *

David was so shocked at what he had read that he fetched his notebook immediately and wrote a letter in return:

August 1893
Limpopo River, Transvaal Republic

Dear Morris

    I have received your letter with much concern. Your personal safety is of far greater concern than the value of the business in KoBulawayo, and I would urge you to flee without any hesitation.

    Please remember that if the Ndebele win and attack KoBulawayo, they will more than likely cut off any escape route, so I encourage you to make your decision with haste. We both know how cunning, ruthless, and powerful they are. What I do not understand is why you have not left already.

    Nguni agreed to help bring the wagons up. When we were in Mafeking he discovered a brother there: a wonderful man called "Daluxolo", who has taught me a great deal about the bush.

    Daluxolo had other friends and relatives in Mafeking who have made up the rest of the team, and yes, they are all Xhosa. How fortunate is that?

    I have set up camp on the south side of the Limpopo River, where I find myself somewhat comfortable, but rather bored indeed.

    I look forward to hearing from you soon.
Your loving brother,
David

He tore the page out and placed it back in the envelope that Morris' letter had come in, crossed out his name, and re-addressed it to Morris in KoBulawayo. In the morning, he gave the letter to Nguni to pass on to the first postal run that was travelling north, before he walked back to the impala carcass and the hole he had dug.

The impala now smelt putrid, and there were a tremendous number of flies buzzing around the flesh of the decaying animal. David had put the impala into the hole overnight to try and prevent hyenas and other nocturnal predators from stealing his bait, but he could smell it before he got to his hide. While attempting to hold his nose, he removed the carcass and placed it back on the lip of the hole before reluctantly climbing into his protective pit and covering his head loosely with twigs and leaves again. He was not looking forward to another day in the hole, but at least it was cool, and after a short while he became accustomed to the rancid odour. In one sense he was glad for the temporary isolation it gave him from the team of men, the oxen, and the passing soldiers, as sometimes it was good just to be alone for a while.

As the day dragged on sluggishly, David's legs and back began to ache. He could not look up for long as his neck hurt when he did, so he spent virtually all the time staring at his boots and stealing an occasional peek out between the meagre cover over the hole to see if any vultures were in the tree branches. It gave him an inordinate amount of time to think about their life so far; the perilous situation his brother was in and how his brother's quick thinking had kept David back at the river and so allowed him to stay with the wagons in safety. He thought about how lucky they had been in their cigarette business in Port Elizabeth, but that they could be on the verge of losing a very large part of their financial worth, all because of an escalating war between the British chartered company and the Ndebele.

Being Polish by birth and Irish by citizenship, David wanted no part of another country's war, let alone anyone's war. Yet the conflict was having a profound effect on their business, their future, and their safety. He thought about his family back in Ireland and wondered if they had received the money that had been sent to them, and if they had moved into a warm and liveable home, free from the ice-cold winters and miserable diet of potatoes and gravy.

His thoughts drifted to the furnace in the foundry where he had worked in Ireland, and the flames seemed to be drawing him in, calling him, smiling, laughing; and then suddenly he bumped his head on the side wall of the hole as his knees buckled. He had nodded off: it was just a dream, his mind playing games. He wanted to laugh at himself, but he felt groggy and ached all over. He reached for his tin water bottle and took a sip of the lukewarm liquid. Suddenly a shadow flashed past the entrance of the hole, darkening it for a split second, startling David. Barely moving, he looked through the twigs that covered his head and scoured the tree branches in his view, but saw nothing, nor heard anything.

Curiosity was getting the better of him, but he restrained himself and did not emerge from the hole.

Only a couple of minutes passed before the dark shadow rapidly crossed the entrance to the pit again, but this time he heard a whoosh as it went past. David froze in anticipation. He was convinced a flock of vultures had arrived, and they were carefully checking the area for danger. Finally, he saw a vulture land on a branch of a tree nearby and his spirits soared. Ungainly in its flight, the giant bird had to flap its wings momentarily as it touched down to get its balance before it was quickly joined by another three of its kind.

It seemed ages, however, before one of the raptors flew down to the edge of David's hole, where it stood nervously surveying the area and stealing glances at the impala carcass that was emitting its vile odour. David felt an overwhelming desire to move the twigs that were disguising him, to climb out of the pit and touch the vulture. As ugly and menacing as it looked, with a hooked beak, bald head, and feathers in disarray, he saw a strange beauty in the raptor and wondered how it could possibly fly.

Suddenly, another vulture arrived and landed right on the carcass. It was only inches from his face, and he was looking up at its belly. He could smell it even through the decomposing antelope. He did not know how to describe that smell, but whatever it was, it was not pleasant, and it seemed decidedly unhealthy. The bird lifted its wing momentarily, and David saw three or four black flies holding onto its feathers. They looked like flies, but they were much flatter than the usual kind that irritated him. Quickly they scurried along the body of the vulture, and like magic slid between the soft feathers and disappeared. He instantly decided that he did not like the look of them, and wondered if the flies were feeding on the bird's blood, which thought immediately gave him the shivers. Within moments of the second vulture arriving, a violent feeding frenzy began. Many birds were suddenly on top of the carcass, screeching and flailing their wings, beating off their own kind, tearing into the flesh of the dead impala. David started to worry that the strange flies on the birds would become dislodged and feed on him.

As the noise escalated, the situation became extremely scary and David became very uncomfortable. So much sand, dirt, and stones were flying into his face that he could not open his eyes to see anything. He wanted to escape the confines of his pit. Suddenly one of the birds found the intestines of the antelope and ripped them out, causing them and their decayed contents to freely spill onto David's head and shoulders, taking with them his fragile covering of protection and seclusion and exposing him to the ravenous birds.

The stench was overwhelming, and David's stomach heaved involuntarily. Not only that, but the vulture's main meal of the day was draped all over him, and he quickly realised that he had to get out of the hole immediately. Throwing his arms out of his earthen confines and bellowing as loudly as he could, he startled the flock of birds, which instantly broke off the frenzy and took to the trees with some ungainly flapping of their wings. Some birds just hopped frantically along the ground, not even making an attempt to take off. David did not waste a second, but clambered directly out the pit and bolted for the tree-line. As he ran, he tugged at his head and shoulders, frantically pulling off the entrails, which automatically wrapped around his feet, causing him to fall clumsily in the dust.

Picking himself up as fast as he possibly could, he ran for cover and only stopped running when he was well and truly clear of the vultures. At that point, he took stock of himself: his dented pride and his disgusting condition. He reeked of putrid meat and decaying animal body fluids, which plastered his hair and his sparse beard, while all sorts of dirt, grit, and dried leaves stuck to his body and clothing. Once again, Africa had taught him that all of the wildlife, including the larger birds, were to be respected at all times. Dejected and embarrassed at the thought of what he would have to tell Nguni and Daluxolo, David trudged back to camp.

Before reaching the camp, however, he made a detour around the back, giving his men a wide berth, and climbed down onto the sandy riverbed of the Limpopo. He made his way further to a pool of still water, well clear of where they had collected the life-giving liquid, as he did not want to pollute their drinking water by taking a swim in it, especially in his disgusting condition. The pond he found was small, and after walking around it several times checking for movement, he was satisfied that no crocodile called it home. He stripped off all his clothing and, totally naked, waded into the cold water and washed himself down. He did the best he could with his clothing before dressing himself and returning to the camp, dripping wet and very uncomfortable.

Nguni and Daluxolo's first reaction was pure horror. But as David started to tell them his sad story, they began to chuckle, and finally laughed openly as the tale unfolded. David's embarrassment did not last long as he started to see the funny side of it, so he embellished the story a little and joined in with the laughter.

"So, my friends," David concluded, "I love the birds of your land, but it seems they do not love me. It is obvious that I may only look at them, but not touch them; neither their eggs nor their feathers. I now carry with me a very big respect for the young men of the tribe who take the feather of a living vulture, for that young man is truly a brave warrior. Braver than I could ever be."

Nguni shook his head slowly in thought. "So it must be then, Boss David."

David was confused with this statement. "What must be, Nguni?"

"The Matabele warrior who called you 'Shaya'nyoni', the 'Fighter of Birds': he has chosen your name well."

David began to laugh. "I still don't like that name, Nguni," he chuckled.

Chapter Nine
Ireland 1893

It was a warm summer's evening in Dublin as Reuben Jacob Langbourne left the synagogue and walked home to see his family. Since his life had turned a very pleasing corner, he was quite happy.

During the previous year, he had received a letter from the manager of a big bank in Dublin, inviting him to present himself without delay. Donning his best garments and taking time to groom his beard, he had made the arduous journey from a rural village to the capital city, a journey he had never enjoyed making.

It had been a great shock when the bank manager had showed him an instruction he had received to give Reuben the tidy sum of £4,000, an amount that was then considered a fortune in anyone's eyes. The money had been dispatched from his two sons, accompanied by a letter written by David in his flamboyant handwriting on the letterhead of the Standard Bank of Port Elizabeth in the African Cape Colony. The letter said that they had created a successful business and had already sold it, part of the profits of which they were sending to the family. The letter came with some conditions, all of which were acceptable. Firstly, Reuben was required to rent lodgings that were comfortable for him and his family, to feed and clothe them, particularly their elder sister, Bloomy, and to send their younger brothers, Louis and Harry, to decent schools to get a good education.

The news got better: the two boys would send the same amount of money every year while they could afford to do so, but that there was no guarantee that this would happen with any regularity.

Reuben was astounded by the amount of money that Morris and David had sent him. Not knowing how two boys under the age of seventeen could possibly have earned so much money in just over one year, he thought that they might have received the money through illegal means and was consequently somewhat reluctant to accept it. The stately bank manager, however, was insistent that he would not take the money back under any circumstances. With some hesitation, therefore, and not without a few tears of joy, Reuben accepted the money and hurried as best as he could to their humble cottage in the countryside, to tell the family what had transpired.

This certainly had been a turning point in their lives, and Reuben had wasted no time. Finding a flat in Wood Quay, Dublin, he negotiated a lease agreement with the landlord and moved the family there as soon as he could. The flat was small but very comfortable, nestled in a narrow lane with many other identical flats built against each other in long lines on both sides of the street. The walls were made of solid brick that were extraordinarily thick, and the roof was tiled with slate. It did not leak in the Irish rain nor allow the icy winds to escape indoors, while the dear little fire in the hearth kept the entire flat warm in winter.

Bloomy's wardrobe had been cultivated by a fine dressmaker, and the boys sent to a well-respected Jewish school nearby, while Reuben had recently married Helena, who just a few days previously had confided in him that she might be expecting a child. All things considered, therefore, Reuben was indeed an extremely happy man. He gave thanks to his Lord every day for the good fortune his two sons had bestowed upon his family. In an attempt to leave the hardships, cold, and suffering the family had endured behind him, he abandoned his first name and took on his middle name only. From then on he was known in the Dublin community and his congregation as Jacob Langbourne.

As he turned into St. Kevin's Parade, he saw Helena and Bloomy standing outside their front door, enjoying the unusually warm summer evening. They were smiling and joyful, giggling foolishly in their cotton sundresses, and it made his heart smile. When they saw him at the top of the road, they began to skip towards him, beaming with happiness. They had never done this before, but he was enjoying the spectacle. When they met up with him, he hugged them both and asked for what earthly reason on this day they might appear so happy.

"We received something quite marvellous today, Father," Bloomy teased, with her hands behind her back.

Jacob returned the smile, enjoying the game. "Well, then, what can it possibly be?"

His beautiful young wife encouraged him further to amuse them. "Come on, Jacob," she urged playfully, "I'm sure a man of your experience can hazard a guess."

"I couldn't imagine anything at all. Please tell me, you little rascals!"

Bloomy whipped out an envelope from behind her back and held it close to Jacob's face. "It's a letter from the boys in Africa!" Bloomy squealed in delight.

Jacob could not contain his excitement. "Have you opened it?"

"No, Father, it is addressed to you. But we have been quite beside ourselves, wondering what they have to tell us in their letter."

"Well, then, let us all go inside and see what it is that they might have to say," Jacob urged, as he took the ladies in his life around their waists and led them back down the lane, clutching the envelope tightly in his hand.

Little Sarah, who was now the cutest little five-year-old, having picked up all the excitement as they burst through the front door, immediately abandoned her dolls, and ran to meet her family. Jacob lifted her to him and gave his youngest daughter a loving hug, after which they all congregated at the kitchen table and sat down. Jacob carefully sliced the envelope open with a butter knife that Helena had handed to him and preceded to read the letter out loud.

1893

Mafeking, Bechuanaland,

Dear Father,

It pleases me to be able to write you this letter to assure you that we are both very well and in good health. First of all, though, we must congratulate you and Aunt Helena on your recent marriage.

We have so much news to tell you, so I will try and say as much as I can in this brief letter.

Since you last heard from us, that is assuming our letter and instructions to the bank reached you, we have travelled by train to a town called Mafeking, which is in the north of

Southern Africa, in a country called Bechuanaland, and which is administered by the British. We bought six wagonloads of general goods, which we took north to a place called Matabeleland, a country ruled by King Lobengula.

We had every intention of walking with our wagon and oxen to a place called Fort Salisbury, but after travelling for three months, we stopped at a settlement called KoBulawayo, where we have halted and opened our trading business, called "Langbourne Bros". Both Morris and I having built two big warehouses by ourselves from logs, mud, and corrugated iron sheets, we filled them with the goods from the wagons. It was a mighty task, and very taxing on our muscles, yet we managed, and are very satisfied with our achievements. They are now the largest buildings in the entire settlement, possibly the entire country. A large sign with our family name now stands proudly in Africa.

Morris has decided that we will be wholesalers and wagon-trader suppliers, a term that I think he invented. Apart from trading from our Sample-Room, we contract traders to sell our goods from wagons around the country. Morris is very clever in his business ideas, a trait that I believe you, Father, instilled in him. What we expected to sell over a two or three-year period, we will now sell in less than six months! So, yes, the business is doing well and is already very successful, which is why I find myself in Mafeking.

I left Morris in KoBulawayo in order to return to Port Elizabeth, there to find a leader for our next wagon-load, and to replenish our stocks. The problem is that Morris remains alone because, although we know that running such a business single-handedly is almost impossible, we cannot trust anyone else to do what I am doing now. We, therefore, need some family members to help us.

Morris has asked that I write to you, Father, and request that you take Louis and Harry out of school as soon as possible and send them here to help us mind the business. We are desperate for their help. Kindly buy them a second-class passage from Southampton to Port Elizabeth. When they arrive, they are to find Mr Jack Shiel, who is the manager of The

Standard Bank over there. He is a close friend of ours and will give them some money. He will also find them lodgings, probably with a lovely lady called Mrs Sonja du Plessis, and they are to await my arrival to collect them. Mr Shiel will telegraph me when they arrive, and I will personally collect the boys and bring them up to KoBulawayo. They may have to wait two or three months for my arrival, as the distances here are truly vast, and communication poor. If they find employment in Port Elizabeth while they wait for me, then they must not shy away from it.

The continent of Africa continues to fascinate me. I do not have time to tell you all that I would like to in this letter, but perhaps another time.

We miss you, our family, very dearly. Please send our love to Aunt Helena, Bloomy, Louis, Harry, and Sarah. She must be getting quite big by now.

Your loving son,
David

The family sat quietly for a moment, digesting what Jacob had read out. Without prompting, he read it aloud to them again. After the second reading, he put the pages down on the table. As she had done a year ago, Bloomy reached over and simply touched the paper, as if somehow making physical contact with her brothers.

It was Helena who finally broke the silence. "Well, by all that's holy: what do you suppose we are to make of that?" Being more down-to-earth and matter-of-fact, she had a tendency to be perfectly forthright.

At this stage, however, they were all in a somewhat confused and emotional state. To have received such a long and personal letter from David in a faraway land that they previously had never heard of made them elated. Yet the distance was so great that even a letter took several months to reach them, so they felt a little sadness, and a powerful yearning to have him with them; to laugh with him, to hug him, and love him as a family should. Now he was asking them to send the remaining brothers away to this unknown land.

This was not how a family was supposed to be.

After another pause, Jacob finally spoke. "I'm happy for them, they bring me much nachas" he said softly. "Though my heart is warmed that they are so successful – beyond all expectations, it seems – I am troubled to send my remaining two sons away."

"What will you do, Father?" Bloomy implored, fearing the answer.

"I don't know. We have to remember, my dear ones, that without their success last year and without all the money they sent us, we would not now be enjoying the life we have at this time. I still remember what we had to endure in that old cottage."

Helena looked at her dry feet and shook her head. "The Lord knows how little I will forget that ordeal, to be sure," she replied. "We cannot deny that He blessed Morris and David with the means to warmth, food, and happiness for us all the way through their bold endeavours and hardships."

"And it seems to me that the Good Lord Almighty will continue to do the same," Jacob added.

"But Louis and Harry are so much younger than what Morris and David were when they left for Africa," Bloomy objected.

"Yes, I agree," Jacob added. "But this time David knows influential people, like a bank manager! And yet, will this man continue to care for the boys? Make no mistake: I do not wish to send my last two sons to Africa. But I am torn in my decision since I do not wish to ignore the request of Morris and David, who are providing for us so abundantly."

"Husband," Helena offered, "Louis will turn thirteen very soon."

Jacob looked at his wife and realised what she was going to say. "You are right. We will send the boys as soon as Louis has had his Bar Mitzvah. He will be as good as any man from that day on."

"But," Bloomy countered, "Harry will still be a boy: he will only be twelve."

"I am sure that Louis will be able to look after him. David spoke of neither trouble nor danger. And he writes that he is enjoying this place called Africa. What is more, the climate is far better, and it seems to produce more than enough food. It must be a safe place, and I am sure it will be a better situation for the boys. I am comfortable with my decision."

Bloomy and Helena nodded their agreement and did not say another word on the subject. Instead, Bloomy stood up and poured some tea that had been boiling on the burner. At that moment, Louis and Harry burst through the front door, laughing and chatting, before greeting the family. They were wearing their school uniform consisting of grey, pinstriped trousers that ended just above their knees; white shirts under a grey woollen blazer and black, brogue shoes. Their long, grey socks had been pulled up neatly to be held in place by tight garters, only serving to enhance their ungainly, knobbly knees.

"Guess what, boys?" Jacob said, breaking up the commotion as his youngest sons turned their attention to their father, "I have something exciting to tell you."

When the evening service had finished the next day, a huddle of Jewish men congregated on the steps of the synagogue, as was their tradition, to discuss the current state of affairs, their families, and their businesses. Business was always a hot topic, but this day Jacob held the centre of attention as he discussed the good news he had received from his sons.

"They walked for three months with wagons and oxen in the African bush to start a business. Can you believe it? They walked for three months!" Jacob repeated excitedly.

"I'm surprised they didn't fall off the end of the world," one of the congregation said with a chuckle. "Where did they walk to, for heaven's sake?"

"To a settlement called KoBulawayo. Have you ever heard of it?"

"KoBulawayo? What kind of name is that?" someone murmured.

"Never heard of it," another man commented, and was joined by a mumble of others, echoing the same sentiment.

"It's somewhere in the north of Southern Africa, a place they call 'Matabeleland'."

"Never heard of Matabeleland neither, nor that other place," a burly man with a bushy beard piped up. Another murmur of agreement followed from the group. Some men said they had heard of this place called 'Africa', but did not know much about it or even where it was.

"My sons have started a business there, and they are successful. Can you imagine having a business in Africa?"

"What's wrong with having a business in Ireland?" another objected.

"Well, all I know is they have built two shops out of wood and mud." Jacob paused. "Can you believe it? Out of mud! Adamah! Now, these two shops are the largest buildings in the country. My sons," he puffed out his chest proudly, "they built the two largest buildings in the country with their own hands!"

The congregation of men talked among themselves in a low hubbub, drawing the attention of other men, who joined in the conversation, constantly being updated by the original group. As the gathering grew larger and larger, Jacob was bombarded incessantly with many questions, and often the same questions. But with only the contents of David's letter to go on, his answers were mostly repetitive, and each time a question was asked, Jacob's answers became a little more embellished. He loved showing off the courage of his two sons, travelling unaided to another, mysterious world and starting up a very successful business. Every father loved to show off his sons, and this was the first time Jacob was able to do so amongst so many new friends.

Jacob Langbourne was in his element; life could not have been any better.

"Two businesses, actually!" Jacob suddenly remembered that he had not even discussed their success in Port Elizabeth. "They started making cigarettes in Port Elizabeth, and sold the business for a handsome profit. Now they are general merchants in another country. All this in two years! Can you believe this?"

"How old are they?" one asked.

"What school did you send them to?" another questioned.

"Do they employ people?" The questions were being fired at Jacob in rapid succession.

"Morris, my eldest, and David, the next eldest, were tutored by myself," Jacob proudly announced. "You know I was set upon by hardships in Poland, like many of you. I could not afford to put them in school. Also, all the moving from one country to another did not allow me to put them in schools, so I tutored them myself."

"Can I send my son to you?" one man piped in, causing a chuckle to stir among the gathering.

"My son, Morris, he is very smart. Whatever I taught him he understood right away. His mathematics is outstanding. He was born to be a businessman, like I once was. Short temper," Jacob put his hands in the air as if in resignation, "but very clever, I tell you."

"Are they looking after you, Jacob?" a small man questioned. The group went silent, anticipating the response from the very question they had all wanted to ask but were too polite to do so.

"Yes, the Good Lord has richly blessed me with two wonderful boys. Now my sons have asked me to send their other two brothers to Africa to help them. They will go as soon as Louis has had his Bar Mitzvah."

The congregation nodded and mumbled their approval. Then, as if by some secret command, the gathering quietly broke up, with all the men shaking Jacob's hand, congratulating him, and some patting him on the back. They were all equally happy for him.

Chapter Ten

Rebellion

The sun was high as David rested under a shady tree. Since his ordeal with the flock of vultures three days prior, he had not left camp, preferring to mend his ego in the company of the Xhosa men and wagons.

"Boss?" Nguni said softly in his familiar, deep voice.

David opened his eyes and looked at him. "What is it, Nguni?"

"Two men are crossing the river. They will be here soon."

David heaved himself up and put on his khaki hat as he walked over to the riverbank. Indeed, in the distance, two BSAC soldiers were walking their horses over the soft sand towards them. David asked Nguni to kindly arrange some boiling water for tea and waited patiently to greet the men in uniform. When they arrived, they gratefully accepted David's hospitality and enjoyed a simple meal made of leftovers from the previous night's hunt.

The news they brought with them was disturbing. There had been a violent confrontation near Fort Victoria that lasted all of about one hour, and then the Ndebele had broken off the assault. The soldiers did not have too many details, but they assured David that the settlement was safe. Half the men involved were then on their way to KoBulawayo to protect the settlement against the possibility of an uprising, while the other half were on their way to Fort Salisbury. Having strict instructions to carry urgent communications back to Mafeking and Kimberley as fast as possible, the BSAC men did not stay long, but left David a letter from Morris, which the younger brother eagerly accepted. He did not read it while they were there, but rather preferred to wait for their departure. When they had finally melted into the bush, he went to sit on his wooden crate overlooking the Limpopo, and carefully pried the envelope open.

Dear Brother David,

I hope this letter finds you well. I am concerned for you, as I can imagine it must be very frustrating sitting in the bush, waiting for something to happen.

It has been very frantic here and everyone has been on edge. Major Seward and I have become good friends, and I often visit him in his office for morning tea and some gossip, the likes of which I find very useful and helpful.

There was a confrontation near Fort Victoria between the Ndebele and the BSAC. Within hours, many Ndebele were killed. The attack was broken off, and the Ndebele have returned to their villages. Although, happily, it seems the war is already over, there is some uncertainty as to whether the Ndebele will attack the settlement at KoBulawayo in revenge. I have been told that King Lobengula respects an agreement he has and will not harm any Europeans, but it seems as if his army is getting somewhat impatient. It is uncomfortable knowing that the royal village is less than a mile away and we could be surrounded in minutes. Nevertheless, the BSAC administration believes this will not happen, and has increased protection for good measure.

I would urge you not to come to KoBulawayo yet, but to hold off for a little until I ask some questions and get a feel for what mood the two sides are in. Business has been good, and we are now very desperate for replenishments. I have worked out that we could make A' 1/2' times profit on the investment we put in so far. If we had this business in Cape Town our profit margin would be less than one-quarter of that, thanks only to the scarcity of goods here. Business is slowing down because stock is running out, and to add to that dilemma, a large portion of our stock is wandering around the countryside—unpaid for.

I long for your return so we can trade properly again, and of course, to see Nguni again.

Your loving brother,
Morris

Although David was very concerned about the hostilities and the loss of life, as well as the impending danger Morris was facing, he had to smile when he decoded the 'A 1/2' from their "black rhino" code to mean 3 1/2 times their initial investment. It was clear that prices in the settlement were exorbitant. It was a good thing for them, but harsh on the inhabitants.

As the days of waiting dragged on, David found ways to keep himself occupied. He remembered that he had bought some fishing hooks from Weil and Co. and spent a good few hours hunting for the small boxes through all the containers and crates that were so carefully packed into the wagons. When he found them, he was disappointed that he never considered buying fishing twine. When he tried to console himself that there was none to buy, he scolded himself for even buying fishing hooks in the first place!

Nevertheless, he fastened a hook to some black-cotton sewing thread at one end of a thin, whippy twig that he had fashioned into a fishing pole with his sheath knife. Daluxolo found some grubs hiding behind a piece of bark on a tree, and they set off to try their luck in the Limpopo River. David was excited at the thought of catching fish when they arrived at a large pond, which the river had left behind when it had stopped flowing after the wet season. The thought of eating fish after a diet of impala and boiled leaves for the last few weeks revived a voracious appetite in him.

It did not take long for a fish to give his hook a bite, but just as quickly as it took the bait, the cotton thread snapped. It was obvious to David that sewing thread would not work. Undaunted, he went back to the wagons to try and find a stronger substitute, but there was none. He became frustrated and despondent. But then Daluxolo told him that there was a certain tree, the bark of which the Tswana people made rope from.

"Really?" David was amazed. "Do you know this tree?"

"Yes!" Daluxolo exclaimed. "They are everywhere."

David looked around at all the trees. "Please, Daluxolo, show me this tree," he said.

Daluxolo led David to a stunted tree that had deep, hard grooves in its bark and dark leaves that were split almost in half, resembling a butterfly.

"I know this tree," David laughed, as he slapped its trunk with an open hand. "You are right! They are everywhere. How do you make twine from the bark? The bark is like rock!"

"The Tswana call this tree 'mopane'," he proudly declared. "The wood is very, very hard. The leaves can be used for medicine, and many birds like to nest in holes in the tree. There is also a very big worm that lives on the tree at certain times of the year. The Tswana people pick the worms off the tree, but they have a lot of hair, which they burn off with fire. Then we squeeze out the juice before we dry them in the sun and eat them later. They make very good food."

"You eat worms?" David was disgusted.

"Yes, very nice."

"So, how do you make twine from this tree?" David pressed.

"This tree is too tough, and we need much time, which perhaps we do not have. I will show you another which is better." Daluxolo walked off in a different direction, with David following, and stopped at very large and exceptionally fat-looking tree.

"I know this tree, too!" David said as he looked at the smooth, pale bark on the trunk.

"You know all the trees because you look at them. But you do not talk to the trees," he said with a mischievous smile.

"Yes, you are right, Daluxolo. I have not taken time to talk to the trees." David was embarrassed.

"This tree," Daluxolo put the palm of his hand on the trunk, "I do not know the name of it, but the Tswana call it 'mowana'. Many years ago these trees were greedy, and they drank all the water that the rain put on the ground. They drank so much water that they became fat, their skin became smooth and tight, and the other trees around it became very thirsty. The other trees became thin and the wood became hard, and even the leaves split in half like a butterfly's wings. The bark became cracked, as you saw, and worms began to live in the cracks."

Daluxolo stopped and put his hand on the smooth bark of the mowana tree and stroked it gently. "Then one day, a giant crocodile came by, and the mopane trees cried. Sometimes they cry so much it is as if it is raining under the tree. The crocodile asked the trees, why are you crying? And the mopane said that the mowana trees were greedy with the water and made the mopane trees thirsty, and made them old, and hard, and ugly. 'Look how fat and full of water they are!' the trees cried. So the giant crocodile got very angry and pulled all the mowana trees out of the ground, turned them around, and pushed them back into the ground, all upside down."

David looked up at the bare branches of the mowana, and Daluxolo was right; it looked like the roots of the tree were in the air, and the tree had been planted upside down.

David scratched his head, partly amused and partly fascinated. "Well, I never!" he exclaimed. "I've walked past so many of these trees and never noticed that it was upside down. I just thought it was a very fat tree!"

"But this tree is very soft," Daluxolo continued, pleased that he had educated his boss further on matters of the bush. "The bark is easy to cut. And if you cut all the bark off this tree, it will grow back and the tree will live. But if you cut the bark off the mopane, it will die. So it is better to use this tree. Inside the bark is twine, and with the twine we can make a net, and then we can catch many fish, not just one at a time with your hook. I will show you how."

That night the men cooked fish over an open fire, and as David drifted off to sleep, he remained in awe of this African land, her people, and everything that lived upon her.

A week later, David was returning to camp carrying a limp impala over his shoulder, its legs and head bobbing in time to his stride, when he found Nguni as always, at the edge of the camp, watching his return.

"I see you, Nguni," David called out.

"I see you, Boss David and I thank you for providing our food for tonight," Nguni beamed. "We had the mail run pass us today."

"Oh good!" David chirped. "Any news from my brother?"

"You have a letter, Boss David." Nguni handed an envelope over to him. David thanked Nguni, took the envelope, and handed over the impala, which Nguni would arrange to be butchered and cooked by one of the herdsmen. David then retreated to his wooden crate to read the letter, as was his custom.

* * *

September 1893

Dear Brother David,

I am the bearer of good news. It appears that the
confrontation near Fort Victoria dealt the Ndebele quite
a hefty blow, and they no longer wish to fight with the BSAC.
The number of dead and injured is unknown, and nobody
here will talk about it, not even Major Seward.
Nevertheless, everything has been calm and peaceful for
about three weeks now, so I believe it is safe for you to proceed
to KoBulawayo. If I could ask you to come with haste, I would,
but I know how difficult the terrain is. Regardless, I would like
to see you again, and certainly we could use the stock.
I have signed up 'K' wagon traders, who are anxiously awaiting
your arrival so that they, themselves, can start their wagon
trading. Abe Kaufman has returned and has sold a good 'A/C' of
his stock. I have managed to restock his wagon, but it has left the
shop desperately wanting.
May I suggest you break camp as soon as possible and commence
your trek north without delay.
I wish you a safe journey. God's Blessings,

Morris

"So," David murmured to himself, "Morris has already rented out the next five wagons, and Abe has sold three-quarters of his stock. Well, I'll be! Business is booming."

He folded up the letter and went to pass the news to Nguni, who was standing over a herder supervising the careful butchering of the fresh impala. "Nguni, my brother tells me the fighting has ended. It is time to leave."

"That is good, Boss David," Nguni smiled.

"Then let us begin to make the camp ready for our departure. Tomorrow we shall cross the Limpopo and enter Matabeleland."

The journey through Matabeleland was much easier and faster for David this time. He remembered much of the route, and his team of men, led by Nguni and Daluxolo, were amazingly disciplined, constantly working as a well-rehearsed team. All the men were happy to talk and chat among themselves, and David felt like he was a part of the group.

When they came across a fork in the trail, David instinctively knew which branch to take. On the odd occasion, he came across the two snapped twigs halfway up a tree that he or Morris had made to indicate that that particular fork was not navigable. He showed these secret signs to Nguni and Daluxolo, who applauded their foresight.

When they passed the place where they had been confronted by the Ndebele scouting party, David related the story to Nguni, who agreed that they had made their presence known as a warning, simply to let the boys know that they were being watched. Why else would they have exposed themselves? Finally, a couple of days later, the familiar smell of open fires and the distinct odours of European cooking greeted their nostrils, sending David's appetite crazy with desire.

After skirting the settlement and leading Nguni and the wagons to the rear of the Langbourne camp, David dismounted and entered the Sample-Room, where he found Morris scrutinising a cashbook with pencil in hand.

"Brother Morris," David said casually.

"David!" Morris exclaimed as he looked up to see his brother in bush clothes, appearing decidedly tacky, with a wild and unkempt beard. He dropped the pencil and bounded over to shake David's hand. "So good to see you: welcome back!"

"You've put on weight, Morris," David smiled, as he took in his brother's healthier shape. "And thanks, it's good to be finally here."

Morris got down to business without a moment's delay and quickly led David out of the Sample-Room. "I hate to tell you this, but: good grief, you stink! Where are the wagons?"

"Around the back," David replied, fobbing off his brother's lack of diplomacy. "I am in desperate need of a wash, a change of clothes, and a solid meal."

"You need that for sure. Get yourself cleaned up, and then go and see Sharon Kaufman for a haircut and a shave. Then come back here, and Nkosazana will have some homemade shortbread for you. Nguni!" Morris beamed when he saw the large Xhosa man and completely forgot about David. "I see you, my friend! Welcome to KoBulawayo. How is your family?"

Nkosazana? David questioned to himself as he watched Morris and Nguni shake hands in reunion and chat away like two school friends that had not seen each other in several years. He looked over to catch Daluxolo's attention and signalled him to bring the wagons into laager. During the long march up to KoBulawayo, the entire team had developed a silent language, using hand signals and whistles. Daluxolo nodded his understanding and started calling the men to action. David knew that Nguni would make introductions in good time, so he silently stole off to their second warehouse, where his bed and personal belongings were located, and prepared to wash weeks of dirt and grime off his body. As he walked in, it immediately struck him how empty the warehouse was; there was hardly any stock left.

A short time later, he was sitting on an old wooden crate with a sheet draped around his shoulders, listening to Sharon Kaufman telling him excitedly how their situation had changed, thanks to the Langbourne boys. Abe had been out for several weeks plying his trade among the remote mining settlements and had returned after selling most of his stock. Morris had quickly replenished his wagon, and he had left for the settlement of Bembezi, about a two-day wagon drive east of KoBulawayo. The business he had conducted in his first outing was more profitable than the two years they had wasted prospecting.

"Then there's my business!" Sharon twittered like an excited little bird. "The fabric I bought from you young men has made my seamstress business very popular. The people, especially the womenfolk, love my clothes, and I can't make enough dresses. It seems I have developed quite a reputation in town already!"

"Well," David managed to get a word in, "you will love what I have just bought for the store. I found some beautiful fabric with exciting colours, imported from England. And the cloth is of a very high quality, fine woven cotton that is perfect for this climate."

"Oh wonderful, wonderful!" the lovely Sharon exclaimed as she snipped away. "I'll pop down to your store later this afternoon and have a look."

"Oh, please wait a day or two. We have not even begun to unpack the wagons yet."

Sporting fresh clothes, a neat haircut, and a clean shave, David returned to the Sample-Room with a definite spring in his step. He felt that his life had been partitioned off into sections; he had been a bushranger and cattle herder that morning, and now he had been transformed into a businessman. He did not know which he preferred, but he knew he loved each chapter of his life just as much as the other. As he approached their camp, he admired the huge sign hanging on the Langbourne Brothers Sample-Room gable and felt proud of it.

When he walked back into their building, Morris had laid on a big welcome. Nkosazana had made fresh shortbread earlier that morning and a hot pot of coffee. He was introduced to Nkosazana, whom he greeted in a polite manner, and asked a little about her and her family. She was dressed in a type of Western European uniform: a pink, one-piece, floral dress that Morris asked Sharon Kaufman to make. When the introductions were completed, she excused herself with a petite curtsy.

"I've asked Nkosazana to cook up a big meal for Nguni and the men," Morris began. "I suggest we eat with the men and express our thanks for their effort. Tomorrow morning, I'll take you down to Major Seward's office and have a cup of tea with him. I do that regularly now. He's really quite a decent bloke when you get to know him."

"Well, I must admit I was a little nervous about him at first, because I never quite knew how to take him," David admitted. He looked around the Sample-Room as he bit into a scrumptious biscuit. "Wow, these are delicious!" he exclaimed, raising his eyebrows in both surprise and delight. Then, looking at Morris with a mischievous scowl, he added, "Better than Mrs Gerran's biscuits."

Morris chuckled. "Oh, I see you got the full treatment."

"Yes, and do you remember where I was when you got the full treatment?"

"Yes, I remember," Morris started to laugh, "but I just couldn't bring myself to tell you when I saw what kind of day you'd had."

Both brothers laughed, and Morris continued by bringing David up to date on all the news. Business had been exceptionally good, and several of their wagon traders had returned, all having had lucrative expeditions into the countryside. Abe Kaufman and an Indian trader had replenished their stocks, but all the others were waiting for David's return as, much to his embarrassment, Morris had simply run out of just about everything.

"But the Sample-Room looks well stocked," David said, glancing around the room again.

"Of course it does, brother! Like I told you, we do not sell stock in the Sample Room; it is merely a place to display one item of whatever we have."

"Yes, I know. And I noticed how empty the warehouse is. At least this time, when we replenish our wagon traders, we won't have to fill their wagons up completely, because they won't be empty this time. So it should be a while before we have to do that tedious run back to Mafeking."

"Well, that's what you think," Morris frowned. "But I'm afraid it's quite the opposite."

"Heavens, no," David was perplexed. "Surely not!" He could not bear the thought of another six-month round-trip back to Mafeking so soon.

"I've already committed five of the wagons to five more traders," he reminded him.

"Morris!" David scolded jokingly. "Don't you ever slow down?"

Morris took that as a compliment, and went on to tell David about the BSAC's intervention in African affairs. It had been almost two months since the disturbances near Fort Victoria, and calm had prevailed. Major Seward had confided in Morris and given him some insight into what was happening. Since Dr Jameson had returned, however, the major had become edgy, not divulging much information, and at the same time being overly friendly and polite. Morris was a little concerned about this, and just could not put his finger on the matter.

"I'm a little worried," Morris admitted. "Something seems out of place, yet I am constantly assured that everything is well. So, we must move on, and that is exactly what we are going to do. Now, as for Nkosazana, she is a godsend. What a lovely lady. She washes my clothes and irons them now. Oh, it is imperative that clothing is ironed because of some fly that lays eggs in wet laundry, and ironing kills the eggs. There can be nasty consequences if the eggs hatch when you are wearing the clothes, believe me. Not only can Nkosazana cook biscuits, but she can also cook proper meals. I have bought an old wood burner from a customer, who has returned to the Cape, and every second day I would buy some groceries from around the settlement, and she would make a meal for me. Now she does the grocery shopping, too!"

"I can see you are eating well, brother," David joked, looking down at Morris' belly.

The following week was frantically spent replenishing their existing warehouse and adjusting the saleable goods in the Sample-Room. In that week, David also learnt Morris' ingenious coding of the costs price, retail price, number of units, and where they were located in the warehouse. Within minutes, David was able to take control of the trading without Morris' help. In the meantime, they replenished their existing wagon traders first, and then took on the next five wagon-trader customers. Although their stock levels took another dent, they still had enough to supply the people of the settlement and the various BSAC officers that passed through. Once they had caught up with the numerous arrangements and backlogs of customers, they gathered Nguni, Daluxolo, and the team together, and arranged for their departure back to Mafeking, and Nguni's further train journey through to Port Elizabeth. Because Nguni and Daluxolo had become a very big part of the boys' lives, it was an emotional send-off. The night before they left, David shot an impala in the bush near the settlement and they ate together, feasting well around the fire. Nguni and Daluxolo sang traditional Xhosa songs, filled with harmony and passion, and then insisted that Morris and David sing something for them. They only knew one song and argued whether it was Irish or Scottish in origin, but stood side by side and broke into a rendition of 'My Bonnie Lies Over The Ocean'. They only knew the first verse and the chorus, and even then, they had to hum through parts of it, but their African friends clapped enthusiastically and the evening went well into the night.

The following day, they gave the men letters to pass on to various friends and business acquaintances and saw them off to the outskirts of the settlement. As they had done before, the team took with them one wagon and enough provisions to see them through to Mafeking. While shaking hands on departure, Nguni became quite serious.

"Boss Morris and Boss David," he said quietly, "Daluxolo wishes to talk to you."

"Sure, Daluxolo," David looked concerned, "what is it?"

"Boss David, and Boss Morris." He looked nervous. "If you need more wagons to come here, then I am happy to bring them. I know the way now. You and Bruno can return to KoBulawayo fast, and I can bring the wagons. If you ask me to come again, I will take Nkosazana for my wife."

"Your wife?" Morris raised his eyebrows in surprise. "Does she know this?"

"Yes, Boss Morris," he flashed his brilliant white teeth in a perfect smile. "She wants to be my wife. We are happy. But now I must discuss this with my father, and he with her father."

"Well, that's wonderful!" David almost shouted. "Congratulations! This is good news."

"Well, I am sure your wait in Mafeking will not be too long." Morris shook his hand in their traditional way. "I am happy for you both."

As the wagon and their faithful team slowly ground their way back south in a soft cloud of dust, the Langbourne brothers went back to their camp and resumed their lives as wholesalers and wagon-trader suppliers. Word had got out that they had been replenished, and trade was constant throughout the next three days before the pace slowed down, and the boys could take stock of themselves and the business. Their last customer that day was a young BSAC lad who appeared to be looking more for company and a little conversation than buying goods, so Morris quickly lost interest in him, preferring to let David entertain the young man while he attended to his journal and cash book.

"No, Dr Jameson is not in town right now. After the fight in Fort Victoria he came back here for about a week, but then took off for Fort Salisbury," the young private said in reply to David's question.

"Oh, that's sad. I was hoping to see him again. He does seem to get around."

"I've been to Fort Salisbury," boasted the soldier. "If you think this place is bland, you don't want to see Salisbury; it is extremely uninteresting and boring. The place is as flat as a pancake, apart from one small kopje."

David tried to sound interested. "What's a kopje?"

"Oh, just a little hill, that's all. At least here we have those massive granite boulders and some hills that we can look at; even that huge rocky outcrop to the southeast: the Matopos Hills."

"Yes, I've seen them, but I haven't been there yet."

"You're not allowed to go there. It's sacred to the Matabele. There's spirits and weird stuff that live there, I'm told." The private shuddered in feigned fear.

"So, what's your next deployment?" David pressed.

"Back to Fort Salisbury, I believe. I hear they want to keep friendly with the Shona, offer them protection from the Ndebele, and they want to secure the middle of the country."

Morris suddenly looked up from his ledger.

"Why would they want to do that?" David continued.

"Haven't you heard? The Portuguese have claimed the east coast of Africa and are pushing inland towards Matabeleland. We've already had a bit of a dust-up with the Portuguese to keep them away from the middle. And if we keep friendly with the Shona, they might help us keep the Portuguese out. If they push through and join up in the north of the country, they will literally cut the continent in half." He slashed the air with an open hand, pretending to cut an imaginary map of Africa along an imaginary horizontal line.

"And further north, the Belgians are pushing in from the west coast. If they make it to the east coast they will also cut Africa in half, east to west." He slashed again. "But the British Army is there holding them back, I think," he said proudly.

"So," Morris cut in, "are you saying the British are trying to force their way up the middle of Africa from north to south, top to bottom, and claim the country as their own?"

"Yes."

"What for? You are only here to mine for gold, not to take over the country, surely?"

"I think that was the original plan, but the Portuguese and Belgians are now well established and we can't have that now, can we? Even the Germans have claimed an area of Namaqualand on the west coast, north of the Orange River already."

"Sadly, the politics don't make sense to me," David objected. "Why do you British have to claim the countries north of here?"

"Well, I'm not sure, really. But I hear Cecil Rhodes wants to build a railway line from Cape Town to Cairo and to do that we need the land all the way to the north," he sighed. "But yes, politics is complicated and confusing. Just look at the colonies of Southern Africa alone: the British and the local Dutch settlers are not the best of friends, are they?"

After the young man had left the store without buying anything, Morris started closing the windows and preparing to secure the wooden door in place. When they were finally alone, Morris pulled David aside and lowered his voice. "What he said troubles me, David," he almost whispered. "It makes sense, actually. If King Lobengula believes the British want to take over his land, then he has every reason to be worried."

"You're right. I'm beginning to wonder if it's not the other way around: that Rhodes and Jameson are looking for a fight, not King Lobengula. But they'll still need a reason to go to war."

"They'll find one, make no error, but I hope we're wrong, David."

Later that night as they climbed into their bedding at the back of the warehouse, David started the discussion again.

"What happens if we are right and a war breaks out?"

"As far as our safety is concerned, we would be in grave danger. We would have to flee as fast as we can."

"I'm telling you now, Morris, I know how these Matabele work. You can be assured they have already planned to cut off our escape."

"We would have to make our escape well in advance and go back another way, an unknown way, if there is such a way."

"What about our business?" Concern was evident in David's voice.

"Financially, we'd be pretty much ruined. We have ten wagons roaming around the countryside that are on loan to our traders. Each wagon is almost fully loaded with our goods, all unpaid for. If they are attacked, looted or burned, we lose everything."

David spoke into the darkness. "There's not much left in the bank in Mafeking."

"I know. I have some money here, but not a lot. We would have to start all over again."

"You know we have just asked Father to take our brothers out of school and send them here."

Morris did not reply, because he had forgotten about that request. They both lay silently in the darkness, pondering what could be done if the situation deteriorated in Matabeleland, and dearly hoping against that, before eventually drifting off into a fitful sleep.

It was the middle of October, and the heat of the summer drained their energy very smartly. The sun came up early in the summer months and mornings were spectacular, with crystal-clear skies and a pleasant freshness in the air. But that never lasted long. By eight o'clock the sun's rays beat down on the earth with relentless energy and sapped everyone of their spirit very quickly. The brothers wasted no time, and were up to watch the sunrise before taking a walk over to Major Seward's office.

As might have been expected, he was delighted to see David after such a long absence, and keen to hear all about his recent journey. Having immediately prepared for them a cup of coffee, he settled down to enjoy their light humour and sharp wit.

"You'll be pleased to know," he said, as he took a sip of his coffee, "that all is well in the land. Dr Jameson is in Fort Victoria right now and making his way down to KoBulawayo with a large contingent of company men and some reservists. Your friend, Captain Marcus Bailey, ought to have been amongst them, but he was assigned to administrative duties and has now been posted to Fort Vic. I thought you might like to know that."

"Wonderful news," David murmured in acknowledgement, although he had been keen to catch up with the captain, since the officer had been so generous in giving David his only supply of morphine when they'd crossed the Limpopo.

"Forgive me for asking, Major," Morris began, looking concerned, "but why is the doctor bringing a large contingent of men with him? Should we be concerned?"

Major Seward flashed a smile that was instantly replaced with a scowl. "You don't miss a thing, do you, Morris?" He took a slow sip of his hot brew. "Actually, I have no idea why he is bringing all these men down here. All I know is that I have been instructed to make camp ready for seven hundred soldiers and reservists."

There was a long silence while everyone digested the conversation. David was the first to speak up. "Such a group will almost double the population of the settlement, will it not?"

"I thought the contingent of BSAC personnel up north was around four hundred," Morris added.

Putting his cup down carefully, the major leaned forward in his chair, crossed his arms on his desk, and looked the elder Langbourne straight in the eye. "Indeed it is, Morris, but for the life of me I can't imagine where the other three hundred are coming from, or why, for that matter. They must be reservists or volunteers."

"Everything is calm out there, isn't it, Major?" David asked.

"Yes. I'm told the Ndebele are in submission, and my scouts have seen nothing unusual. All is well, apart from a random attack on a group of prospectors yesterday. A rider came in last night with a message that a group of four prospectors, about thirty miles west of here, were murdered by a small Ndebele raiding party. It happens occasionally, but very rarely, and I've sent out a reconnaissance team to investigate."

Morris sighed, "I must admit, Major, all this activity does make me a little nervous."

"Never fear, Morris. You will all be quite safe in the settlement. We are well defended."

"That may be so, but virtually all our business interests are not in the settlement."

The major thought about that for a moment. "True," was all he said before he was interrupted by a soldier who appeared at the door of his tent. "Yes? What is it?" he demanded.

"Excuse me, sir," the soldier apologised. "A rider has just come in with a message. A prospector, his wife, and an infant were brutally murdered, presumably yesterday, by Ndebele warriors."

Major Seward looked at Morris and David in turn, then back at the soldier, his dark pupils flashing with anger. "Where?" he snapped.

"About twenty miles south of Bembezi, sir."

There was a short pause as the major played this information through his mind. "Get Captain Rudge into my office on the double. Dismissed," he bluntly commanded the soldier, who immediately turned on his heel and disappeared, and then turned to address the Langbourne brothers,

"I'm afraid, chaps, that this is not random. I'm now sure that these are coordinated attacks and that the Matabele have started a rebellion. Something is going on out there between the Ndebele, Dr Jameson, and Mr Rhodes. I don't know what it is, but nothing is making sense. If you'll excuse me, I think I have an emergency on my hands."

Without hesitation, the brothers bade the major farewell and left his tent. They set a fast pace back to the shop, adrenalin pumping through their veins.

"What the hell is going on, Morris? Have you any idea?" David asked his brother.

"It's hard to tell. I think when the BSAC intervened in the Ndebele affairs they provoked them, and now they are rebelling. I think a war is about to start, and I think Jameson and the top brass are aware of it."

"He said that last attack was south of Bembezi." Horror was etched in David's voice. 'Abe Kaufman is in Bembezi."

Morris was very concerned. They had reached the Sample-Room and he started unlatching the door. "We have to get a message to him to get back here without delay."

"I'll go," said David firmly. "I'll take Bruno. It's not that far, so I could get there later this afternoon and be back before morning."

"It's too dangerous," said Morris quietly.

"What choice do we have? We can't just do nothing!"

"All right, but be very careful. Who knows how close the impi are to Bembezi now? You'd better hurry."

David quickly changed into his bush clothes and put his precious bottle of morphine in the saddlebag, along with a spare box of ammunition for his Martini Enfield. He mounted Bruno and took off immediately towards the east. Morris went back inside and sat down at his makeshift desk and opened his ledger. He stared through the page in front of him, not even looking at the numbers sprawled across the lined sheet.

"Oh, dear Lord," he said aloud. "If this is a rebellion, we are in big trouble."

Chapter Eleven

Pandemonium

David rode hard to Bembezi, carefully scouring the bush on either side of him for Matabele warriors. It was only about 25 miles to Bembezi, but he was hoping against all odds that he would find Abe before he got there. The further away from KoBulawayo he rode, the more dangerous it became, and even now the thought rankled that he might be too late.

When he was almost there his prayers were answered, because he saw in the distance a wagon slowly grinding its way towards him. As he got closer, his heart leapt for joy—he had found Abe Kaufman!

David panted as he pulled Bruno to a rearing halt at the head of Abe's wagon. "Abe, thank the Lord I have found you!"

"David, how good to see you!" Abe said, a worried look on his face. "What's the matter?"

"The Ndebele people have started a rebellion. They are killing every European settler they find. We have to get back to KoBulawayo for protection, and fast! Grab whatever is valuable to you, while I outspan your oxen and release them." David was about to dismount, when he stopped before he could even swing his leg over the saddle. "It's too late; they're here!"

From over the crest of a low, grassy hill appeared about 300 Ndebele warriors in full battle dress, spears glinting in the bright sunlight. When they saw David and Abe, they let out a bloodcurdling cry and charged down the hill towards them.

"Get on my horse. Now!" David shouted as he looked around for an escape route. "Now!" he demanded ferociously.

When Abe turned to grab something out of the wagon, a sharp crack just above his head made him duck involuntarily and stop in his tracks, as a bullet from an Ndebele Martini Henry passed inches above him. This was almost immediately followed by a hollow thud from the direction it had been fired from.

"Abe!" David screamed at his friend with such ferocity it almost sounded like a growl. Abe needed no further encouragement, and in a split second, he was up onto Bruno. David spun his horse round to flee the fast-approaching warriors. There were another two cracks in the air above their heads as the bullets began to fly, and then a sound like a wet slap as a lead bullet slammed into the side of one of the oxen. Horrified, David heard the beast grunt and turned in time to see it instantly drop to its knees.

"Go! Go! Go!" David yelled at Bruno, who instantly took off at a blistering pace. There were more overhead cracks and another wet slap before David and Abe crested a small hill and the warriors disappeared from view. David set a fast pace for a few more minutes to get some distance between them and the enemy before slowing down to allow Bruno to regain his energy and maintain his stamina.

David was relieved, but shaken. "That was too close for comfort!"

"Thank you, David, thank you," was all Abe could say as he looked back over his shoulder to make sure they were well clear of the Ndebele.

"Are you alright?" David asked.

"I think so." Abe started patting his body. "Oh dear," he moaned.

"What?" David was concerned at the tone of his voice.

"I think I have been shot in the leg."

"Are you in pain?"

"No, I can't feel any pain, but there is blood all down my left leg."

David turned slightly and looked down at Abe's leg. He could not see any damage. "Maybe it's my leg," he said lifting his leg in the stirrup and feeling his calf. "No, I seem to be alright."

But then it dawned on him. "Bruno," he said quietly.

A minute later he pulled Bruno up and stopped. After David and Abe had dismounted, David soon found the source of the blood. The bullet had travelled between Abe and David's left legs, missing them both by the breadth of a hair, and penetrated the saddle. From there it had entered into Bruno's body but had not exited.

"I'm sorry, boy," David said sympathetically, stroking his muzzle. "How did you even get us this far?" he cooed.

"Is it bad?" Abe nervously looked back over his shoulder.

"From the angle they were shooting at us I would say he's had a lung shot. Yes, I think it's very bad."

Just then, as if on cue, Bruno went down on one knee, then the other, and then lay down, rolling onto his side. Some frothy blood sputtered from his nostrils before he stopped breathing. David looked back from the direction they had bolted and saw a plume of smoke rising from behind the crest of the hill.

"They're burning the wagon, Abe. I hope you can run. They'll see the blood trail and will be coming after us very soon." David ripped open the saddlebag and retrieved the morphine, the bullets, and his rifle, and then signalled Abe to follow him as he started running in the same direction they had been heading when Bruno died.

After about three minutes, Abe was panting badly. "David, wait up. I can't keep up with you. I'm not fit enough," he complained.

David realised that neither of them would ever outrun the Ndebele warriors. The warriors were trained for this, and it would only be a matter of time before they caught up with their fugitives.

"You're right, we're wasting our time." David stopped and looked at his surroundings as he caught his breath. "We have to use our brains."

Looking ahead, he saw an outcrop of granite rocks. "These warriors are excellent trackers," said David, "but the one thing we have to our advantage is they will be in a hurry to catch up with us, so they won't be looking at the ground too hard. Can you make it to those rocks over there, another two hundred yards?"

"Yes, no problem," Abe panted, and they both set off for the grey rocks.

"Follow my footsteps. When we get to the rocks, stay on the rocks!" David called to Abe as they neared the outcrop. The moment they stepped on the rocks, David stopped and turned to face where they had come from.

"Wait here!" David hissed, then sprinted up the rocky hill about 20 yards. He deliberately pressed his shoe into a very small patch of dirt between two rocks, leaving a small portion of his tread easily visible, but only to the trained eye, before running back down the rocks to where Abe stood, bent over, clutching his knees as he tried to catch his breath.

"Come on; we'll head back now. Stay in my tracks as best as you can. But now we have to hurry!"

The two fugitives ran straight back to where Bruno lay, continued past his lifeless body, and ran back over the tracks the horse made by about thirty yards. At that point David turned sharp right and picked his way carefully down the gentle slope, taking care to tread only on exposed rocks.

"Hurry," Abe urged, "I can hear them coming!"

"Sure," David acknowledged but did not look up. When he got to the bottom of the gentle decline, he turned left and followed what was the bed of a very small, dry stream for another 30 yards, again stepping carefully only on the rocks, until he found a bush no higher than knee height.

"This will have to do." David nervously crouched behind the sparse vegetation. "Get down here and don't move." He laid his Martini Enfield on the sandy soil and tore some dry, dead grass from the ground, sprinkling it over the weapon. He then instructed Abe to do the same, but sprinkle it over his head. When they were both done camouflaging themselves as best they could, they curled up tight and listened to the approaching warriors virtually singing as they ran, getting closer by the second.

"I'm hoping that when they see Bruno they will be distracted and stop looking for signs on the ground," David whispered to Abe. "Once they pass Bruno, they will surely track us to the rocks and not expect us to have doubled back. They will hopefully lose our tracks there and spread out looking for us in that direction. If that happens, then we make a run for it."

"And if it doesn't?" Abe was sounding desperate.

"We will have to fight our way out. Now quiet, don't move, here they come."

About twelve warriors appeared over the crest of the hill, wearing their full battle dress, with feathers attached to a band on their head enhancing their height significantly. Leopard tails dangled like a skirt around their hips, and armbands with more feathers were tightly bound to their upper arms. They each carried a stabbing spear, with long, wide blades that were held menacingly by their sides, and an oval shield made of brightly patterned Nguni cowhide. They ran in time to each other, matching footfall with footfall. It was chillingly obvious that they were well trained and disciplined.

On seeing Bruno's body they let out a shrill scream of excitement. It was clear they had wanted blood, and a fearful chill ran down David's back. He prayed his plan would work and they would miss their footprints doubling back on themselves. As the warriors passed their concealment behind the bush, David had even stopped breathing.

They were so close he could see each warrior's facial features. He noticed that they were staring intently at Bruno's location, and not watching the ground. David assumed that these twelve men were simply the tracking party, or the killing party, the bigger group staying behind at the wagon. When they passed him his hopes rose ever so slightly, but still, he was petrified.

They stopped at Bruno's body, and one of the warriors checked through the saddlebag while another walked ahead slightly and studied the ground. Suddenly, David saw one of the spearmen at the rear of the group turn around and start looking at the signs on the earth immediately behind him. David's heart sank as he realised there was a very strong chance he would notice that they had back-tracked. But suddenly the lead warrior screamed and pointed his spear upwards and towards the rocky outcrop. To David's absolute relief, the man at the back spun around, and the chase resumed.

"Don't move," David hissed through his teeth. He was sweating profusely, and realised he had unconsciously wrapped his hand over the stock of the rifle, still covered in dry leaves and grass. The troop arrived at the granite rocks and immediately split up and started searching the ground for any sign of which direction their quarry may have fled. They slowly made their way to the top of the stony hill, and then one by one started disappearing over the crest. As soon as the last warrior's feather headdress slipped out of view, David jumped to his feet, grabbing his Martini Enfield at the same time.

"Come on, we don't have much time," he spat at Abe. "We have to get to the top of this hill and over the crest right now. Quick!"

The two men wasted no time, putting their heads down and running up the long, gentle hill behind them. There was hardly any cover, and as much as David wanted to look over his shoulder to make sure that they had not been spotted, he thought best to keep his head down and run for the crest as quickly as possible. It seemed to take forever to reach the summit, but when he did, he ran for a small clump of bushes and dropped behind the meagre cover it provided. A francolin that was resting under the bushes took off in fright, startling David. Abe was right behind his rescuer.

"Did they spot us?" Abe asked anxiously between his ragged panting.

David peered through the sparse leaves. "No, I don't think so. But when they realise that we have tricked them they'll backtrack swiftly, I'm certain of that. Come on; we have to keep moving." He stood up and turned to run further away from the Ndebele when suddenly he saw something that took his breath away and he dropped to the ground heavily, taking Abe with him.

"Oh my Lord!" David cried.

Abe looked down the rear side of the hill and his jaw dropped. "Oh my Lord God Almighty," he whispered to himself.

At the bottom of the hill were thousands of Ndebele warriors, running in step with each other and moving from their right to their left. David and Abe were looking at the tail end of the regiment. The front of the impi could not be seen as it crested another hill and disappeared over the edge.

Abe sighed. "We're finished now. How many, do you reckon?"

"Thousands," said David grimly. There must be three or four thousand men that we can see. Who knows how many more are over the top of that hill."

David looked back over his shoulder. They were in a terrible situation. If the killing party came back over the granite outcrop, they would be exposed to their view, and they could not crest the hill they were on, or a thousand warriors would see them. David was thinking fast, and he could see Abe was getting just as desperate as himself.

"I have an idea," David whispered, "but it's risky."

"I don't care." Abe's voice quavered in fear.

"We can't stay here or they will see us, for sure. But those men down there are not looking for us, yet. They are running towards Bembezi," David looked at the direction the mass of men was heading. "In fact, they are running straight at the smoke from your wagon. That's caught their attention."

David looked behind again. Mercifully, the killing party had not returned yet, but he was sure that the two of them had only seconds remaining. "You see that rock over there?" He pointed to a small rock no more than a foot high and only three yards ahead. It was located marginally over the crest.

"Yes?"

"We are going to leopard crawl over to it very slowly. You hear? Very slowly. Any quick movement and those men will notice us. When we get to the rock we will be out of view of the small group behind us. Let's go, but very slowly."

They only had three yards to navigate, but it felt like three miles. And all the way they were totally exposed. When they reached the rock, they kept their faces to the ground. They both felt that if they looked up they might make eye contact with a warrior, and then it would all be over. After a full five minutes, David very gently peeked out over the rock that gave them some life-giving seclusion. The army had passed, and just a few of the less fit stragglers were vanishing over the next crest.

"There's our ticket out of here," David whispered.

"Where?" Abe was very anxious.

"At the bottom of the hill. We will hide our tracks in their tracks. They will never find us now; the ground is well trampled." Abe was about to get up, but David held him down. "Wait, I have to go back over the ridge to get my rifle."

"What? You left your rifle?" Abe was shocked.

"I couldn't bring it with me in case the sun reflected off the barrel. They would have noticed that. Wait here!"

David sidled back to the crest and carefully lifted his head up. The killing party had returned and were already walking back to Bruno's body. They stopped about halfway back and studied the ground carefully, then, noticing something, they ran past the dead horse and studied the ground again. David scuttled back to Abe as quickly as he could, grazing his elbow on a sharp piece of quartz rock.

"Quick, they have picked up our trail. They'll be up here in minutes. Run!"

"What about your rifle?"

"They can have it!"

They scrambled to their feet and ran down the slope as fast as they could. David took the lead and signalled Abe to follow him. He took a slightly diagonal run at the trail left by the passing army, as if heading in the opposite direction to them, but as soon as they reached all the trampled grass and twigs he suddenly stopped. They were very exposed.

"Abe, quick, take off your boots! Hurry!"

Abe grappled with his boots and tore them off his feet. David did likewise and then motioned to Abe to follow him. He changed direction and ran after the army, towards the billowing smoke of the wagon.

"Where the hell do you think you're going?" Abe protested through his panting.

"They expect us to run that way. We have indicated we are going that way, but we're going this way. Run like hell! We only have a couple of minutes before they come over that hill."

Grasping their boots, the two ran along the wide track made by the Ndebele army. After only fifty yards David turned sharp right and cut across the track, heading up the next hill. Abe started to lag behind, and David began to hiss at him to keep up. Their lives depended on getting over the next crest. He looked up at the crest and suddenly realised that Abe was just not going to make it. David might have made it had he been on his own, but if Abe were discovered, he would be too. He had to find an alternative plan.

There were no trees to hide behind and no rocks big enough to conceal them. At that moment they were very vulnerable. David expected the killing party to come over the hill at any second, and then all their efforts to hide their tracks would have been in vain, ending right there on the face of an open hill. The hairs on the back of his neck began to prickle, and butterflies raged in his gut.

Then he saw a tuft of grass, straw-like, brittle and coarse. It was all the cover he could find. He realised that just a tuft of grass would be exactly what they needed, something no one would expect two scared fugitives to hide behind. Grasping Abe by the scruff of his neck, he swung him around and pushed him to the ground hard. Abe hit the dry earth with a jarring thud and grunted. David quickly ripped at some dead grass lying on the ground and showered his companion with the debris, trying to break up his bodyline and camouflage him as best he could. It was a terrible attempt, but he was desperate and running out of ideas and time. David then dropped heavily on his stomach behind another tuft of dry grass no bigger than a football and made a half-hearted attempt at throwing dead grass and straw over his back and head.

"Don't move!" David growled in desperation. He looked back at the hill they had just run down and saw the feathered headdresses of three or four of the killing party bobbing over the edge, immediately followed by their heads, and then the rest of their bodies emerged.

"They're here," David whispered through gritted teeth. Dust and fine particles of dry grass caught in Abe's throat and he stifled a cough, not even daring to lift his head. "Shh…" David warned, and then the two lay as still as they could.

David watched the warriors pick up his rifle and heard them raise a loud cheer. Then they fanned out and picked up their spoor, causing the warriors to run down the hill, following their scuff marks and boot prints, the broken bits of dried grass, and upturned stones. He was amazed at how quickly they could pick up their tracks: the warriors were like bloodhounds, detecting something that was invisible, like a scent. When they arrived at the bottom of the two hills and picked up the evidence of the passing army, they gathered together to discuss their next move.

The leader pointed to the top of the hill where they had found the rifle and drew a line with his arms to where they stood, before appearing to convince his troop that their prey had headed in the opposite direction from where the army was heading. The warriors all appeared to agree, and took off in the direction David had tricked them into believing they had gone. It was equally obvious that they would have tried to escape in that direction because it was in the same direction as KoBulawayo, their home and protection. Falling into formation, they took up the chase again, and just as David was about to breathe a sigh of relief, a soldier at the rear of the pack must have called out, because they all stopped and turned to face him.

"Now what?" David mumbled to himself, but Abe did not even flinch.

The warrior was talking and gesticulating, and David thought he could understand what he was trying to say. He was pointing over the hill, towards the granite outcrop, and then pointing away from it and then back, seemingly retracing their search movements. The moment the soldier tapped his head with his finger, David knew what he was saying.

"Oh no!" he said hoarsely.

"What?" Abe mumbled, keeping his face to the soil.

"One of them thinks we are smart. He has realised that we are good at bush craft and almost fooled them in our backtracking, knowing that our trail would be lost in the army's path. He thinks the trail we laid down the hill is a decoy and now they are arguing about it."

"Oh no, oh no," Abe was almost crying.

"They have split up. Half of them are heading east, the other half are heading west," David continued with his commentary. "Don't dare move, Abe."

All David wanted now was to see the westbound group pass his location and crest the hill. As they ran, they scoured the hillsides looking for clues, but thankfully they saw nothing as they jogged past the two men, chasing the large army that had passed only minutes earlier. The easterly group had vanished out of view just before, and David and Abe continued to lie absolutely still for another full minute.

When David finally thought it was safe, he leapt up and roughly pulled Abe to his feet. Turning to face the top of the hill, they made a dash for the crest. Once over the top, they quickly laced their boots back onto their cut and bleeding feet and then ran to get as much distance as they could from their bloodthirsty enemy.

Since David constantly stopped and checked the way ahead before moving on, progress was slow, Abe kept a watch at the rear – although he did not know what he would do if a warrior tapped him on the shoulder with the point of a spear. When night fell, David chose a secluded position between some boulders, where he figured that they were very close to the route from Bembezi to KoBulawayo.

"We'll sleep here tonight. We should be safe," he reassured his friend.

"How far do you reckon it is to KoBulawayo?"

"At this rate, about two or three days. But I think what we will do is find the route home in the morning. We should be close. Then we'll wait for a passing BSAC troop to come by and rescue us."

"What makes you think we will be rescued?" Abe questioned.

"By morning my brother will be having kittens with worry. He'll organise a search-and-rescue party."

"And what makes you so sure they'll listen to him?"

David laughed. "You don't know my brother. He can be extremely persuasive."

* * *

By mid-morning, David and Abe were sitting concealed behind some rocks along the KoBulawayo-Bembezi route. David felt that he could have easily walked back over the course of the day, but their narrow escape had unnerved him, and he did not want to risk any chance of meeting up with more Ndebele along the way home. In any case, he was sure Morris would convince Major Seward to send out some well-armed men in search of them.

He was right. By mid-afternoon, a troop of six riders was spotted heading their way, kicking up a small cloud of light brown dust behind them. David and Abe remained concealed until the last moment, when they stood up and walked into the middle of the track, waving the men down.

Introductions were made, and David warned them against going any further. The men needed no encouragement, instructing the two fugitives to share horses, and then immediately did an about-turn and headed back to KoBulawayo.

It was almost dark when they rode into the settlement and halted at the BSAC parade square. Morris, Sharon Kaufman, and Major Seward were anxiously waiting for them, worry etched all over their faces. Sharon looked distraught and burst into tears when she saw Abe. David casually dismounted and greeted his brother and the major.

"Thank you for rescuing us, Major Seward," said David in heartfelt gratitude.

"Think nothing of it, young Langbourne. So, I'm assuming the rescue was necessary? I wasn't too sure if you had simply decided to spend the night, but your brother convinced me to send some men after you."

"It was indeed," David said gravely. "You have no idea how bad the situation is out there."

"Where's Bruno?" Morris noticed the missing horse. "Killed, sadly. Shot through the chest."

"Shot?" Morris exclaimed loudly in shock.

"Yes. We were so lucky to get out alive. Everything is gone; the wagon, the stock, Abe's money, the oxen, my rifle. What you see is what we came out with. Major Seward, there is a massive problem out there. I personally witnessed an impi of about four or five thousand warriors, maybe six or seven thousand, who knows? They stretched over the hill; I couldn't even see the start of the column. I reckon a quarter of them had Martini-Henrys. They were marching in the direction of Bembezi, and they clearly wanted blood."

Even in the dim light of the kerosene lamps, the boys saw the colour drain from the major's face. He looked mortified.

"What's wrong, Major? What did I say?"

"They'll all be in Bembezi tomorrow!"

"Who?" Morris asked curtly.

"Jameson and all his men. Almost the entire company. About seven hundred of them," Seward stammered. "It's going to be a massacre."

David waited nervously in the Sample-Room the following morning. He was waiting for Morris' return from his visit to Major Seward. He was pacing and planning ways to escape the settlement the moment he felt the situation was about to become dire. Finally, Morris returned, looking rather relaxed.

"So?" David enquired impatiently.

"Nothing. Absolutely nothing. Seward has strengthened the guard around the settlement, but that's all."

"What about in the royal village? What do his spies have to say?"

"They call them scouts, not spies," Morris corrected his brother. "All calm, it seems. The king is surrounded by his elite army, which is normal. So, no news at all."

Nkosazana brought them their morning tea. As they began nibbling on a fresh, buttery piece of shortbread, Morris asked David to recount exactly what happened the previous day. David had been too tired to tell Morris much when he'd arrived, but gave him just the basics. Now, in the safety of their Sample-Room, David recounted some of what had happened to Morris, who sat and listened in horrified silence.

"David," Morris finally spoke when he was done, "You're damned lucky to be alive. I can't believe what happened to you. That is shocking. I also can't believe how you outsmarted them." Morris was so proud of his brother, even though the thought of almost losing him had shocked him to the core.

"I'm still wondering if we should make a run for the Transvaal or Bechuanaland. There's no hope in hell that the BSAC will win this, they are far too outnumbered; seven hundred as against six or seven thousand.

And of those, about two thousand have Martini-Henrys and massive amounts of ammunition."

Morris gave his brother a serious look. "If we make a run for it, we will lose everything, you do know that?"

"I'm wondering if we haven't lost everything already, apart from what's in here." David waved his hand around the Sample-Room. "Abe's wagon, all his remaining unsold stock, and all the cash he had made for us has gone up in smoke. We can't ask him to repay us; it just wouldn't be fair. Don't you agree?"

"No, we couldn't," Morris sighed. "He's lost everything, too."

"There are another nine of our wagons loaded to hilt out there. If our traders come across any Ndebele they will be killed if they can't escape, and the stock will be looted and burned. We'll lose everything."

"I asked the major to send troops out to warn them and protect them, but the traders never told us where they were going, and our traders are not the only ones in danger. There are a lot of prospectors out there. Seward has already dispatched troops. If they find our wagons, they'll protect the traders. Sadly, our wagons will have to be left behind. I'm really worried for them, David. And what a stupid idea of mine." Morris shook his head in dismay.

"Not a stupid idea at all," David defended his brother. "In fact, a brilliant idea, which was working well. It's just that politics and war don't mix with business, and nobody expected that to happen." He smiled at his brother reassuringly, but that was brief. "I can tell you one thing for sure: if the Ndebele attack the wagons, I very much doubt our traders will make it out. Abe and I only escaped by the skin of our teeth. The Lord was watching over us."

"Let's wait until we know how the rebellion is going. You never know; they might negotiate their way out of this before it gets out of control."

"Morris," David said sternly, "I know these people. If there is an attack at Bembezi and they win, they will be on us so fast. The very first thing they will do is surround the settlement and cut off our escape. If we don't flee quickly enough, we're dead. I'm even concerned that Nguni and Daluxolo did not get far enough."

Morris was not looking relaxed anymore. "All the more reason to keep very up to date with the major," is all he said.

On the following morning, events unfolded at an incredible pace, which left the entire settlement in confusion and deep anxiety. Word got out that there had been a massive attack at Bembezi, and a large crowd gathered on the BSAC parade square, incessantly babbling among themselves and waiting for some sort of announcement from the Administrator. Around mid-morning, Major Seward strode out of his tented office and stood at the edge of the parade square in full uniform. Being short in stature, he could not see over the heads of most of the assembled settlers, so he ordered a wooden crate to be brought for him to stand upon.

"Chop-chop! Hurry up!" he bustled, as his assistant steadied the crate. When he stood on the crate, he stood as tall as he could, puffed out his chest, and addressed the men and womenfolk of the community at the top of his voice.

"Ladies and gentlemen!" he bellowed, his eyes turning to slits as he stared at the people. "Yesterday, a column of British South Africa Company men were intercepted and attacked by King Lobengula's impi at Bembezi. Our men were proceeding from Fort Victoria to KoBulawayo to offer us protection against the Ndebele, because it appears that we settlers have fallen out of favour with the king's army.

"We are therefore now officially at war with the Ndebele nation!" he thundered. There was a ripple of murmuring that spread through the crowd. He continued, "Many lives were lost in the attack, and it is estimated that some two thousand, four hundred Ndebele warriors were killed." He paused as another, louder mumbling rumbled through the assembled masses and waited for the noise to peter out. "The BSAC lost four men."

A deathly hush spread through the parade square. A lone, confused voice called out over the heads of the people, "Only four?" The gathering remained silent, waiting for the major's answer.

"Yes, only four men. The Ndebele are now in retreat. News of the battle was received in this camp late last night by horseback rider. We expect King Lobengula will hear of his army's defeat by a messenger runner any time today."

The major raised his voice a few notches. "We do not know what the king will do when he learns of his defeat. He may attack this settlement, or he may flee, or he may surrender. Dr Jameson and his men are in pursuit of King Lobengula to seek a surrender. I implore you all to go to your camps, urgently, and return here within the half hour. Bring with you any weapons and ammunition you may have, as well as some provisions and blankets. Tell your neighbours; leave no one out there. The company will close ranks around the parade square to offer you the best protection we can. Do not!" he yelled, then paused, scouring the wide-eyed population with thin lips and beady eyes. "Do not, under any circumstances, attempt to flee for the Transvaal or Bechuanaland. Your safety is not guaranteed beyond the limits of this parade square!"

Another desperate rumble erupted from the group as men, women, and children quickly turned to vacate the parade square and go to their camps.

Suddenly a violent explosion rocked the ground from the direction of the royal village. A second later, a shockwave ripped through the settlement, tearing leaves from the trees and causing birds to take off in fright. Dogs bolted from their owners, and a kudu bull came crashing through the trees, horns pressed firmly against its back, head high in the air as it fled past the settlers, who now stood motionless in their tracks with only their faces turned in the direction of the explosion.

Then, silence reigned. The only movement was from Major Seward, who overbalanced as he tried to look over his shoulder at the commotion and heavily stepped off his crate. Like everyone else, he stood still and stared blankly at where the explosion had come from. Above the trees, not far away, a very large plume of black smoke gently rose into the sky.

There was more deathly silence as everyone looked in confusion at the spectacle of billowing smoke rising gently, spectacularly, towards the clouds before a new sound began: the sound of rain pitter-pattering gently through the tree leaves. The noise intensified slightly before people realised it was not rain falling on the leaves, but stones and bits of debris. A log the size of a man's arm went twisting in the air over their heads, making an eerie whooshing sound.

"Hurry!" bellowed the major at the top of his voice. People began shouting and running in every direction, some knocking others over in their panic to find their loved ones or fetch whatever weapons they had, or simply to get away from the shrapnel that rained down upon them. And as they ran, more explosions erupted from the king's royal village.

Morris and David crashed through the door of their warehouse and rummaged through their trunks, retrieving their revolvers and whatever ammunition they had. They were panting and filled with mortal fear. Not wasting time to buckle the leather holsters around their hips, they ran out of the building.

"Where's Nkosazana?" Morris shouted to his brother.

"I don't know! I'll check the Sample-Room!" he yelled, and ran for the next building as sounds of hundreds of gunshots could now be heard from the village. He found Nkosazana cowering behind a table laden with fabric, panic smothering her entire being. "Come!" he demanded.

"No!" Nkosazana shook her head in defiance. "King Lobengula is very angry. His anger and his voice shake the ground."

David stared at her, trying to understand what she had said. He decided there was no time to explain these things to her. "That is why we need to go where it is safe. Come with me; I will protect you."

Cautiously she stood up, and David gently took her hand. "Come with me," he encouraged calmly. Once they were back in the daylight, he saw Morris scanning the bush for trouble. He looked very nervous.

David gave a short, sharp whistle and Morris spun around, signalling David and Nkosazana to follow him. Within thirty seconds they were back on the parade square. Pandemonium reigned, with settlers milling about, talking, shouting, and some even crying. In the distance, gunshots and explosions went off all the while.

"Quiet!" a loud and very authoritative voice yelled. The crowd went silent and looked to the voice. It was Captain Charles Rudge. He was standing on the crate that had been used as a podium only minutes earlier, his right hand sporting a heavy bandage and protected by a white cotton sling wrapped over his shoulder.

Taking charge of the situation, he directed the women and children into the centre of the parade square, placing all men with weapons around the perimeter for protection. The Maxim machine gun had been moved back from its concealed position, and for the first time, the civilians had a look at this interesting contraption that stood on two legs. It was located on the eastern edge of the parade square, pointing in the general direction of the royal village, and manned by two BSAC soldiers. Half a dozen British soldiers were instructed to stand at the western edge and direct all the stragglers who ran in for shelter and protection to the middle.

David took Nkosazana and placed her in the centre of the gathering, telling her to wait for him, and then he joined Morris on the perimeter. They buckled up their holsters and waited at the ready, expecting a marauding flood of Ndebele to come tearing through the bushes. A weird but calm silence began to settle over the gathered mass of humanity.

"Listen up!" Captain Rudge called out loudly and very clearly. "We don't know what is happening over there, but brace yourselves for an attack. Men with weapons, do not, I repeat, do not open fire until I command you to do so. I repeat once more, do not open fire unless I command you to do so, as you may hit friendly forces!" He punctuated this sentence with a very stern pause between each word.

"What the hell is going on?" David whispered to his brother.

"I wish I knew. It seems even they don't know what's going on." He nodded his head towards Captain Rudge.

The eerie silence descended again. A baby cried, and a dog barked, but apart from the distant shots and muffled explosions, no one spoke.

As night set in, all able-bodied men took turns in protecting the BSAC camp while the women and children nervously tried to sleep under the stars. There were only a handful of soldiers in camp at the time, and now the civilians were expected to do their duty. An orange glow from the royal village gently lit up the darkening night sky. By midnight the gunshots and explosions had petered out and virtually stopped, with just the occasional shot being heard. The orange hue in the sky, however, lasted all night, only to be replaced by the very welcome early morning rays of sunlight. Morris sidled up to David, who was sitting on the dusty ground, nodding as he fought off much-needed sleep. He had hardly slept the previous night, and now the fatigue was setting in with a vengeance.

"Hey, brother?" David whispered.

"Good morning," Morris smiled, forcing his eyelids open. "Looks like we got through the night without incident."

"Yes, it seems so," David agreed. "I must admit, I was very scared."

"Yes, me too. When this is over, I think we must head right back to Cape Town. This is not our war."

"I agree. After what I went through, and what I saw in Bembezi..." his voice trailed off. "This is not what we came to Africa for."

"We took a risk, and it looks like it didn't pay off. We can start again."

"I actually don't think we will get out of here alive, Morris," David confessed. "They may have won in Bembezi three days ago, but what if they went after King Lobengula yesterday and lost?"

"What makes you think they lost?" Morris was almost too frightened to ask that question.

"Well, listen." He nodded his head in the direction of the royal village. "The fighting has stopped, not a shot being fired now. And yet, not a soul has returned to the settlement. Not a single BSAC soldier. They know where we are. What if they were lured into a trap, and every one of them has been killed? We would be next, not so? The Ndebele would have surrounded us by now and will attack when the sun is high."

Fear gripped Morris. He had not thought of that.

"Riders coming from the north, sir!" a man called out, startling everyone.

On the edge of the parade square stood a structure that the Langbourne brothers believed to be an unfinished windmill. The wooden structure, tapering to a point high above the ground was always noticeable, but it had no blades. Now the brothers realised it was a lookout tower, not a windmill.

"Friend or foe?" Captain Rudge bellowed in his strong English accent.

"Look," David prodded his brother in the ribs with his elbow. "He's using one of our telescopes!" He felt quite proud of that fact.

The watchman on the tower peered through the brass telescope for a moment before looking down at the captain. "Friend, sir! Doctor Jameson and his troops. Hundreds of them!"

"Hold your fire! I repeat, hold your fire!" Rudge yelled urgently at everyone. A palpable sense of relief swept through the gathered population.

About ten minutes later, literally hundreds of BSAC troopers rumbled into camp on their horses and took up positions around the perimeters. The civilians, including Morris and David, were herded into the middle, and the BSAC took effective control of the situation. The brothers found Nkosazana and were joined by Abe, Sharon, and their two sons. Sharon had been crying, the tears causing streaks of dust down her cheeks. Speculation was rife, and wild rumours were being created almost every minute. The company men were not in any hurry to keep the populace informed, but disciplined and firm orders were being shouted out to the troopers, moving them into positions and making ready for an imminent attack.

"Morris," David pulled his brother aside. "If Jameson just rode in from the north with all his troops, he was never in the royal village. What was all that commotion we heard, then, the explosions and the shooting? Just what the hell is going on?"

Morris shook his head. "I have no idea, brother," he said, looking at all the soldiers running around the immediate camp.

Major Seward finally stood on the now-famous wooden crate and called everyone to attention. "Ladies and gentlemen! I have been informed that the disturbances we heard yesterday and last night had nothing to do with Dr Jameson and his troops. He and his men are all well! Their losses tragically remain at four men only, which they sustained in the Battle of Bembezi!" He looked around at the expectant faces all about him. "I ask you to wait here, for your safety, for another hour. Dr Jameson is now in camp and has sent some scouts to the royal village to assess what has happened. I will let you know the situation within the hour. Thank you!" he finished and promptly stepped heavily off the wooden crate.

Four hours later, Dr Jameson mounted the wooden crate and announced that his scouts had confirmed that King Lobengula had fled. In the process, the king had torched the royal village, destroying everything. Every house and hut had been burnt to the ground and all his royal treasures, including his vast stock of elephant ivory, had perished. All ammunition and explosives he had amassed in terms of the treaty he had with the British had also been deliberately destroyed, and that accounted for the massive explosion they had experienced the previous day, and later all the ammunition exploding. He further announced that the BSAC would be mounting a patrol to pursue the king, capture him, and demand his unconditional surrender. Without the king, the Ndebele tribe was in disarray, and the Matabele rebellion was now over. The British South Africa Company were assuming administrative control of the country from the Limpopo River in the south to the Zambezi River in the north, with immediate effect. The company founder, Mr Cecil John Rhodes, would be visiting KoBulawayo to assess the situation.

Just then his speech was suddenly interrupted by the watchman on top of the lookout tower. "Riders approaching from the south, sir!"

Everyone turned their gaze to the top of the tower. The watchman was peering through his brass telescope in the opposite direction this time. The settlers had forgotten he was still up there.

"Friend or foe?" Captain Rudge bellowed from somewhere in the crowd.

"Friend, sir!" he yelled smartly. "Company men, supported by hundreds of King Khama's soldiers. About seven hundred men, sir! All armed."

"Who is King Khama?" Morris asked no one in particular.

Phil Innes had been standing beside Morris. He bent down to his ear and whispered, "He's the king of Bechuanaland: a fierce supporter of the British."

Dr Jameson continued with his speech. He assured the assembled group that they were well protected now and that it was safe to go back to their tents and continue their lives as usual. He would have an important announcement on the parade square at ten o'clock the next morning, and encouraged all settlers to attend. As the assembly broke up, Morris, David and Nkosazana walked back to the Sample-Room.

"Morris, I need some sleep, desperately. I've been on the go for two days now," David yawned. "The shop's yours today."

"I also need some sleep. Let's not do any trading today."

David grumbled, then in Xhosa he spoke to Nkosazana, "No work today. We will meet tomorrow."

"The king is no longer angry?" she asked timidly.

"The king has run away," David replied forlornly, then looked at Morris and reverted back to English with a tired and confused look on his face. "I don't understand something here; am I right in thinking that as of this moment, Matabeleland is no longer ruled by a Matabele king, but by a British Queen?"

Morris scratched his head in confusion. "Nothing makes sense anymore."

Chapter Twelve

Rebuilding

Although the rainy season had been due to start, by ten o'clock in the morning in early November the BSAC parade square was already blistering hot. Yet, despite the dry heat and fierce sun, soldiers stood at the ready in full uniform around the perimeter, and settlers milled expectantly in both small and large groups. There were almost as many military men as there were civilians. While the women were fanning their brows, the children playing in the dust and the babies all crying, the civilian men were all in deep conversation. Some moved anxiously from one group to join another, listening to what others had to say, and asking after friends and colleagues who were still out in the land and unaccounted for.

Morris and David saw a group that had congregated around Phil Innes, who seemed to be holding the floor, while all those around him appear to be nodding in agreement. Since Phil had become recognised by numerous settlers for his vast knowledge on all matters, his advice was often sought on a number of subjects, so the brothers wriggled into the group to hear what he had to say. He and some of the other men were theorising about where King Lobengula had fled to, and whether he would regroup and mount a counterattack. Some of the other men believed he would not dare, after losing so many men to so few BSAC soldiers.

"I still think the Ndebele impi are all bark and no bite," one citizen commented.

At that moment, David felt a heavy hand land on his shoulder with a dull slap. "They are most certainly not!" Abe Kaufman cut in. He had seen David in the group and walked up behind him. "This lad saved my life a few days ago. We were attacked by about three hundred warriors. If it wasn't for David Langbourne," he slapped him on the shoulder again, "we would be dead. They are exceptionally well trained in tracking and warfare, and they are very strong, fit, ruthless and brutal. I saw it first-hand with my own eyes."

"What happened?" someone asked.

"They wasted no time in opening fire on us, killed my oxen, set my wagon alight, killed David's horse and hunted us down. We only survived because David outsmarted them. No, I tell you, they mean business. I owe my life to young David here."

David was embarrassed and did not know where to look. He was saved further embarrassment when Dr Jameson walked out of his tent and strode to the lookout tower. The entire population of settlers on the parade square went silent and turned to watch him in anticipation. The doctor climbed up three steps of the tower so that he could see past everyone's head, and carefully turned to put his back to the structure and face the people.

"Ladies and gentlemen!" he began. "After our intervention between the Shona and Matabele disputes, we expected the Ndebele nation to rise up against us. As a result, we sent seven hundred reinforcements from Fort Salisbury and Fort Victoria to protect this settlement, but we were attacked at the Shangani River. King Lobengula sent nearly four thousand of his warriors to engage us, but sadly, they lost over one thousand five hundred warriors, and we lost four of our respected men. A week later we were attacked again, this time by over six thousand warriors, of whom two and a half thousand warriors lost their lives, while we received no casualties." The doctor took a deep breath and paused, allowing these lopsided numbers to register.

"When the king learnt of these defeats," Jameson continued, "he decided to flee with his high command, and it would appear that it was his policy to leave nothing behind, so he torched his entire village. I have personally inspected the village, and I can confirm there is nothing left whatsoever. Everything within has been burnt to the ground.

"We do not know if the king and his high command will rebuild their army, but we will not allow that to happen. As a result, I am sending a patrol to pursue the king, capture him, and negotiate a surrender and peace accord with the Ndebele nation.

"Until then, the British South Africa Company is assuming administrative control of Matabeleland and Mashonaland.

"Furthermore," he paused and shifted his footing on the lookout tower, "as from today, we will begin relocating this settlement to the site of the destroyed royal village." A low rumble rose from the group. "This will give the BSAC a much stronger ability to protect you.

"The BSAC administration will start the relocation process. We will stake out the plots and demarcate streets and avenues. Once we are ready, all registered settlers will be notified to vacate this camp and move to stands that we allocate to you. This process will take two to three weeks. Therefore, I urge those who have not registered with the registrar to do so today. I hope that is clear."

The crowd nodded in agreement and mumbled among themselves.

"I ask that you go about your daily lives now, and take comfort that, not only are all hostilities over, but also you are protected by the company." With that, Dr Jameson climbed down the lookout tower and walked back to his tent. Phil Innes, Abe Kaufman, and the Langbourne brothers turned to face each other.

"I still think I'm going to leave for the Cape," Abe said sadly. "I'm broke, and everything I have done has been for nothing. I've had enough of this country, and it almost killed me, too."

"I'm staying!" Phil seemed rather upbeat. "I think things are going to improve. Think about it: if seven hundred of these men can take on seven thousand warriors and beat them in one day, when news gets out to the world, their reputation is going to do crazy things." He waved his hand at the bush behind him. "This country will be deemed to be as safe as houses, and with the prospect of gold, people will flood in here. No, I'm staying. I feel business will be really good soon."

"We were planning on leaving," David said. "Like Abe, we took a big risk and failed. We might have enough to start again, but we need to stack the odds in our favour."

"First we need to find out if any of our traders survived," Morris continued. "Our final decision rests on what we can salvage from this debacle."

Morris and David left their friends and returned to the Sample-Room to talk about their own future. Their finances were in very poor shape. They had no idea if they had any wagons or oxen, and all the stock that went with them were let out on credit, so nothing had been paid for. Their warehouse was about three-quarters empty, and they no longer owned a horse. To make things worse, within a week they would have to vacate the two buildings they'd erected and build new ones in the new settlement if they wanted to continue with the business.

Morris worked out that they would have to borrow money if they wanted to continue trading in KoBulawayo, and Mr Savage at the Standard Bank in Mafeking would take great personal delight in declining any application they made for a loan. Their only hope would be Julian Weil. They hoped he would give them credit to buy his stock, but Mr Gerran would not part with a wagon if it were not paid for. They also thought he might not part with a freshly baked piece of shortbread, if he knew he would not get a sale. Furthermore, they would need money for salted oxen and a team of herders.

"It all depends on how many of our traders made it. Even the wagon-trading side of our business is threatened. We don't have enough to buy wagons," David sighed.

"No doubt about it, David, we are in trouble. All we can do now is open our doors and sell what we have in stock. Give customers discounts; let's just sell through what we have and collect what we can."

"We need to ask the BSAC chaps to keep an eye out for our wagons."

"I'll have a chat with Major Seward. I hope he will help."

After two days, sales were almost non-existent. It seemed that everyone was feeling the same as the brothers, and biding their time to see what the new KoBulawayo would bring. To top it off, Major Seward was nowhere to be found. Morris finally lost his patience and decided he would walk down to the ruins of the royal village and find him physically.

"You coming?" he asked his brother as he walked out the door.

David followed him out of the Sample-Room. "I don't think we are allowed."

"I don't care." Morris shrugged his shoulders as he walked off.

"Alright, I'd like to see the village, and there's not much chance of a customer coming in..." his voice trailed off.

There was a hive of intense activity going on at the old royal village. Everything had been flattened. There was soot and ash and debris strewn across a very wide area. Nothing stood higher than two feet in the entire village, except for a small concentration of BSAC tents somewhere near the middle, and a flagpole bearing a flag with the BSAC insignia.

They walked to the tents with a purpose in their stride. The soldiers around them took no notice, but continued with what they were doing. One team were clearing away the burnt and charred debris, leaving the entire area covered in a variety of shades of ashen grey, while another team were pegging plots with broken spears and attaching numbered tags to them. As they got closer to the new BSAC headquarters, the ground had been better cleared, and streets and avenues had been demarcated with pegs and ropes. Finding their way to the first tent, they simply followed a roped-off straight pathway, obviously soon to become a street. The boys were impressed with all the organised activity.

They found Major Seward standing by one of the tents surveying the area, hands on his hips and with a furrowed brow. When he saw the brothers approaching, he broke into a friendly smile and signalled them to join him.

"What do you think?" he asked proudly. "Looks great," David lied.

"Major Seward," Morris immediately got down to business, "we are very concerned about our wagon traders and our wagons out in the field. We were wondering if any of your men might have come across them."

"I can understand your worry, Morris," the major replied, "but rest assured, we have scouts all over the place already, checking on prospectors and miners. If they come across your wagons, I will be sure to let you know what their situation is, either good or bad."

"If we have lost many wagons, sadly, we will have lost our entire business," Morris informed Seward. "None of the stock on the wagons had been paid for. Our traders could not afford to pay for the stock at the time, so they took it on credit, and that included the wagons and oxen. We were hoping to give them a start in the business world. If we lose them, we will be out of business."

The major looked very concerned. "I understand your predicament."

"It was a risk," Morris continued, "we understood that, but we did not expect a rebellion. This could break us. If we now have to buy land and build another shop over here, well, we simply cannot afford to do that. We are already making plans to return to the Cape and start again."

"Chaps," Seward said after a short pause, "there's not much we can do for you out there, but, confidentially between you and me, we will be offering stands at exceptionally low prices on very favourable terms. I think you should wait a week or two before you make any firm decision. Within two weeks, you'll know what the situation is with your wagons and your traders, and we'll be in a better position to know what we can offer you to relocate."

Morris and David thanked Major Seward for his sound advice and decided they would hold out a little longer. He pointed them to a tent not far away, where an old acquaintance of theirs, Captain Marcus Bailey, was stationed. At the sound of his name, the boys became excited to see him. He had now been assigned to allocate stands and plots to the settlers as soon as they cleared the debris away and to mark out where the streets would be.

"We now have the opportunity to create a town with a structured format; no more of these higgledy-piggledy paths and random campsites," the major said with enthusiasm.

The boys bade him a good day and headed over to the tent where they hoped to see their old friend, Marcus Bailey.

"Oh," David stopped and turned to the major, who was once again standing with his hands on his hips. "Is this going to be the main street of the new KoBulawayo?" he called, indicating the roped-off path they were walking along.

"Yes, indeed it is. I haven't decided on a name yet. Would you like me to name a street after you?" he smiled.

"Uh, no… not necessarily." David instantly became embarrassed. "I just thought it might be a lot wider, you know, perhaps wide enough to allow a wagon and team of twelve oxen to do a U-turn."

Seward stared at him. A nasty scowl crossed his face, and his eyes and lips turned into slits.

"Sorry," David quickly apologised, "just a suggestion," and then quickly resumed his walk down to Captain Bailey's tent.

"Morris! David!" Marcus exclaimed as they entered his tent. "How wonderful to see you two. Welcome!"

The three of them were delighted to see each other. They quickly exchanged news on how the other had been since their last meeting at the Limpopo crossing. It had been over eight months since that day. Marcus had joked about David's discovery of how a hippopotamus marked its territory, and David again thanked him for the morphine, which he was pleased to say he had not needed to use, and also for his introduction to Dr Jameson. Morris joked about the incident where he and Dr Jameson had played a trick on Major Seward with the jack-in-the-box, and that had Marcus engulfed in raucous peals of laughter.

Since that time, Marcus had been stationed at Fort Victoria, assisting with the administration of the settlement, until the rebellion had broken out, but had now been posted to assist in the relocation of the KoBulawayo settlement. Their name had come up in a discussion he'd had with a colleague who had also been posted to Fort Victoria, Captain Grant Dent.

"Oh yes, we know him. Really nice man," David enthused. "What news of him?"

"Well, both he and I missed all the action down here, but he has been ordered back here by Major Seward to help with the rebuilding of this settlement. He should be here in a week or so."

This was good news for the boys. "I cannot understand how so few of you could win against so many of them. They, too, were armed with Martini-Henrys."

"The BSAC had three Maxim machine guns. Terrible weapons, each one so devastating, and each worth about five hundred men, they say." He looked bewildered.

Suddenly a loud and bloodcurdling scream cut through the camp.

"Blimey!" the captain shouted and drew his revolver from his belt, running for the tent door. "Stay here!" he commanded the brothers as he tore out of view.

Silence reigned. There were no more screams, no gunshots, and no shouting. The brothers anxiously peered cautiously around flaps in the tent, even getting down on all fours and lifting the bottom of the tent an inch or so, dreading what they might see. They were beginning to sweat nervously while ten whole minutes passed before Marcus finally returned to the tent to the two very nervous brothers. He looked extremely flustered.

"What happened?" Morris asked nervously.

"It's just Major Seward throwing a tantrum." He shook his head disapprovingly. "Sorry about the concern. He wants to quadruple the width of every street that we have already pegged out. He wants a wagon and a team of sixteen oxen, no less, to be able to make a U-turn. This will set us back days, I can tell you. I swear that man has a screw loose somewhere."

David just looked at Morris and smiled.

Two weeks later, the rains had set in with a vengeance. The Sample-Room and the warehouse leaked badly, and pails were dotted throughout. The ground became a quagmire of mud in places, and the women tended to stay in their homes, their long dresses not being suited to this type of environment. In the late afternoons, black clouds would roll in and unleash torrents of rain and intimidating lightning. The flashes in the night skies were spectacular, but the real damage was inflicted simply by the wind. A sudden gust of wind would invariably bring a tent down, or tear a roof off its structure. When the settlers had built their homes, they had never given a thought to the impact of a gust of wind. Nevertheless, the community all helped each other where they could.

For the Langbourne Brothers, however, business was not so good. Their customers hardly came into the shop not only because of the bad weather but also because of the uncertainty of a mass exodus to the new settlement that the BSAC was designing with some degree of secrecy. The only business that seemed to be doing well was Phil Innes's hardware store. He was fast running out of screws, wire, and the tools required to keep the fragile dwellings upright and as waterproof as possible.

Word had come in that one of the Langbourne wagons and its trader in the north of the country had not been affected by the rebellion, and was due to return to KoBulawayo within the month. All other wagons had been lost in similar circumstances to Abe Kaufman, but two traders were sadly not so fortunate, the rescuers getting to them too late. This news devastated the Langbourne boys.

With this information, Morris calculated that with nine of the ten wagons that did not survive, they were in very serious difficulty, but that in time they could eventually recover. However, recovery would be extremely slow, and they would not get into a profitable position for many years to come. As the boys sat in their Sample-Room facing each other with a bucket catching drips between them, they discussed their future plans, whether to stay and try again or to return to the Cape and start anew.

"It's been a bad year for us, David," Morris lamented. "If you take what we started with at the beginning of the year, and deduct what we have today, we have lost just about everything."

"How were we to know there would be a rebellion? If there had not been this uprising, we would have been very successful and rich right now."

"Yes, three times richer than when we started. Wagon trading was a bad idea."

"No, it wasn't!" David objected fervently. "Your idea was brilliant! It worked, didn't it?"

"Yes, of course it worked," Morris agreed reluctantly, "but it was risky. And the risk didn't pay off."

"But not because of our doing, or your doing. If the British hadn't taken on the Ndebele we would have been three times richer in just one year, and that, brother, is an amazing achievement. We were only just starting; next year we would have bought more wagons, and more stock. We would have been as much as seven times richer, and we would have been able to continue to support the family."

The mention of the family silenced them for a while as they cast their thoughts back to Ireland. They would not be able to send any money back to them this year. The sound of water dripping in the pail exacerbated their sadness.

"Well, we've let the family down," Morris broke the silence, stating a fact.

"The main reason we came out here was to support them. They should understand why we can't this year," David said forlornly. "What a pity. We were doing the right thing, seriously we were. We were even going to expand and…" he broke off and sighed. "Oh dear!"

"What?" Morris looked at him curiously.

"We asked father to take Louis and Harry out of school and send them here."

"Oh no." Morris dropped his chin to his chest in resignation. They had completely forgotten about their brothers. When things were going well, they had high hopes. And then when things took a sudden turn, they had been very distracted. He looked up at David. "Is it too late to get a letter to Father and tell him not to send them?"

"It's too late. It takes about four or five months to get a letter from here to Ireland. By the time it gets to Ireland, Father would have put the boys on the ship," David sighed. "They're coming, Morris, like it or not."

Morris thought about this for a while. "Then we are responsible for this. We have to make it work." He stared at David.

They went into an intense discussion about how they would bring themselves out of the mess they were in. They would need money to buy a plot in the new settlement for another store, and even more money to buy wagons and stock. Almost all the wealth they now possessed was tied up in some cheques, a little cash, unsold goods, one wagon somewhere in the bush and hopefully one wagon had made it to Mafeking with Nguni and Daluxolo. Mr Savage of the Standard Bank would never lend them money, not in a thousand years; but Julian Weil had offered to give them credit once. Morris felt he might still make that offer. Perhaps Mr Gerran would rent them wagons?

They would have to buy a horse, another rifle, and oxen. Basically they would have to start from scratch. But they were convinced they could do it. They knew how to trade, they knew what worked and what did not, and they'd proved it worked. It was just a matter of time before they could recover and forge ahead, providing they used their money wisely.

"And money, my good brother," Morris said, flashing a smile for the first time in weeks, "is what I know best!"

"So then we are agreed; we stay and make another go of it."

"Yes. It's quite safe, now that the war is over. It will be hard work, but once our brothers join us, it should get a lot easier. I have plans for them." Morris shifted his weight on the box he was sitting on. He looked down at the carton and studied it for a moment. "What's in this box?" he asked David.

"So that's where it is!" David smiled. "It's a box full of playing cards, American-made. Just slipped my attention, mainly because you use it as a chair all the time."

"Well, they won't sell, if they are not displayed," Morris scolded his brother, as he stood up and proceeded to open the box. "You paid £5 for the box, if I recall."

"Yes, it was £6 for the carton, but I got Mr Taylor down to £5, and there are one hundred and sixty packets in there."

"So how much per box?"

"Oh, come on, Morris," David sighed in frustration, "I don't know. They were around one shilling per pack before the discount. I don't know, about ten coppers per pack? You work it out."

"Well done, brother, you are quite correct," he smiled. "I don't know why you bought these, because they won't sell. Have you seen anyone playing cards in the settlement? Nobody plays cards here."

David sighed again. "Well, maybe nobody plays cards because nobody has cards."

"Well, if that's the case, then let's take a punt and sell them for 10 shillings each."

"Are you mad?" David exclaimed, sitting bolt upright. "That's more than ten times the price we paid for them!"

"If we sell them all, we will make a lot of money. We could buy a couple of horses with that."

"More than a couple. You're crazy. Who in their right mind would pay that much for a pack of cards?"

Just then a tall gentleman in his mid-thirties ran into the entrance of the shop, holding a light jacket over his head. His boots were wet and splattered with mud. He was tall, good-looking, and sported a trim and neatly manicured moustache. He wore a loose, beige, cotton shirt with short sleeves and a darker shade of beige trousers.

"Good afternoon, gentlemen," he announced as he ran his fingers through his hair, shaking raindrops to the earthen floor. "My word, it's wet out there! My apologies for storming in here, dripping wet." He smiled generously, with a very pleasing face.

Since the newcomer seemed to simply ooze friendship, the brothers took an instant liking to him.

"No problem at all, sir, welcome. Come on in," Morris greeted him.

"I'm looking for a gentleman called David Langbourne, said the visitor.

"That would be me, sir," David introduced himself, curiosity invading both brothers.

"My name is Robert, but my friends call me Bob. There's talk around the settlement that you outsmarted a party of Matabele warriors that were hunting you recently. Is that correct?"

"Yes," David replied cautiously. "I didn't know people were talking about that."

"Oh yes, you've created quite a name for yourself," he smiled. "I wonder if you would mind if I was so bold as to ask you to recount how you did that. The reason I ask, because I know you are going to ask me why I ask, is because I find bushcraft fascinating, a sort of hobby of mine, and I've never met anyone who has outsmarted a killing party of trained Ndebele warriors."

Being somewhat humbled, David looked to Morris for support, who simply nodded. They pulled up another wooden crate, and the three of them sat around the bucket and talked. It turned out that Bob had come up to KoBulawayo with King Khama's reinforcements from Bechuanaland the day after the royal village was destroyed. Because he was a BSAC soldier and had spent a lot of time in the bush, often for long, boring, and wasteful periods, much like David, he had acquired a keen interest in the wildlife, the plants, trees, and insects, and the African people, in order to keep his active brain occupied. He was particularly interested in how the African people survived in the bush with so little, and how each tribe had their own survival techniques and methods. Tracking held a special fascination for him. But although he often practised tracking animals and humans in the bush, he had never thought to cover his tracks and hide, as David had done. He was therefore very interested in learning from David.

When David began to talk, it was not just Bob who listened intently, but Morris, too. Morris was flabbergasted at what David came out with, as he had not heard him tell his story this way, and in such detail. David recounted every little facet, how he had hoped that – when the warriors had seen the dead horse – they would have been momentarily distracted and would have stopped looking for signs as they approached Bruno's body. He had therefore backtracked in their footsteps to the position where he thought their attention might have been diverted, and then immediately bolted in another direction. David told how he had sprinkled dried grass over their bodies to break up the shape of their heads and shoulders, and how he had taken off his boots when backtracking in the army's path. He explained the deceptions that he had been forced to create, having so little cover to work with; the false leads; and the use of rocks to hide their footprints, all at the same time having to lead an unfit man who had no idea of bush craft whatsoever.

Morris thought he knew his brother well, but then suddenly realised that there was much more to him than he himself had realised, and that he was very proud of him. David spoke about his time waiting at the Limpopo River and how Daluxolo, from the Xhosa nation, had shared his interests and had taught him how to track, and how to use plants as medicine, or how to catch fish with nets made from the fibrous bark of certain trees. They had spoken about Xhosa and Zulu folklore around the fire at night, and he had learned many of their customs. He, therefore, confessed that he owed most of his knowledge of Africa and bushcraft to this man. Piet van Tonder, on the other hand, a farmer he had met in Patensie near Port Elizabeth when they'd first arrived in Africa, had taught him how to hunt, but it was Daluxolo who taught him about the bush. He spoke about their incident with the ostrich, and the thorn bush that literally had captured Morris. Bob laughed at the story and told them he too had been a brief victim of that bush which they aptly called a "wait-a-bit tree". The story of his vulture "hide", the hole in the ground had both Morris and Bob in stitches of laughter.

David was ecstatic that he could talk to someone who understood the things he loved. He was finally able to talk intimately to a person about how his mind worked in the bush, the anxiety and fear he had to deal with, and how he faced death. The words just poured out of David. Having never heard his brother talk so much before, Morris was entranced by David's animated face and gesticulations. It was as if a world of frustrations, joy, fear, and happiness all at once tumbled out of his inner being.

With the darkness of night finally approaching, Bob invited David to join him with another colleague on a two-day expedition to explore the hills of the Matopos, not far from the settlement. He said that they might use the time to learn more from each other about the arts of tracking and bushcraft in Africa.

"I heard we are not permitted there," said David, "Those hills are sacred and filled with spirits and things."

"That's why I want to explore there. I don't believe that, mind you," he said with a wink. "And in any case, it was King Lobengula who forbade anyone to go there, and he's not around anymore."

When David agreed but explained that he did not have a horse, Bob did not think it was much of a problem, and said he would borrow one from the company for the two days, being quite convinced that nobody would object. On the following day, therefore, David met Bob at the parade square with a saddled and ready horse, and they took off for the sacred Matopos Hills on horseback. They were accompanied by Bob's friend, an equally imposing gentleman.

The Matopos comprised a massive set of unusual granite boulders, piled high upon each other, the rocks smooth and grey, with hundreds of intricately coloured lichens growing on their surfaces. Bob reported that the Ndebele name for Matopos meant "bald heads" a name that seemed very apt. Since it was at that time the rainy season, the rocks were extremely difficult and dangerous to climb, due to their slippery surfaces, but the outcrop commanded a special beauty that captivated the three men entirely.

They mostly travelled on horseback, stopping occasionally to dismount and study an unusual footprint, or an exotic flower, or pick at a shiny piece of rock or stone. Because the rocks were so slippery, however, they simply could not venture deep into the hills, so they skirted around outcrops as best they could. It was clear that there was a labyrinth of crevices that would make up pathways into the interior, but they felt it was best to err on the side of caution and so agreed not to venture too deep inside. Besides, within the silence and mystique of the hills, they all experienced in equal silence an eerie feeling that something unseen was watching them from within its shadows.

Nevertheless, they returned home on the following day, having thoroughly enjoyed the outing. David felt they had all learnt from each other, and longed to revisit the outcrop again one day when it might prove drier and his courage a little bolder. After he thanked Bob for the excursion and handed back his horse, he returned to the Sample-Room, where Morris met him waving a small, brown envelope in his hand, and looking very pleased.

"What's that?" David asked.

"Read it." He handed the envelope to his brother, but withdrew it suddenly. "Actually, I'll tell you what it is: it's a plot of land that has been allocated to us in the new KoBulawayo settlement."

"And is it where you want it?"

"Well, we don't have a choice, but it seems to be on one of the main roads that they are calling Abercorn Street."

"But can we afford it?"

"Am I wearing a sad face or a happy face?"

David laughed at his brother. He could tell things were going to come right.

Activity between the two settlements rapidly moved into fever pitch. Wagons were loaded, and household goods were relocated the short distance to the new development. Wooden pole and mud huts were abandoned, with only usable material being salvaged. For the Langbournes and Phil Innes, the logistics were terribly difficult. First, neither had wagons to help move their stock and possessions, and just as importantly, neither had tarpaulins to cover and protect the goods when they moved from one plot to another, while the arrival of the rainy season made the move all the more difficult. Some of the original pioneers claimed that this was the heaviest rain they had seen in the short time they had been there, and the road between the two settlements became a quagmire of mud.

It was a most frustrating time for all involved. Tempers flared, and friendships were put to the test. David had to split his time between the task of moving and keeping Morris' outbursts under control. Wagons and tarpaulins were in such short supply that even renting them proved to be almost impossible. The Langbournes could not move their stock until they had a dry, safe place to store it, and they could not create a dry area without their corrugated iron sheets that were protecting them in the original Sample-Room. It was very frustrating, even for David's calm temperament.

Then some shocking news rocked the population of the settlement. While Major Alan Wilson's patrol had been chasing down the fleeing King Lobengula and his elite army, they had crossed the Shangani River but had then been ambushed and surrounded by the king's rear-guard. Three members among the 37 had broken out to summon reinforcements, but the Shangani River had been swollen by the torrential rains, and they had become trapped on the wrong side of the river. The remaining men had fought on bravely, but when their last bullet had been fired, the survivors stood together and sang "God Save The Queen" before being overrun by the Ndebele impi, who had slaughtered them with their short, stabbing spears. King Lobengula had thus managed to escape to the north of the country, his whereabouts unknown.

This news further disturbed the already fragile situation in the settlement and pushed Major Seward, Captain Bailey, and all the other BSAC officers to the limit. Nerves were frayed, and diplomacy was somewhat in short supply, but somehow, over time, normality returned with the end of the wet season.

Morris and David were simply unable to trade for almost two months while they relocated their business. They still did not have a home, as they had used the warehouse for sleeping quarters, but that was at least one less worry they had with the logistics of moving. They had wanted to build a bigger warehouse and Sample-Room, but without any available roof sheeting, their warehouse and Sample-Room was limited to the same size they'd had in the old settlement.

In the first week of 1894, their hard work finally paid off, and the famous "Langbourne Bros. Sample-Room" sign was proudly carried by David and Morris over their heads and placed above the door to the new shop. Immediately after they had re-opened for trade, they began to plan for a trip to Mafeking in order to rebuild the business. Although David was obviously the right person to go down there, because of his knowledge of bushcraft, horsemanship, and hunting, it was Morris' negotiating skills and business relationships with Mr Weil and Mr Gerran that would be needed. It was therefore agreed that Morris would make the journey as soon as they could buy a suitable horse.

The new settlement was certainly far better than the old one. Since neither a tree nor a blade of grass was visible in the entire area, the vast expanse of flat, cleared land allowed people to see past many of the structures, giving the impression that the settlement was actually quite sparse and under-populated. Together with the unbelievably wide streets, which actually looked quite comical, and drew much light-hearted criticism from the residents, the settlement appeared decidedly empty.

Phil Innes had been allocated his hardware store's position right opposite Langbourne Brothers. His plot was so much larger than before, however, that he had been forced to spread his wares as far apart as possible, which only served to make his business appear under-supplied, untidy, and not worth visiting – more like a dumping ground for scrap metal, as a passer-by once commented. Phil was understandably not happy with his new location – despite the fact that he was pleased with the massive stand he had been given. In the end, he painstakingly moved all his stock closer to his small thatched mud-and-pole office on the site, and that made it look a lot more inviting to his potential customers, although he was still left with what appeared to be a rather large and empty backyard.

Much the same applied to Morris and David. Their allotted stand was huge, but, since all their goods were housed under the roofs of their two buildings, the premises somehow seemed very small and isolated. They had a third building on the premises now, located at the rear of the stand, and that was the typical circular, mud-and-pole, thatched home for Nkosazana.

Within two days, Morris had bought himself a horse, paid mostly from the profits of the Bicycle playing cards, and had joined a mail run for the gruelling ride down to Mafeking. David, Phil, and Abe walked down to the new parade square, with its freshly painted flagpole, to say farewell to Morris and after he and the four riders had departed, the trio of friends sauntered back to Phil's hardware yard and boiled up a jug of water for tea. They were quite relaxed that day, and Abe found three wooden boxes that they used as chairs. He placed them on the ground outside Phil's hut.

From the other side of Abercorn Street, Nkosazana watched them pour their tea into enamel mugs and take a seat. Feeling it was the right thing to do, she promptly placed six shortbread biscuits on a chipped enamel plate and walked across the road to give them to the men. They laughed when they saw her coming towards them. She politely curtsied when she handed them to each of the young men with her beautiful and charming smile. They all thanked her profusely for her consideration, Abe clapping his cupped hands in a traditional sign of grateful thanks.

"You'll get a reputation, David," Abe laughed at his good friend. "You should be in the catering business!"

"I wish there was a decent place where we could congregate. In Port Elizabeth, there was this amazing place, The Grand Hotel…" David sighed as he recalled the wonderful memories. "It was at the same Grand Hotel that Langbourne Brothers was born."

David looked across Abercorn Street at their large sign that hung over the door to the Sample-Room, and then went on to relate some of the stories of The Grand from their past, which, in reality, was not that long ago.

"Maybe we should build a place like that right here," Phil mused.

"Impossible," David interjected. "You need bricks and mortar. You could never build a structure more than one storey high with logs and mud. You definitely need bricks and mortar."

Phil took up the conversation, and gave his friends a fascinating lecture on the history of bricks, how they first had been used; how in ancient times they had added straw to the bricks as a filler or for insulation, and how the curing time could be improved and hardening increased with the use of a fire-based kiln. His facial expressions and hands became quite animated in the telling of the history of brick-making, and it kept his friends captivated and enchanted.

"So," David interrupted, "why don't we three go into a partnership and manufacture bricks? Heaven knows this place could use bricks!"

"Permanent structures are not permitted in this country," Phil objected.

"I know that, but that was the rule laid down by the king. My understanding is that the BSAC make the rules now. That's why we are sitting right here on this spot." David tapped his shoe in the dirt to make a point. The men stared at his foot and the print the sole of his shoe made on the damp earth.

"If they will give us permission to build, then I would like to build a proper shop," Phil announced, "with a grand shop front that expands the entire width of my stand."

"Of course, and so would I, and a dozen others around us feel that way too, that is for certain." David gesticulated around the settlement at all the open spaces. "I'll bet the BSAC want more permanent offices for their administration, and we could certainly use some hotels and eating establishments. We need a place where businessmen can meet, exchange ideas, and forge friendships and partnerships. We need different places of worship: churches, synagogues, that sort of thing; a hospital. The demand for bricks would be insatiable."

"I'm a prospector at heart, and not a good one, I must admit. But I know a little about rocks and soil," Abe said softly. "There's a lovely clay patch on the east side of this settlement that I found yesterday. No hope of finding any gold or gemstones there, but perfect for clay bricks. You, Phil, could show me how to make bricks and how to build a kiln, and David, you understand business."

"Yes, I could show you how to make the tools to cast the bricks, and how to build a kiln to cure them," Phil smiled. "That's the easy part."

"And I know exactly who to speak to in the BSAC to get permission and an allocated stand," David said with a wink. "But first, we need to formally agree that we will partner up. We need to decide what each of us will do, and how we will share any profits or losses."

"I say we split our partnership three ways equally," Abe suggested.

"I agree," Phil concurred.

"Then I will draw up an agreement on a piece of paper that we must all sign. It's the right thing to do; my father told me business deals always need to be written down, agreed upon, and signed by all those involved."

As everyone was in agreement, they shook hands and toasted their new partnership with the last dregs of their weak, black tea.

"Major Seward, sir," the orderly interrupted.

"What is it?" the major grunted. He was standing with arms behind his back, scrutinising a map on his desk.

"Mr David Langbourne and friends are outside. He would like a minute of your time, sir."

"Good show, bring him in." He looked up, and, without waiting for David to enter, called out to him. "David, come in, come in!"

David bounced into the tent, followed by Phil and Abe, who sauntered through, looking a little nervous.

"Good morning, Major Seward." David smiled and shook his hand. "May I introduce you to two of my friends, Mr Phil Innes and Mr Abe Kaufman?"

"Innes?" He shook Phil's hand. "I've heard of you. Hardware, is it?"

"Yes, sir, and thank you for my plot. Most suitable, and greatly appreciated," he bent the truth a little.

"And Kaufman…" He shook Abe's hand. "Your wife, does she…?"

"Yes, sir, the hairdresser."

"Yes, yes, of course, I've met her. Splendid lady; cuts some of the men's hair. Highly recommended! Take a seat, gentlemen. What can I do for you?"

"Major Seward, my friends and I would like to form a business partnership, but our partnership depends on some matters relating to the future decisions of the BSAC."

"Such as…?" the major was quick to respond.

"We noticed how well the settlement is being laid out," he began, throwing in a little flattery for good measure, "and we sort of wondered what the BSAC's intention was for the settlement. Specifically, will we be allowed to build permanent structures now that the king is no longer in power?"

"That has been considered, David, but the person who ultimately makes those decisions is Mr Rhodes, in Cape Town. Of course, he passes those decisions on to the Administrator, Dr Jameson, who advises me. Right now, I have not been advised of what direction the settlement is going in as far as permanent buildings are concerned. Why do you ask?"

"Well, Mr Innes here knows the methods used to manufacture bricks, and…"

"Bricks?" The major's eyes turned to slits as he glared at Phil.

"Yes, sir." Phil suddenly sat bolt upright and nodded confidently. "I know everything about bricks, sir."

"And," David continued, "Mr Kaufman has worked with earth all his life. He was a miner and a prospector, and with my knowledge of business, we believe we could make a perfect team to manufacture and sell bricks. If the company wishes to develop the settlement into a small town, for instance, we would like the company's permission to manufacture bricks."

"Sir," Abe spoke up, which caught David by surprise; he was usually a very timid man and did not say much at the best of times. "The other reason we need your permission is because I have found a very suitable patch of clay on the east side of the settlement that would make top-quality bricks. We would like to stake a claim on that land so that we could set up the factory and kilns. The bricks would be of the highest quality."

"Furthermore," David added excitedly, "we would extend the Langbourne Brothers pricing structure to the BSAC, should they have the need to purchase bricks." He knew that would spark the major's capitalist tendencies.

"Interesting," the major said slowly. "Please wait here a moment," he said, and left the tent with a frown, while the three friends exchanged glances. Phil and Abe looked worried, but David smiled and winked. They smiled back.

About three minutes later, Major Seward entered the tent with Dr Jameson. All three quickly stood up and greeted the doctor, making appropriate introductions.

"You haven't had need for that morphine yet?" the doctor asked as he shook David's hand.

"Thankfully not, although it goes with me wherever I go," David laughed; he was very relaxed in the doctor's company.

"The major tells me what you three would like to do with your partnership. A splendid idea, I must say. We are looking for innovative and progressive members of the community," he commended.

"Thank you, sir," David responded.

"Now, the issue is that I have not had a direct instruction from Mr Cecil Rhodes, but," he paused, "last time we communicated, I received a strong impression that he intended for the settlement of KoBulawayo to become an established town."

The three friends smiled; this was very good news.

"I would suggest to you," the doctor continued, "that you go ahead and begin your venture in earnest. I will grant you a plot on the east side of the settlement for the purposes of mining the clay that you have found and manufacturing the bricks. If, for whatever reason, Mr Rhodes decides not to develop this settlement, then you must be of the understanding that I will revoke the grant, and you three will have no claim against the BSAC."

"We accept that, Dr Jameson. Thank you," David beamed.

"Good show," Jameson flashed a broad smile. "Major Seward, please be so kind as to draw up an agreement reflecting what was discussed here today. Good luck, gentlemen, and thank you for your pioneering attitude. I would venture to presume that you three are the very first to formulate such a partnership in this community." Then he shook their hands warmly and left the tent, before returning abruptly and putting his head back inside the tent. "Oh, I forgot to ask. David, you wouldn't have any more of those jack-in-the-boxes, would you?" He smiled and winked at Major Seward.

"Sold out, I'm afraid, Dr Jameson." Both David and the doctor allowed a laugh to escape while the major's face began to take on a slightly scarlet hue.

"What was that about?" Phil asked as all the men took their seats again.

"Private joke, Phil," David said, and stole a glance at the major. He was glaring at David, but David just smiled back.

"Right, gentlemen," Major Seward began. "I need you to go down to the registrar's tent and see Captain Marcus Bailey. I think you know him, David?"

Just before David could answer, Abe quietly interrupted, "What's a jack-in-the-box?"

David and the major locked eyes, then Seward started to chuckle softly. The chuckle became a chortle, and then both David and the major began to laugh heartily, leaving Abe and Phil looking very confused.

Captain Bailey's tent was across a wide, dirt road named Selbourne Avenue, which had been demarcated by pegs and ropes. Cutting across the various plots by stepping over the sagging ropes regardless, as everyone else seemed to be doing, the trio soon found the captain hard at work at his desk. Another four soldiers were also shuffling papers, filing, and doing a host of administrative duties in his tent. The captain was very glad to be able to take a break from his work to see to the newcomers' needs. They all sat on makeshift chairs and told the captain of their plan to form an equal partnership in the brick-making business. They told him that they had been instructed to register their claim once it had been established and to register their business.

"Well, I can certainly register your business now," Captain Bailey explained. "But the claim will have to be done once you point out to one of my officers where it is. You can do that tomorrow, if you wish."

"That sounds good to us," David agreed, nodding to his partners, who nodded back in agreement.

"Alright, name of the business?"

"Ahh, we didn't think of that, did we, fellows?" said David, looking at his partners, which drew a sarcastic smile from Bailey.

"You choose," Phil replied. "You're the businessman amongst us."

"Alright, what about 'KoBulawayo Bricks'?" David suggested. "Actually, drop the 'Ko' and just call it Bulawayo Bricks; that has a nice ring to it."

Everyone agreed, and Bailey started writing it down in a ledger. Just then, someone walked into the tent and all the soldiers, including Captain Bailey, leapt to attention, with one soldier shouting, "Sir!" David, Phil, and Abe instinctively stood up and, not knowing what to do, simply stood absolutely still in nervous fear.

"At ease," came the friendly reply, and everyone gently sat down again. David looked over his shoulder. It was his friend, Bob.

"Bob?" David exclaimed, before noticing the insignia on his collars. "I mean, Major!"

"David!" he cried, smiling and shaking his hand vigorously. "Fancy seeing you here. He's not giving you any trouble, is he, Captain?" he asked, directing his question at Captain Bailey.

"No, sir," Bailey replied promptly.

The conversation became very relaxed, and the boys explained what they intended to do. Bob was very charismatic and had the entire tent in stitches of laughter. David had taken a strong liking to him from the start, and now he could see why. Everyone in Bob's presence enjoyed him. He engaged with those he spoke to and made them feel special, needed, and alive, with a purpose in life. He eventually excused himself to allow the others to get on with their important work.

"I'm looking for a Captain Grant Dent. Can anyone point me in the direction of his tent?"

"Two tents down on the right, sir," Captain Bailey announced.

"Excellent, thank you. He has a most delightful telescope, I believe. I want to find out where he bought it. As you were, gentlemen," he said, and stepped out of the tent.

"Major!" David called him back quickly. "I gave it to him. If you call past my shop, on Abercorn Street, I have one left, which I will reserve for you."

"That's very kind of you, David. I will certainly call on you for that instrument, indeed."

"But please, sir, do yourself a favour and continue to call in on Captain Dent. You will be pleased you did. He's a good man."

The major smiled and nodded his appreciation with his hands behind his back, and with a shallow bow, walked off towards Grant Dent's tent.

David could not contain his excitement. "I didn't know Captain Dent was in camp!"

"He arrived yesterday from Fort Victoria," Captain Bailey said. "I didn't know you knew the major. What did you call him? Bob?" He looked shocked.

"Yes," David replied. "That's what he told me to call him. Who is he?"

"He's a very smart man. Very smart," Bailey repeated. "He has a really long surname, so we call him 'B-P' for short, Robert B-P, not Bob. Heavens no! He's also a very talented artist. Spends every spare moment he has sketching in a notebook of sorts."

"I can well believe that. And I can also tell you that he knows the African bush better than any other European I know. What does B-P stand for?"

"Baden-Powell, I think," one of the other officers in the tent interjected, while scratching through some paperwork. "Here it is: Major Robert Stephenson Smyth Baden-Powell."

They looked at the officer blankly before Bailey guided them back to the business of registering Bulawayo Bricks. Their ownership having been divided equally into thirds, both Abe and Phil registered in their own names, but David wanted his share registered under the name of Langbourne Brothers and not his personal name. He had to explain to Abe that this meant the business was still owned by him as a one-third partner, but simply represented by a company name, which implied that he and Morris had no more or fewer votes than Abe or Phil. The men accepted this agreement, and they signed the document appropriately after paying a small fee. They then left Captain Bailey to call on Captain Dent.

David's day was getting better by the minute. He had met up with four very good friends, all within the hour, and had formed a business partnership with two other good friends. Although these people were much older than he was, this did not mean a thing to him, since they always respected him as an equal, without hesitation. He had mixed often with older people in the past, and so was actually more comfortable in their company than those younger than himself.

Seeing Grant had been very special for David, since he had been concerned that his newfound friend might have been killed or injured in the rebellion, but Grant assured David that he had missed all the action. He had been ordered to replace someone at Fort Victoria Headquarters at the last minute, which had been a great reprieve. He was also very happy to be in KoBulawayo, as the people seemed friendlier. They agreed to meet later that evening at Langbourne Brothers. David would ask Nkosazana to prepare a meal for them, and they could catch up on all the events that had recently taken place, and reminisce about their long journey down to

Mafeking.

Later that afternoon, Bob came to visit David at the Sample-Room. He gave Bob the last remaining telescope but refused any payment for it. He said it came with one condition: that he should take time every so often to observe the African birds and wildlife, and not just for an enemy soldier. Bob accepted the telescope, in his turn, on condition that David accept his brass compass and new pocket knife, a precision device that had two razor-sharp blades which folded into the handle, one blade larger than the other. It had been made in Switzerland and was their latest model. He told David that, often when he was alone in the bush, he would whittle at a straight piece of wood and create a walking stick, sculpturing the head of a person or animal on the grip. He said he would like for David to try that on occasion instead of looking at birds! He also gave him a quick lesson on how to use the compass to keep him on the right track and prevent him from getting lost in the bush.

David agreed to practice whittling walking sticks, and said he would go one better and design a practical walking stick, one that was as tall as himself. It would have a small fork on the head without a handgrip, but would prefer to place a separate handgrip, which he would fashion out of twine, in the middle of the stick.

"I would rather call that a staff, not a walking stick. How would that be practical?" Bob asked curiously.

"I would use the stick to flip logs over from a distance in the event that there might be a scorpion hiding underneath, or an agile snake. I would then hold its head down with the forked end until I had made a safe escape. And even better, if I were to be attacked by another ostrich, I would catch its neck in the fork and hold it, and keep its deadly toenails away from me while I found my way out of the situation. I have given this a lot of thought, believe me!" They both laughed. "You do have a wild imagination, young David," he chuckled, as he walked out of the store, flashing him an unofficial salute in the air.

Chapter Thirteen

Full Circle

Morris dumped his bag on the floor of the room at the lodging David had recommended, causing a small plume of light-brown dust to billow around his knees, and then walked over to the tiny mirror that hung on the wall. It had begun to mottle, and had a crack down one side. His beard was untidy after nearly three weeks of neglect, but he had a full growth. He picked at a piece of straw that was tangled on the side of his jaw and, deciding that his beard was not dignified enough, he walked down to the bathroom with his razor and a towel, had a good soak in the tepid brown water, washed his hair, and gave himself a good, clean shave.

Although he was exhausted from the hard push on the last day of the journey, he wasted no time in putting on a suit and walking down to Weil and Co. to find his good friend, Julian. When they met, Julian was so delighted to see him that, instead of ushering him into his office for refreshment, he immediately took him down to a new hotel just one block away that had recently opened. There Julian bought him tea with fresh scones and homemade strawberry jam, which they enjoyed outside on the wide verandah.

"You are looking decidedly thin, Morris. The ride must have been tough. We need to fatten you up!" he joked without smiling. "What happened? I have heard the news from Matabeleland, terrible news."

"It was not good, Julian," Morris confided. "It was very scary, I must admit."

"But you were not hurt," he stated, which sounded like a question, because he always seemed to lift the accent on his last word.

"No, no, we are alright, thank you. But we suffered big losses. We lost nine of the ten wagons we had, all filled to the hilt with stock. Burnt to the ground; lost it all: our oxen, our horses, everything. And sadly, we lost two of our traders, killed in the rebellion."

"And David? Is he alright?"

"Yes, he is well. He is an amazing chap. He was attacked by over three hundred Ndebele and outsmarted them on foot when they gave chase. I admire him, Julian. He could have been killed. He was rescuing one of our traders; a chap called Abe Kaufman."

"I've met Abe, I know him. Good Jewish fellow. A bit..." he held his hand in the air, palm down, and rocked it from side to side. "A bit, well, I'm not sure what to make of him. He needs some courage in his veins. His wife, though, Sharon... Well, there's a lovely lady. She has ambition. Chutzpah! I like her, very attractive woman. We are related."

"Oh!" Morris was surprised. "What's chutzpah?"

"Courage, or gall. The Americans say 'gumption'. She's got it all right: chutzpah! You haven't heard that word, Morris?" he asked, almost condescendingly. "Good Yiddisher word, chutzpah. You, Morris, you have chutzpah!"

Morris squirmed as he started to feel embarrassed. "Alright," was all he could think of saying.

"So, what brings you here?"

"I want to rebuild the business. Matabeleland is calm, the conflict is over and there is money to be made again. I'm looking to take another six wagons of stock up with me, and the problem is that this time I no longer have the money to pay for it."

Julian choked on his tea. "Another six wagons? You are brave, Morris. How are you going to finance this?"

"I want to ask you to give me credit."

Julian looked Morris in the eye. He took another sip of tea and took a long look at Morris, before taking a deep breath. "You have chutzpah, Morris; I'll say that."

* * *

As Morris walked past a building-supply business, he was smiling as he glanced into their yard. The meeting with Julian went better than expected. Just as he was about to kick a stone off the walkway, he noticed a lone worker walking through the piles of construction material. He quickly returned his attention to the path and hoofed the pebble out of his way.

Suddenly, he stopped and looked back along the path. Retracing his steps a few yards, he stood outside the entrance of the building-supply business. Piled on some racking was some bright and shiny, galvanised iron, roof sheeting, just like those they had used to build the Sample-Room. Morris immediately walked in and the owner, the lone man whom he had seen walking around the yard, approached him. Morris quickly introduced himself and showed an interest in the roof sheeting. He was sure that Langbourne Brothers could use the sheets, if they expanded on their recently acquired plot. But if not, he could make some money out of them, as they were in high demand and desperately scarce in KoBulawayo.

"I'd be interested in purchasing half your supply, sir, if half would fit on one wagon." Morris ran his hand along the shiny, smooth surface of the top sheet. It was blazing hot, so he quickly left it alone.

"Half of what you see there would comfortably be carried on one wagon, sir," the owner said with a very friendly smile.

Morris quickly negotiated a price, and just before they agreed, Morris upped the quantity he might be interested in, if the owner were to discount him a little more. After more haggling, they agreed on a better price per sheet.

"Excellent!" Morris exclaimed excitedly and then became serious and sad. "The problem is, I don't have a wagon. Lost them all in the Matabele rebellion. You heard all about the Matabele rebellion, have you?"

"Yes, I did." He looked very serious, in keeping with Morris' serious look.

"Nasty stuff, that. Very brutal. Thousands of lives lost."

"So I heard."

"You wouldn't have a wagon that could deliver these sheets, would you?"

The owner looked to his left, and under a huge pile of rusting scrap metal, old wooden planks and dead plant matter was a dilapidated wagon. Morris had already spotted it.

Before he could answer, Morris continued, "If you could deliver these sheets for me, I'll give you one-quarter of the cash up front, and the remainder on delivery." They had not even discussed payment terms yet, and just as Morris thought the owner was about to object to the one-quarter down payment, he threw in a distraction, "I need it delivered to KoBulawayo."

That comment completely threw the owner. "To KoBulawayo?" he nearly shouted in surprise, and instantly forgot about the unhealthy payment terms. "That's a three-month trip just to get there!"

Morris ignored that remark because he was now on a roll and he knew that the man needed the sale. "I'll tell you what," he said, "I've got about six wagons of other stock going up in a few days' time. If you lend me your wagon, I'll add it to my convoy, and you won't have to go up yourself. It also won't cost you a penny. My herders will take care of it and bring it back to you with a cheque for £5 for the use of your wagon. Just think; instead of it rusting away under all that junk, you have an opportunity to make £5 out of it; for nothing!"

Morris walked out grinning. He had just bought a stack of items that he knew he could sell for a fortune, and he had negotiated some really cheap transport. Furthermore, he had paid just one-quarter of the cost to secure the deal! By the time Morris had to pay for the full amount it would be at least six months down the track, and by then, he would have long sold the sheets for four times the price he paid for them.

"Now that's good business sense!" he said under his breath.

The next stop was to enjoy a lovely cup of tea and some scrumptious shortbread biscuits with Mr Gerran. He already had one wagon, safely returned and parked by Nguni and Daluxolo behind one of Weil's warehouses, but he needed to convince Gerran to let another five go without payment. Morris knew that the negotiations were going to be tough, but he was looking forward to the challenge, as he could feel in his bones that he was going to convince Gerran to make the sale. After all, he felt like some shortbread biscuits! By the time he walked out of Gerran's Coach Builders, Mr Gerran believed he had just concluded the best deal of his life, yet it was Morris who stepped onto the gravel pavement grinning from ear to ear with a distinct spring in his step.

The last stop of the day was at the Standard Bank subsidiary branch to deposit what little cash and cheques he had with him. Unfortunately for Morris, Mr Savage was patrolling the floor, glaring at his staff as he entered the door, and he could not ignore the manager, as much as he might have wanted to.

"I see you have returned," Savage looked down his nose at Morris, avoiding a cordial greeting.

"Good day to you, sir. Yes, I have. I need to make some deposits, if you will excuse me," Morris turned to walk over to a teller.

"Come into my office, please, Mr Langbourne."

Morris was not sure how to take this, but nodded his agreement and walked with Mr Savage to the office, where he was invited to sit while the manager called a teller over and instructed the young lady to process the deposit. Noticing a large, leather-bound ledger lying open on the manager's desk, Morris stole a glance at the numbers neatly written with a flourish in royal blue ink, but without a single correction in sight. Once Mr Savage was seated he took up the conversation.

"Did you get tangled up in that awful confrontation which the BSAC chaps experienced with the Ndebele recently?"

"Yes sir," Morris kept his answers to the point. He wondered if Savage wanted to ask him for information about the north.

"And your business? Was that affected by this disagreement?"

Morris had a feeling that Savage had heard. "Yes, we were badly affected."

"Have you lost much?"

Morris now knew he must have been talking to Gerran or Weil. "Almost everything, sir," he confessed.

"You know that Mr Weil is a valued customer of this bank and a personal friend of mine. If you were to purchase goods from him on credit, it would be my duty as his financial advisor to counsel him against risking any money in your future business, should you decide to continue with this folly of yours in Matabeleland."

Morris' blood boiled and he tried desperately to calm himself.

"Sir," he said through gritted teeth, "you are entitled to give advice and guidance to your clients and friends, if they ask you for it, of course, but your interference, or influence in their business decisions based on whom they are dealing with would be construed by me as being totally unprofessional, and a deliberate interference by yourself, based purely on personality differences, and my assessment of your professionalism is in deep doubt at this moment in time as it is."

Savage took a deep breath, leaned forward with his elbows on the open ledger and stared hard at Morris. "I don't have to take this from an immature and arrogant little whippersnapper such as yourself. Why, you are barely nineteen years old! You have no right or authority to question my integrity and professional standards."

Morris corrected him indignantly. "I am seventeen years old, sir. Perhaps I have no right to question your authority, but age should not be a factor in determining authority, professional standards, or integrity. For instance, take that list of deposits you have written in that ledger," he nodded at the open ledger under the manager's elbows. There were about fifteen handwritten entries, all in pounds, shillings and pence, which were totalled under a thick blue ink line at the bottom.

Savage moved his elbows off the ledger and covered the numerical entries gently with his open hands. "I beg your pardon, sir, these entries are confidential."

"Indeed, I would hope they are. Yet I am sitting across the desk from you, and I can read the numbers, albeit upside down, and I can see at a glance that you have incorrectly added the numbers, the difference being in favour of the bank and not the client. I am now obliged to ask myself the question as to whether that error is indeed just that, a simple error executed by one of simple mind, or whether it is an error deliberately perpetrated on your behalf to defraud your client. Sadly, I am inclined toward the latter.

"Now, if you are obliged to raise the matter of integrity, or professional standards, how is it that I, a seventeen-year-old whippersnapper," Morris coldly punctuated the description with gritted teeth, "how may I add up the value of a set of numbers in my head, and not just ordinary numbers, but pounds, shillings and pence, whilst reading them upside down, no less. Whereas you, sir, cannot obtain a correct figure at leisure with the aid of a pencil and while sitting with the numbers in front of you, the right way up?"

"You cannot add these values up in your head. Don't play games with me, lad," Savage scolded. "The total is correct," he said, while looking at the numbers apprehensively.

"Actually, I beg to differ. You have eight shillings and tuppence in favour of the bank written down there. Be that as it may, while it is not for me to question your integrity or professional standards, would it be professional of me to discuss your accounting errors with your clients around town? I would believe a matter of reputation is at stake here, Mr Savage. Would it not be intriguing for Mr Weil to find that his daily takings were eight shillings and tuppence short just in yesterday's banking alone?"

Mr Savage's face had turned a deep red, and he ground his teeth in fury. He was just about to stand up and say something when the young teller returned and handed Morris his deposit slip with the official bank's stamp across the final total. Morris checked the slip quickly and thanked the lady as he stood up to leave.

"If you can't keep your own accounts in order, sir, how can I possibly trust your integrity? Eight shillings and tuppence, Mr Savage. I suggest you check your work. Oh, and please don't worry about me asking for a loan; Langbourne Brothers are quite capable of rebuilding the business without the help of your bank. Good day to you, sir."

Morris turned his back on Mr Savage and walked out the door, smiling uncontrollably. He desperately wanted to turn around and watch Mr Savage snatch a pencil and rework his arithmetic in order to test Morris' claims and to realise that he had made a mistake, or even better, that Morris had been correct, but his pride held him back. He knew he was right, and suddenly he couldn't wait for his next encounter with the surly bank manager. In fact, he thought he might call in the next day simply to check his balance for the fun of it.

Ten days later, Morris shook hands with Daluxolo and his team of herders and bid them farewell, watching them leave the northern boundary of Mafeking in a cloud of dust. Daluxolo was keen to go back again as he wished to see his future bride. There were seven wagons loaded to the hilt, all under the competent leadership of Daluxolo and in control of a team of experienced Xhosa men. He had negotiated some wonderful deals with Gerran and Weil, and he did not need to borrow a cent from Mr Savage. Interest rates on his various credit terms were favourable, and the trading conditions were better than he expected. He had enough roof sheeting to quadruple the size of their warehouse, which was already the largest structure in the settlement, and Matabeleland was stable again, protected by a prestigious and now famous paramilitary force. He felt more confident about Matabeleland than ever before.

Morris had planned to ride north with the BSAC mail run the following day to join David in KoBulawayo. Since Daluxolo and his men had done this trip before, they knew the way, so Morris was comfortable that they would manage the journey without incident. As the last of the men and beasts disappeared from view over the crest of a low hill, Morris stood in the silence and gave a personal thanks to his Lord for protecting and guiding them through these testing times. He also gave special thanks for protecting his brother when he was attacked. He missed David, and wanted to get back to KoBulawayo as quickly as possible.

A bird let out a shrill screech, and Morris looked over his right shoulder to find it. He was standing by the cemetery on the northern edge of town, in the same place where they had made their original decision to go to Matabeleland. That was exactly one year before, and they had come full circle. So much had happened. Only one year ago they had enjoyed a healthy bank account and enough stock to open a lucrative business. Now they had lost virtually everything. There was hardly any money in the bank, and all their stock, their wagons, and oxen were on credit.

Morris shook his head slowly. It was a sobering thought that Africa could do that to a person in just one short year. But then he accepted that the land had its own rules and men simply had to live by them. He was reminded that, when they had fled the poverty of Ireland, he had owned nothing to his name. Now, not even three years later, he had less than nothing to his name: he owed all the big players in town a lot of money. But they had given him a second chance, based mainly on his reputation.

Morris took a deep breath and held it for a moment before exhaling gently. About to turn eighteen, he felt invigorated, confident, and anxious to get back into business once more. He looked at the open expanse of Africa that was once again calling to him, and silently reflected on the past year. He remembered a discussion he had held with David, while standing on that very spot the year earlier: that they would either walk out of Matabeleland very wealthy, or poorer and worse for wear, but greater in experience. It seemed the latter was the case.

If I could make £75 000 in just one year in Port Elizabeth, when business was not affected by war and politics, Morris thought to himself, *then I could make a lot more up north now that things have returned to normal.*

A melodious and lonely call of a distant Fish Eagle drifted over the open land. Morris looked up at the clear blue sky and saw the speck of the majestic bird effortlessly soaring high above the plains. It was flying north, towards Matabeleland, as if giving him a sign.

"Watch me now," Morris nodded at the bird and smiled momentarily. His mind was racing like never before, and he had a fire in his heart. "I'm going to build an empire."

Langbourne Brothers were back in business!

TO BE CONTINUED…

LANGBOURNE'S

EMPIRE

At around noon, a short gentleman wearing a long-sleeved pale yellow shirt and dark brown slacks arrived at the Sample-Room and poked his head inside. "Mr Langbourne, sir?" he asked timidly. "Yes, indeed, come in Sir. How can I be of assistance?" David stopped what he was doing and approached the man.

"Herbert Bachmayer at your service, sir. I come from the new Posts and Telecommunications Office. I have a telegraph message for you that was delivered last night by the BSAC postal run."

David's heart skipped a beat. "Oh, fantastic!" he almost shouted. He wanted to snatch the envelope out of Mr Bachmayer's hand and rip it open.

"Perhaps I could ask you to place your signature here," he produced a small book with lined pages in it, "to acknowledge receipt of the telegraph, of course."

"Certainly," David agreed and quickly scribbled his signature in a spot that had been neatly indicated with a tiny 'x' by the name Langbourne Brothers.

"I believe this may be one of the last telegraphs the BSAC postal run will deliver," he said with a smile.

"Really, why would that be?"

"Well, as you know, there is a network of telegraph wires that connect most of the towns south of us, but the cable stops at Mafeking, along with the end of the rail line. However, Mr Rhodes has funded a telegraph line to connect Mafeking with Fort Salisbury, up north. That line is now complete and working, and they have taken a branch from that line and are heading towards KoBulawayo. The line is now only six miles away, and soon the KoBulawayo office will be connected. Very exciting news for the citizens of KoBulawayo if I say so myself," he beamed. "Unfortunately we are still not connected to the rest of the world. I doubt that will ever happen, but certainly, we will be connected to all the main towns in the Cape, Transvaal, Bechuanaland, Free State, etcetera, etcetera."

David was very impressed. This would be a huge game changer for their business. The ramifications were immense, and he needed to tell Morris as soon as possible. He thanked Mr Bachmayer and politely saw him out the door. The moment he left, David dashed into the warehouse to find his brother.

"Morris! Guess what?" he exploded excitedly.

"What?" Morris was visibly annoyed, and quickly turned his attention back to his ledger where his pen had scratched through a number when David startled him.

"Two bits of news: firstly, a telegraph has arrived, and secondly, in a few days a wire will arrive in KoBulawayo that will connect us to all the big towns south of us."

This caught Morris' attention, and he immediately put his pen down. "You know what this means, David?"

"Yes, for starters we will be able to communicate with Louis in the East London office."

"And we can order goods from Weil without going down there every time we need to replenish our stocks."

"The possibilities are endless!" David was almost beside himself with excitement.

"What's in the telegraph message?" he nodded at the envelope that David was clutching tightly in his hand.

David tore it open and read the irregular typeface that punctuated the coarse surface of the dull postal paper. "It's from Jack Shiel in Port Elizabeth!" His face lit up with joy. "Our brothers have arrived, safe and sound."

"Well that is also good news," Morris stood up from his desk and slapped his brother on the shoulder. "They say good news comes in threes. Two pieces of good news in two minutes is not bad, brother."

Just then there was a knock on the wooden doorframe, and the brothers turned to see who it was.

"My apologies, gentlemen," Mr Bachmayer timidly poked his head through the doorway again, "I forgot to advise you that Mr Honey of The Standard Bank asked me to mention to you that he would be grateful if Mr Morris would pop down to see him later this morning."

Morris looked at David, "I dare say that might be number three," he grinned, leaving Mr Bachmayer looking a little confused.

David thanked Herbert and sent him on his way, then, turning to Morris, he lowered his voice to almost a whisper, even though there was nobody else in the room, "Do you think Mr Honey has approved our loan?"

"I'm sure he has," Morris also spoke in a hoarse whisper, "then, mark my words, we are going to make more money than you could ever imagine, because, believe me," he frowned seriously, "nobody is going to stop us now. David, we are going to build a business empire, and it begins right now."

ACKNOWLEGEMENTS

Once again I acknowledge and thank Scarlett Rugers for her design and layout of this, my second book – a wonderful lady to deal with, and to Chrissy at Damonza for the internal layout for this second edition.

I also acknowledge the relatives and friends of the Langbourne family, whose memories of the brothers, and their history, allowed me to write both 'Langbourne' and 'Langbourne's Rebellion'.

My best friend, Martin Robinson, with whom I grew up with in Africa, I give many thanks for his valuable advice and feedback as the book progressed. For this I am extremely grateful. I thank another good friend, Phil Ineson, for his technical advice on the weapons used in the story.

My sincere thanks to Cindy Kramer for her mentoring, suggestions and guidance, always reassuring and constantly there for me. I'd be lost without her. I'd also like to thank Wendy Meyer for casting a vital 'old school' eye over my work, and to John and Cherie for their comments on the manuscript, and to my newfound cousin, Steve Landau for his proofreading abilities.

My thanks also to my editor, Mike Kantey of Watercourse, Plettenberg Bay, for his belief in my books.

A very special thanks to my partner, Sharon De Bruyn, for her undying encouragement, enthusiasm, feedback and suggestions, and for accompanying me around Southern and Central Africa whilst I researched some of the history behind the story.

Finally, and most importantly, my thanks to you, my readers. I truly hope you enjoyed the story.

ABOUT THE AUTHOR

Alan Landau was born in Salisbury, Rhodesia (now Harare, Zimbabwe) in 1959. In 1978 he joined the British South Africa Police (formally the BSAC). At that time Rhodesia was entangled in a civil war that ended in 1980. After serving in the new Zimbabwe Republic Police for a short time, Alan retired to enter the commercial world.

Alan worked in Zimbabwe's widely known tobacco industry for five years before joining his father and ultimately taking over the family business when his father retired to the UK. Later on, Alan was involved in the travel, tourism, hotel, property, financial, and retail sectors. His service to his community took the form of Rotary International with a committed focus on the Rotary Youth Exchange Program.

Having migrated to Brisbane, Australia, in 2001, Alan bought a franchise in the retail sector, which he successfully ran with his late wife and two children. In 2012 he sold the business and went into semi-retirement. He now pursues his hobbies of writing, travelling, wildlife safaris and ornithology with his wife, Sharon.

More about the author can be found as follows:
Web: www.landaubooks.com
Twitter: @landaubooks
Facebook: www.facebook.com/landaubooks
Instagram: landaubooks

The Langbourne Series

Based on a true story, the Langbourne series follows the lives of four intrepid brothers who journey to Africa in 1891. Without parents, friends, or family, they disembark the ship at Port Elizabeth and set their minds to making enough money to support their destitute family in Ireland. But Mother Africa has ideas of her own.

A Landau Books Publication
www.landaubooks.com

"To Brave Men"
by
Alan P Landau

Based on the true story of the Shangani Patrol, delve into this enthralling narrative as the haunting tale of the ill-fated Shangani Patrol unfurls with gripping intensity.

Embark on a journey alongside the audacious Fred Burnham, whose adventurous spirit knows no bounds.

Meet Major Allan Wilson, a valiant officer navigating the harrowing perils of war with unwavering courage.

Discover King Lobengula, a complex figure embodying both ruthless tyranny and diplomatic finesse, leaving an indelible mark on his people.

Witness the loyalty of Mjaan, Lobengula's steadfast Induna, tested to his limits.

Set in 1893, against the backdrop of a war-torn southern African landscape, the remarkable bravery of these men echoes through time, reshaping the course of history. Immerse yourself in a world of bravery, sacrifice, and unbreakable human resolve in this captivating and unforgettable tale.

"Of Sand and Stars"
by
Brenda Kate

In the vast Australian outback, FBI agent Mandy Richardson and an enigmatic Australian astronomer kindle a forbidden romance while unravelling a sinister plot. Their combined knowledge uncovers a scheme for mass destruction, forcing them to navigate dangers and reconcile loyalties. Racing against time and torn between duty and desire, they must conquer ruthless adversaries and protect humanity. Prepare for a thrilling journey where love defies rules and survival hangs in the balance.

Another Landau Books Publication
www.landaubooks.com